Death in
the Abstract

Also available by Emily Barnes:

The Fine Art of Murder

Death in the Abstract

A Katherine Sullivan Mystery

Emily Barnes

CROOKED
LANE

NEW YORK

Published in the United States by Crooked Lane Books, an imprint of The Quick Brown Fox & Company LLC.

Crooked Lane Books and its logo are trademarks of The Quick Brown Fox & Company LLC.

Library of Congress Catalog-in-Publication data available upon request.

ISBN (hardcover): 978-1-68331-122-5
ISBN (ePub): 978-1-68331-123-2
ISBN (Kindle): 978-1-68331-124-9
ISBN (ePDF): 978-1-68331-125-6

Cover design and illustration by Matthew Kalamidas/StoneHouse Creative. Book design by Jennifer Canzone.

Printed in the United States.

www.crookedlanebooks.com

Crooked Lane Books
34 West 27th St., 10th Floor
New York, NY 10001

First Edition: May 2017

10 9 8 7 6 5 4 3 2 1

Chapter One

Georgia O'Keeffe had brought me to New Mexico the first time in 1990—well, not literally. By the time I made my pilgrimage, she'd been dead for four years. But I reasoned that if I couldn't actually meet my hero in the flesh, at least I might be able to channel her spirit in the place she loved best. The Southwest had set her creative soul on fire; her canvases came alive with brilliant corals and turquoises. Such vivid colors; landscapes unlike any place I'd ever seen in Minnesota.

I'd talked about the "someday" I'd go West—when there was extra money, when my workload lightened up a bit. I talked about it so much that my dear husband finally had enough and bought me a round-trip ticket as a surprise. So I got on a plane, rented a car, and celebrated my thirty-sixth birthday blissfully alone. For one whole week, I wasn't a wife or mother; I was an artist. It was the best birthday I can remember.

I strolled Old Town in Albuquerque and bought silver jewelry from natives displaying their creations on woven rugs spread in front of them. In Santa Fe, I ate tacos and drank sangria in a café, feeling like a local as I watched tourists barter with vendors. I read pamphlets and checked maps. It was all very educational and beautiful, but I didn't feel the inspiration I'd hoped would engulf me.

As I drove north to Taos, I wondered at my disappointment. Maybe I'd seen too many quaint adobes or gotten over the excitement of spotting cactus and sage. But then I saw the Sangre de Cristo Mountains. I'll never forget that moment. The sun was behind a fluffy white cloud edged in pink, the only cloud in the sky. The mountains appeared navy blue, capped off with brilliant dabs of snow. I steered the car onto the shoulder and just stared. No one had to tell me that Taos was called the "Soul of the Southwest." I felt it inside me. And twenty-five years later, I still do.

*   *   *

It was one of those perfect days that happen far less often the older I get. Nothing hurt or ached. My clothes seemed to fit just right—no tugging, no label scratching at the back of my neck. As I walked toward the wooden picnic table, about a half mile from the main house, every part of me was happy.

But glancing down at my worn boots, I had to admit I did miss crunching gold and red October leaves beneath my feet. There really aren't seasons in Taos—well, not like back home in Edina.

The table was in an isolated area on the southern boundary of the colony. There were paint spatters across the sun-bleached top, and I wondered how many masterpieces had taken shape there. I was so content that I would have whistled, but I never mastered that particular art.

I'd been painting for about an hour when I heard Judy Lowenstein. Couldn't miss her—she was belting out a show tune a la Ethel Merman.

"Yoo-hoo, Katherine!" she shouted before getting to the verse.

There was no place to hide, so I waved. "Hi, Judy." *Please*, I thought, *please don't stop*. I tried sending her a telepathic message to keep walking.

But apparently, Judy wasn't tuned in to my frequency.

"What a beautiful day," she said, coming around to have a look at my painting.

"Perfect," I said and nodded.

"I thought the muse would visit while I soaked up some nature. Is it okay if I sit awhile?"

The last thing I wanted was to listen to Judy chatter all morning. But I'd been taught to always be polite, and old habits die hard—if ever. "Sure." I wiped my brush, then swirled it around in the bowl of water sitting on the table next to me.

She picked up the hem of her long pink skirt and walked around to sit on the wooden bench. "Thanks. I won't stay long. After all, we're all here to create. We all need our space. But that guy in cabin three . . . does he ever come out? I've been here eight days and I've only seen him once. He must go into town to eat or else he'd starve."

I dabbed my brush into a blob of deep purple. "Every artist works differently, I guess."

Harmony Village is a "creative colony," designed to encourage the artistic spirit. Ten small cottages circle a larger one where the owner, Bridget Ryan, and her husband, Will, live and work. Both are award-winning sculptors and two of the nicest people I've ever met. Breakfast is served in their large kitchen every morning. The rest of the day, we're on our own where food is concerned. In the evening, guests are invited to gather in the Ryans' great room for a social hour where drinks and hors d'oeuvres are served. Artists can register for a few days, a week, or a month, whatever they feel they need. Throughout the years, I'd met novelists, composers, playwrights, actors, and even a ballet dancer.

"Huh, I guess you're right." She took a deep breath, looked up at the lapis sky, and fell silent.

At first I thought she was meditating. The air resumed its calm. I was just starting to get comfortable with her being there when she started again.

"Well, I for one find that I need people to get the creative juices flowing. How can writers be expected to write realistically about life if they don't go out and experience it?"

Realistically? Judy wrote romance novels.

"To each his own," I said.

"You must have some great stories. I've never met a police chief before."

"Retired police chief."

"But I heard you just solved a murder. Didn't a woman get killed in some mansion last spring? You were retired then, right? So are you a private eye now? Isn't that what a lot of retired cops do? Become gumshoes?"

"No, I'm not a private eye—not exactly. I did some investigating for my daughter, who was representing a man accused of the murder. It was just a one-time thing."

"You're too modest," Judy said. "Have to toot your own horn nowadays. Promote yourself. Has anyone ever approached you about writing a book? It would be great—inspire a lot of women out there. Girl power is a hot topic now."

As she talked, I remembered our first meeting, how she had grabbed my hand into an aggressive shake, announcing, "Judy Lowenstein, *Love Comes Softly*." It had taken me a minute to realize that along with her name, she was announcing the title of her latest novel.

"No book. There are more than enough inspirational women out there to cheer on the younger generation. And I've always believed that every woman has to find her own way. But maybe a TV movie. That would be nice. And if Susan Sarandon is too busy, I could play myself." I wondered if she knew I was joking. From the look on her face, she didn't.

I concentrated on my landscape, trying not to laugh.

"So you live up here year-round?" she asked, changing the subject. "I was told no one could sign up for more than a month at a time."

"I worked out a deal to buy my cottage. And I travel back and forth to see my family often, so I never have to worry about losing my spot here."

"That's nice. And is there a man in your life now? You're a widow, right?"

"Yes. My husband got shot in the line of duty about five years ago. And no, there's no man that I'm interested in now."

"Well, you're still an attractive woman. You must get hit on all the time."

Still? Judy looked to be about twenty years younger than I, so she probably did think of me as old.

"I have my moments. How about you?"

"Oh, I married the boy next door. We've been together twenty years now. We have four great kids: Joanie, Jill, Joyce, and Jack." Before she could take out her phone to show me the family album, I turned to clean my brush.

"So there's no one special?" she persisted.

"No, there isn't, Judy."

"Please, don't call me Judy. I prefer Faith—Faith St. Charles. That's my pen name. A more fitting name for a romance writer, don't you think?"

"It's nice."

My phone chirped as I was putting away my supplies. When I picked it up, a picture of Nathan appeared above his number on the screen. I smiled.

"I have to take this," I told Judy . . . ahh . . . Faith.

"It's a man," she teased. "I can tell. You're blushing."

Chapter Two

Nathan Walker is a very . . . special friend. He's charming and intelligent, understanding and . . . okay . . . it doesn't hurt that he looks like Denzel Washington. We talk or e-mail several times a week when I'm in Taos, just to catch up on our news. Whenever I'm in Edina, we get together for a dinner or two. But there are two obstacles we both have to overcome before anything serious can ever develop between us: my husband and Nathan's wife.

Sully had been on the force a few years when Nathan was assigned to his squad. The fact that Nathan was black seemed to rub some officers the wrong way. When Sully saw what was going on, he requested they become partners. And that, as they say, was the beginning of a beautiful friendship. But the friendship ended abruptly when Sully was killed. Survivor's guilt did a real number on Nathan. It took a few years, but he was coming out of it when his wife, Terry, died of cancer. I'd come to think of Terry as a very dear friend and still miss her. The four of us would barbecue in the summer, go to the movies; we even spent a few vacations together. Maybe someday those two lovely ghosts will disappear, and the guilt will lift, but for now, Nathan and I are content to be just close friends.

"Nathan," I said anxiously, "hi."

"Katie, this is Rosie."

I answered so quickly that I hadn't noticed the call was coming from Nathan's business number and not his private cell phone.

"Hi, Rosie. What's up?"

"Can you talk?"

I glanced over my shoulder at Judy. "Not really. Is something wrong?"

"Call me back when you're alone. I'll tell you everything then. Okay?"

"Give me half an hour."

Judy could see I was upset. "Bad news?" she asked as I put my phone away.

"I'm not sure, but I have to go back and make a call—it's personal."

She must have seen the panic in my eyes. "Go. I'll gather all your stuff up and bring it to your place later."

"That would be great," I said and grabbed my tote bag. "Thanks so much!"

* * *

As I hurried, my mind conjured up all sorts of scenarios that would have prompted Rosie to call me. None of them were good. And soon my pace went from rushed to frantic.

After Nathan retired, he bought a security business from another police veteran who decided he'd had enough of Minnesota winters and moved to Florida. Knowing that he needed a staff, Nathan rounded up four people he referred to as his "crew." Rosie, a nickname Nathan had given her because she reminded him of Rosie the Riveter, was a master locksmith and B&E expert. In her early fifties, she's one tough cookie. I had worked with her on an investigation last spring and came to respect her many talents.

What could have happened that she and the rest of the crew couldn't handle on their own? I wondered. Over and over, my imagination played out horrific possibilities. *No,* I told myself, *don't go there. Wait. Wait to hear the facts.* How easily I slipped back into the comfortable skin of a cop. Facts are hard and cold. No getting around them. But the flurry of hypotheses you have to work through to get to them is what wears a person down.

Finally, I was at my front door.

After catching my breath, I sat in a chair by the window and dialed.

"Katie, thank God! Guys," Rosie shouted, "she's on the phone!"

I could hear voices in the background.

"I'm putting you on speaker."

"Who's there?" I asked.

"Polly, Brock, and me. E.T.'s out installing an alarm system."

I shouted a hello, and they responded in solemn tones.

"So what's going on?" I asked. "Are you guys okay?"

From the sound of it, they seemed to be trying to decide who should deliver their news to me. Then a male voice blurted out, "Mr. Walker's gone!"

"Brock! You couldn't have done that a little more delicate?" Rosie asked.

Brock was the muscle of the group—a huge man with a huge heart.

"Sorry."

"What do you mean 'gone'?" I asked. My heart started beating in my ears. I tried ignoring the thumping and concentrated on what they were telling me.

"No one's seen him since Friday . . . That ain't like Mr. Walker, know what I mean?" Brock said. "An' he was a no-show at work yesterday."

"Do you know what he did over the weekend?"

"We don't have a clue," Polly chimed in.

"Did you go to the police?" I asked.

"Well," Rosie started, "first off, we're not sure how many days he's been gone. It ain't as though we socialize on the weekends. We all do our own thing."

"And isn't it true that Nathan would have to be a threat to the public or himself before they'd get involved? Or be missing forty-eight hours?" asked Polly.

"That statute has actually been changed in Minnesota, but Chief Bostwick has chosen, at his discretion, to keep it alive in Edina," I told her. "Have you've been to his house?"

"That's the first place we checked," Rosie said, obviously agitated. "There was no sign of any foul play."

"Don't worry, we was real careful not to disturb nuthin', like you showed me," Brock said reassuringly.

"All of you went?"

"Hey, Katherine. It's me, Polly. There wasn't any need for all of us to go. It was just Brock and me." Machines and animals are Polly's passion. There isn't a computer out there she can't hack into.

"What did you find?"

"Nathan just had a tablet in the house. You know, to check e-mails and stuff, but the heavy-duty computers are at work. He has two here, in his office."

"Nothing on any of them?"

"Nope," Polly said. "Maybe he just wanted some time alone and went off by himself? Do you think we could be overreacting?" Polly's analytical mind was having trouble dealing with the emotional aspects of the situation.

"Come on, Pol," Rosie said. "You know as well as I do that the boss ain't that kind of dude. He'd never just go off and leave us hangin' like this."

"Of course he wouldn't."

"I don't care about statutes or rules." Like a dog with a bone, Brock just couldn't let go of the question of calling the police. "After being on the force for all them years, that ain't fair. They should give him special consideration—what's it called? Professional courtesy? Something like that."

"They should," I commiserated, "but that's not standard procedure. They have to prioritize, work on more important cases first. People go missing every day, Brock. We used to get half a dozen calls a week. Cops get jaded."

"When's the last time you talked to him?" Polly asked.

"About a week ago. He seemed fine, nothing unusual."

Brock piped up. "So now what?"

"Nathan's the puppet master," Polly said. "Without him, we're just a bunch of specialized brains. We're lost here without him."

I could only imagine the frustration they were all feeling.

"Katie, will you help us?" Rosie asked. "We've gone as far as we can on our own. We need some . . . guidance, ya know?"

"Of course I'll come. Let me check flights out of here and I'll call—"

"I got it," Polly said. I could hear her clicking away at computer keys. "Is tomorrow morning at eight too early?"

"You can't get something tonight?" I hadn't wanted to scare them, or myself, but kidnap victims were usually murdered within the first twenty-four hours of being taken. And there was no chance I'd be sleeping that night. Better to do something productive.

"There's a flight leaving out of Santa Fe at six tonight. But I don't know how you can—"

"Text me the information," I said. "I'll be on it."

After I hung up with them, I dialed Nathan's cell phone. My call immediately went to voicemail.

"Nathan, it's Kathy." He was the only person who had ever called me Kathy. "Everyone's worried sick about you." I sounded more stern than afraid. "Please call me. You know I'm always here for you . . . well, not here, in Taos. I'm taking a flight out tonight. I'll see you, I hope . . . tomorrow." I softened my tone. "If you're in trouble, I'll help. I'll do anything you need. Please, Nathan. Call me." I knew I was rambling but couldn't stop myself. Before I got beeped, I quickly added, "If you get this message, know that I'm going to find you."

Chapter Three

I called Lizzie from the airport while waiting for the announcement to board. After telling her about my conversation with
Nathan's crew, we both ended up with mixed feelings regarding my trip. I was going to see my beautiful daughter and
grandchildren, which would be fun, but the underlying reason
I'd be coming was almost too frightening to even consider.

Figuring we were done, I started to say good-bye when
Lizzie hurriedly mentioned she was leaving tomorrow for a
legal convention in Baltimore and would be gone for five days.

"Why didn't you tell me sooner?" I asked.

"Because my being away doesn't have anything to do with
your visit."

"What about the kids?"

"They'll be staying with Tom, at his apartment in town."
Tom was Lizzie's ex, the children's father. "You'll have the
house to yourself for a few days, and hopefully, when I get
back, Nathan will be home safe and sound. Right?" Her voice
sounded weak when she asked me to agree with her.

To make us both feel better, I went along with her hopeful scenario. "Right. He probably just went off without his phone. He's always forgetting it."

My daughter complains all the time that I analyze every person and situation to death. Since my retirement, I've been trying to do better. But part of me will always be a cop. And thank God for that, or I wouldn't even know how to begin looking for Nathan.

"I'd pick you up at the airport, Mother, but . . ."

"Not to worry. I'll take a cab. It'll be after eleven by the time I land, and knowing you, there's last-minute packing to do."

A heavy sigh, and then she said, "Okay, I'll give you this one."

"See you soon, Lizzie."

"Mother?"

"Yes?"

"Stay safe . . . please." It was something she'd said every day when I was on the force.

I answered with my predictable response: "I always do."

* * *

Lizzie met me at the door before I had a chance to knock. "The kids are asleep. You can see them in the morning."

I'd taken only four or five steps into the room, still clutching my purse in one hand and carry-on in the other, when she grabbed me into her arms and squeezed.

"Don't worry, Mother, you're going to find Nathan," she whispered into my ear. "I know you will."

Her concern was so sincere, it touched my heart, and I almost gave in to the moment and cried.

We stood there, just being close. My shoulder muscles eased a little. It felt good to relax. But we both knew when it was time to end our pity party and broke the embrace after a minute.

"You must be exhausted," she said. A single tear rolled down her cheek. "I got your room ready. There's wine in the fridge and fresh coffee, whichever sounds better. Are you hungry?"

"Let me kick off these shoes, and then a glass of wine would be great. Maybe a sandwich?"

"No bread. How about soup?"

"Great." I headed for my room while she walked toward the kitchen. "I'll be right there."

The frantic, wild woman I saw staring back at me from the mirror was scary. I thought I'd been doing a good job of hiding my fear. Maybe a stranger couldn't see it in my eyes, but I could. And I knew Lizzie must have seen it too. Even though my little girl is a competent, thirty-eight-year-old attorney and mother of two, she still gets upset knowing I'm upset. So I got out a comb and forced my lips into a reassuring smile.

She was sitting at the table when I walked out. I hadn't noticed her pink pajamas in the living room. The palm-tree and martini-glass print didn't quite seem like Lizzie's style and somehow that amused me.

"Love your pj's," I told her as I pulled out a chair.

"A present from Randy. To make up for the trip we were supposed to take to Hawaii for my birthday. Men can be so . . . so . . . stupid sometimes."

"Your birthday was three months ago, and it sounds like you're still mad at him."

"He opened another gallery, over in Bloomington. For months he was running back and forth. To the bank, to the new property, visiting exhibits so he could meet new artists he wanted to feature."

"I'm impressed," I said. "Sounds like he's really trying to make a go of his business."

Lizzie sighed. "Oh, he's working his butt off. And I'm very happy for him. But why, of all the days in the year, did he have to hold the grand opening on the weekend of my birthday?"

"It was thoughtless of him," I had to admit. "Especially if you both had this big trip planned."

"Two months!" she said. "All the details were set eight weeks before he decided the opening had to be that Saturday."

"What did he have to say for himself?" No matter what he said or what my daughter thought, I knew it was a classic example of passive-aggressive behavior. Looked like Randy hadn't changed all that much.

Randolph Pierce and Lizzie had known each other since high school. If the word had been invented then, you would have said he suffered from "affluenza." He misbehaved because he had no boundaries; his rich parents indulged his every whim. But after attending college in New York, he came back a mature, likable man. Well, until he was charged with murdering an employee. The last time I saw Randolph was at a party in his art gallery, celebrating his release from jail after Nathan and I turned the real murderer over to the police.

"At first he said he forgot. Can you believe it?" she practically spit the words out. "When he saw I wasn't buying that explanation, he said the event coordinator he'd hired only had that weekend open on their schedule."

"I'd say you have every reason to be angry."

"Half of me is the grown-up, telling myself that there'll be other vacations. And the other half, the unreasonable girl-friend who just wants to get out of this town and go lie on a beach, is pissed off."

She made me laugh. "Ahh, it's those voices in your head that'll do you in."

Lizzie opened the bottle of wine and nodded. "I hear ya. But enough about my silly problems. How are you?"

"Well, I've had time to make a plan and that always helps. First thing tomorrow, I'll go to Nathan's office and talk to his staff, catch up on what they've done so far. Then I'll see Bostwick and file a missing person's report. And I want to check out Nathan's house for myself."

Lizzie filled my glass and rolled her eyes. "Sounds like a full day. But don't count on Chief Bostwick giving you a warm welcome. He's been a very busy boy."

"I'm well aware I've never been his favorite person, so no welcome is ever expected. But what's he got going?" I asked.

"Last week a woman's body was found in a shallow grave out back of the old Coleman place. The paper's been full of it. But I keep forgetting that you're not much into local news these days. You know, most people, when they hit their sixties and retire to someplace normal, like Florida, usually subscribe to their local paper. Just to keep up with friends . . . family." She got up to ladle out a bowl of soup from a pot on the stove. But I knew she was also trying to hide that smirk that took over her face whenever she teased me.

"If you're waiting for me to buy a condo in Miami and lie around the pool, studying obituaries all day, you have a long wait, Daughter Dearest," I said, playing along. Then getting back to the subject, I asked, "Have they identified that woman?"

"Yes, two days ago," Lizzie said, walking back with a steaming bowl and a spoon in her hands. "Carolyn Watson. She and her husband lived out in The Oaks—off of Valley View Road. Did you know her? Or her husband, Sid?"

Having been born in Edina and having lived here most my adult life, I searched my memory but came up blank. "Nope."

"Well, you can check out the news tomorrow . . . or maybe your old pal Bostwick will fill you in."

"Yeah, right." Now it was my turn to do the eye-rolling thing.

The soup, creamy potato with broccoli, was one of Lizzie's specialties. It was meant to be a comfort food, but I knew nothing could comfort me until I got to work looking for Nathan in the morning.

Chapter Four

The glowing red numbers on the clock by the bed seemed to light up the room like a spotlight. I sat up, grabbed my phone, and dialed Nathan's number—again. This time, I couldn't leave a message like the dozen other times before. This time, his mailbox was full. But at least it was still a working number, which meant that it could be tracked. *Come on, Nathan,* I thought, *send me a message.* Concentrate.

We'd talked over the years about the mental connection between family members and close friends. Many times, we knew what the other was doing, even when we were miles apart. We joked that he was a strong sender. His mind had always been so focused and precise. I, on the other hand, was more sensitive to emotions and thoughts of others, which helped when I profiled a suspect. And that particular talent put me in the role of receiver.

I couldn't get comfortable, no matter how much I adjusted my pillow or blanket. All I could think about was Nathan. Was he sleeping? Was he hurt? Hungry? I promised myself that until this was finished, I wouldn't even consider the possibility that he might be dead. I wouldn't let the thought invade my brain. He was alive and I'd find him.

But I couldn't do anything until the morning.

Sleep. The time will go faster if you sleep, I told myself. But I couldn't even manage ten minutes with my eyes closed.

Frustrated, I got up and threw on some clothes, then crept out of the house.

* * *

The security lights were on outside Nathan's house. Daffodils that had been there the last time I'd visited were long gone. But the orange and burnt-red chrysanthemums Terry had planted years before still came back every year. The house looked neat and undisturbed from the outside.

We'd exchanged keys during my last visit. I took mine out and opened his front door. The crew had gone over the place, and I had no reason to doubt they'd done a thorough job, but I needed to see for myself.

I went from room to room looking for something—anything that might help find Nathan. Everything seemed to be in its place. There were a few dishes in the kitchen sink, probably left from the last morning he'd eaten breakfast here. His clothes hung neatly in the closet; his bed was made. Drawers were closed; the lamps hadn't been overturned. I walked around keeping my hands in the pockets of my jacket, thinking I was doing a routine search, but when I saw Nathan's slippers in the bathroom, I lost it. He'd gotten up the last morning he was in this house, thinking everything was normal in his world. Ate breakfast, took a shower, got dressed, and left for the office, same as every day. But it hadn't been the same.

I ended up in the living room. There was a picture on the wall, by the TV, of the four of us. Sully and Nathan clowning around, Terry and I laughing at them. Two of us were gone now. But I refused to let Nathan make it three. Sinking into the large recliner, cursing my tears, I sat there trying, with every part of me, to imagine where he could be. What was he doing?

* * *

I'd managed to get a few hours of sleep after returning from Nathan's but kept jerking awake. Finally, around 6:00 AM, I gave up trying.

My granddaughter, Chloe, loved surprises. At thirteen, one year younger than her brother, she was a happy little girl. But Cameron, who suffered from Asperger's, did not function well when his routine was disrupted. As much as I wanted to see my grandchildren, maybe it would be better if I just got ready and left. Lizzie could prepare them by saying I was in town visiting a friend and I'd see them later that night.

Getting out of bed, I tiptoed toward Lizzie's room. Light was streaming from beneath her door.

"Can I come in?" I asked softly as I pushed the door open a crack.

She pulled me into the room. "You're up early."

I told her my plan; she agreed not to mention anything about Nathan to the kids.

"They've known him all their lives," she said. "It would be upsetting to hear he was missing. You're right; it'll be better just to say you're here to visit a friend. You have your keys?" she asked, stepping into her shoes.

She was referring to the spare keys to her house and my Grand Cherokee. Sully had bought the jeep right before he was killed. It took a while, but now I enjoyed driving the vehicle around town whenever I visited.

"Yep. Have a safe trip, and please call me when you get there."

"No worries, Mother."

We hugged a quick good-bye, and I headed for the garage.

*   *   *

The sun was coming up as I drove toward Nathan's office. I hadn't even thought about breakfast, but my stomach had and was grumbling. As I sat at a stoplight, I spotted a small shop, the only business on the block that looked open that time of the morning. A bakery. It was a sign from Dad. Whenever I'd get upset or frightened, he always brought me chocolate donuts. I pulled over and went inside.

The warm fragrance of cookies and cakes sent me back to my childhood. For the moments I stood giving my order, I felt comforted.

Returning to the car, I carefully put the box in the passenger's seat while pangs of guilt jabbed at my heart. Was I trying to avoid starting my search for Nathan? Had I just wasted valuable time? I slammed the door and walked around to the driver's side, angry at myself.

Chapter Five

Situated in the corner of a strip mall, Nathan's office was lit up inside, but the large sign announcing "Walker Securities" was dark. Rosie's motorcycle was parked in front, flanked by an older car and a van.

When I pushed the front door open, you would have thought I was Santa Claus with a bag of presents instead of a lady with a box of food.

"How did you know we'd be here?" Polly asked. "You don't have a key, do you?"

"No."

"So how were you going to get in?" Her pretty face scrunched up in a confused expression. She knew everything there was to know about any electrical device. She was as high-tech as they came. But until she'd spent some more time in her skin and out in the world, she wouldn't be able to understand the concept of gut instinct. Disconnecting, swimming freestyle, going rogue. But she'd learn.

"They were afraid to call you too early," Rosie started as she rushed toward me, "but I told 'em Katie will probably be here before us. Then I remembered you don't have a key, so I got my butt outta bed."

"I think she slept here last night," Brock said, taking the box from me. "'Cause when I got here an hour ago, that hog of hers was out front. Sure glad to see you, Katherine."

"What happened to all your hair?" I asked. "Last time I saw you, you had a beard and lots of hair up there." I pointed to the top of his head.

He rubbed his bald head. "It was a hot summer. An' I needed a change. Ya know?"

Recognizing the lettering on the box, Polly looked pleased. "Caldwell's Bakery—they're the best." The small dog she held in her arms barked. "You remember Herbie, don't you, Kate?" The adorable pooch had been rescued by Polly from a testing lab.

"Of course I do." I scratched the dog behind one of his fluffy ears.

We all walked to the large desk in the reception area. The only thing on its surface was a pile of pamphlets listing various products and services Nathan's company offered. Brock put the donuts down, and the rest of the crew rolled their chairs over.

"Let me get Herbie settled, and then I'll bring some coffee," Polly said as she headed over to a pet bed in the corner. "I've been spending every minute here. It's put my schedule out of whack. The poor pooch gets frightened when I'm not home at night. If the boss knew I brought him here—"

"It's okay, Polly." I smiled and sat down.

I could feel fear rippling off all of them. After years of dealing with crime victims, I thought I'd gotten used to tension-filled rooms. But this was something entirely different. This time I was personally involved, not just an impartial observer.

"Where's E.T.?" I asked.

"He's got a meeting out at the library. Some of their computers went missing. Sad, huh?" Rosie asked. "A library has to have surveillance? Those kinds of places used to be safe when there were just books inside. But not no more." She shook her head. "Poor guy ain't doin' too good since the boss ain't here."

"E.T. would have a fit if he knew we had these." Polly put a coffeepot on the desk and held up a stack of Styrofoam cups. "Bad for the environment and all. But who has time to wash cups all day, every day? Certainly not the men around here, that's for sure." She raised a pierced eyebrow and looked sternly at Brock.

When everyone had a full cup and a donut in front of them, there was no more avoiding the subject. I got the feeling they were embarrassed; the three of them seemed almost ashamed they had needed to call me.

"Today's day three that Nathan's been missing—three work days," I began. "You saw him on Friday, and today's Wednesday. Of those five days, we only know his routine in this office. There's no way we can account for what he does on the weekend or at home. But it isn't like Nathan to miss three days of work. Correct?"

They nodded.

Polly brushed long bangs out of her eyes. "But of course, we're all worried that he's been in trouble all five days. He could have been kidnapped or . . . hurt . . . right after work on Friday. Or he ran into someone on Saturday, or . . ."

"For now, let's stay with what we know, okay?" I looked around the table. Everyone nodded glumly. "Was everything okay on Friday? Did Nathan look good? Did he seem upset about anything? Angry?"

"Same as ever. He was his old self," Brock said.

"Can one of you get me some paper and a pen?"

Brock jumped up and grabbed a legal pad off a nearby desk. Rosie took a pen out of the drawer in front of her.

"Here's what we know: Nathan's been missing for three days. His house hasn't been tossed, right?"

"Right," they said together.

"Where's his car?" I asked.

"Not here," Rosie said as she grabbed another donut. "And not at his house. We checked the garage, walked around the block, looked in every yard and driveway in the area. No sign of it."

"How did you guys get inside his house in the first place? Did Nathan give you a duplicate set of keys?"

Everyone sat quietly until Rosie spoke up. "Come on, Katie, you know there ain't a lock I can't pick." She shrugged and cracked a smile. "It's what I do."

Nathan told me once that it was the reason he'd hired her. Even after learning she had a criminal record—petty theft, breaking and entering—along with known connections to some unsavory characters, he added her to his crew.

"Polly, have you found his phone? There's a GPS chip in all of them, right?" I asked hopefully. "That means we can track his location or the last spot he was when he made a call."

She moved uncomfortably in her chair. "Sorry, but it's not exactly like you see on those crime shows. As a person moves over a long distance, their device switches from tower to tower. We could narrow down a location to a wide area, but a single reading won't give an exact location."

I tried not to show my disappointment. "Well, at least we have a place to start, right?"

Polly nodded. "Mr. Walker met with three clients last Friday. We contacted all three and found out he made every appointment. But he always comes back to the office at the end of the day to do his paperwork. He didn't do that on Friday."

"To be honest, none of us was here neither," Brock said. "None of us gave him a thought. Then he didn't show on Monday. Tuesday—nada. Somethin' bad happened or he'd be here." When he turned away from the table, I thought the big guy was going to break down.

Trying to draw attention away from Brock, I continued. "I'll need the files on those clients. And any others who have made complaints or caused trouble."

They all rolled their eyes and nodded. "Mr. Waterton," they said in unison.

"Nothing's ever good enough for that bastard," Rosie told me. "He's been a pain since day one."

"His mother died last year, and he got a bundle in insurance money," Polly said. "E.T. spent a whole day with him, suggesting the most effective units and where they could be placed that wouldn't mess with the decor. Finally, it was agreed that our number five security package would be the best."

"But he wasn't satisfied," Rosie said as she smoothed back her pompadour. "Nothing could ever satisfy him."

Polly agreed. "Nothing. He must have called here at least four times a day. Oh, at first, he was nice and polite. But after a week, he turned into a demanding monster. I don't know how the boss kept his cool."

"Looks like I'll need his file, too. Hard copies would be so much easier for me to work with." I had run out of patience years ago with computers controlling working hours. Or sending my progress off into a black hole, forcing me to waste time duplicating my work. No, paper never let me down. Give me a nice, clean manila folder, and I'm a happy camper.

Polly got up and wiped her fingertips clean. "I'll get those right away. But you don't honestly think that a little old man, a man who came in here using a walker, could hurt the boss?"

"Oh, he wouldn't have to raise a finger. His money would do all the work. You'd be surprised how cheap a criminal goes for these days. But let's not get distracted. We have to concentrate on motive. Who would have a motive to harm Nathan?"

Chapter Six

I looked over the files Polly had laid out in front of me. "Open the office at the regular time, and continue as you normally would."

"But there has to be more I can do. Maybe I could—"

"No. There might be someone watching. We want to give the impression that we have things under control. Okay?"

"I guess."

"And I'll need you here to coordinate our calls."

That seemed to appease her for the moment.

"I'm going with you, Katherine. And I'm gonna be stuck to you like glue, so no complaints. The boss would want me to keep you safe," Brock said, crossing his arms, daring me to contradict him.

"Do you have a gun?"

"Gimme a break here. I ain't some amateur."

"And what am I supposed to do while you two go chasing around town?" Rosie asked.

The front door suddenly banged open, and E.T. came running in. "I found his car! It's parked behind Bredesen Park. I didn't touch a thing, don't worry. I traipsed all over that park but couldn't find a sign of the boss. From what I could see, though, the inside looked okay. Nothing seemed to be missing. And there wasn't any . . . blood. Oh, hey, Mrs. Sullivan!" he managed between gulps of air. "Come on. I'll show you."

Polly handed him a small bottle of water. "What were you doing out there? You were supposed to be on a call."

"He don't want no one to know, but he's been drivin' around town every chance he gets—lookin' for the boss. He don't sleep much anyways, so it makes him feel useful," Brock said as we all focused on E.T.

"What does it matter how I found the car? I just did. Now come on, we have to get back there before any evidence gets compromised."

He was right. Every minute we wasted was one more minute a stranger could come along and unintentionally get their prints all over Nathan's car. Or an animal could leave DNA that would muddy the investigation.

I looked up at Brock, who stood beside me, zipping his parka. "We'll take my jeep," I told him.

*　*　*

E.T. sat next to me while Brock took his place in the middle of the back seat, leaning forward to catch every word. E.T. talked nonstop, pointing, directing me toward the park. He was agitated and frustrated. He'd pulled his long thin hair back in a ponytail. What looked like a stone hung from a leather cord around his neck. His bony fingers worked the buttons on his wool pea coat nonstop. This was definitely not the same man I'd met earlier in the year. True to her word, Rosie did not stay behind. She followed us on her motorcycle.

That man was calm and reflective. He'd been added to the crew because of his feng-shui knowledge, which allowed him to install alarms and monitoring systems in subtle, unobtrusive places in customers' homes or businesses. He was a vegetarian proficient in martial arts. And while he'd go to any lengths to avoid a confrontation, this man looked ready to explode.

"I retraced the boss's call sheet from Friday. I was scheduled to go with him that day, but there was a protest over at the courthouse, and I'd promised some friends . . . I should have done my job. I'll never forgive myself—"

"Hey, man, stop beating yourself up. You ain't doin' no one any good," Brock told him.

"He's right," I said as I steered toward the entrance of the park.

"Not here," E.T. said. "Go around there." He pointed to a side road.

Bredesen Park covers 206 acres. There's a two-mile trail to walk or bike around the area. Nine Mile Creek runs through it. In the center is a nature reserve with an assortment of animals. But it was the marsh and pond trails that worried me. Nathan could be hurt or, worse yet, in a watery place where we'd never find him.

I'd driven about half a mile when I spotted Nathan's car in an isolated area. Because it was dark green, it blended in with the fir trees surrounding it and was difficult to see at first. Once I parked, the three of us got out of the jeep without a word and headed over to the Nissan. Rosie pulled up alongside the car on her bike, removed her helmet, but stayed put.

I'd grabbed a handful of latex gloves Nathan kept in his office and now handed each man a pair, then took one for myself.

"I'd say it's been here for at least two days. A car doesn't get covered in this much grit and bird poop after just one day," I said, peering in the driver's window. "No sign of an attack. The upholstery isn't torn—no dirt or blood."

E.T. stood by the back window. "Like I said, everything looks fine."

"Any chance the keys are in the ignition?" Brock asked as he shielded his eyes from the sun and stared in at the steering wheel. Then he answered his own question: "Nope."

"You two are going to do a search of this entire area. One of you walk the perimeter. Slowly spiral around, working toward the center. The other one start in the center and slowly work your way out. Be as thorough as you can. You both have your phones?"

They looked at me like I was crazy for asking.

"Good. Stay in touch. We came here together; we're leaving that way. Call if you find anything . . . any little thing that looks wrong could be important. While I give the car a good going over, Rosie can start canvassing the neighborhood. There's got to be at least one person who saw something."

Both nodded, seemingly relieved that they had a definite job to do, and left.

Alone, I walked around the vehicle, inspecting every inch of it. I looked at the treads of each tire, inspected the hood, and scrutinized the doors from every angle for a dent, a scratch . . . anything . . . all the while, hoping I'd catch something that would lead us to Nathan.

Chapter Seven

I waved at Rosie to join me. She looked so cool on that bike, and I thought back to what Judy Lowenstein had said about girl power. If she wanted a strong female character to write about, she should meet Rosie.

Escaping Chicago, running from a thieving husband and his cronies, she'd had to make a new life for herself. And it wasn't until her ex was behind bars, sentenced to twenty years for armed robbery, that she felt completely safe. I found Rosie a truly inspirational woman. Maybe the millennials who read Judy's books would too.

"Wow," she said when she reached me. "Whoever hid the boss's car did a damn good job. It's a wonder E.T. ever found it."

"I thought that while I examine the inside of the car, you can start going door to door in the neighborhood, ask if anyone saw something."

She looked down at herself, slapping dirt off her black leather jacket. "Do you think people will wanna talk to someone who looks like me? I mean, I don't exactly look like a Girl Scout or an Avon lady, do I?"

She was right. "Well, you don't look threatening. But I see what you mean. Maybe you could go back—"

"Oh, no. I need to be out here . . . doin' something."

"Yeah, I know. Okay, let's start with the car. Do you think you can open it up?"

She unzipped her jacket and took out a small leather pouch. "Hold out your hands," she told me.

Using my hands like a table, she laid the slender satchel on my palms and then rolled it out. There were six silver tools, each in their own pocket. She bent down, studied the lock, and then reached out for two picks.

She worked for less than a minute before I heard the lock pop. With a broad smile on her face, she took the pouch from me and replaced the tools to their proper place. Then she stuffed the kit into her jacket. "There ya go."

I handed her a pair of gloves. "I've gone over the outside of the car, but you have a look while I'm inside. Nothing is too small to ignore."

"Gotcha."

The first thing I noticed was that there was no odor—good or bad. Nathan kept his car clean, so there were no receipts, mail, or trash of any kind. But wouldn't there be a clipboard or work orders somewhere? Typically, a customer signs a form when work's completed on a project. From cable installers to plumbers, every service person I'd ever dealt with needed my signature to prove they'd been there and done their job. Most came with paper—real paper and a pen. And all of them left a receipt. The same had to be true of the way Nathan did business.

I checked the mileage and made a mental note of it. Maybe, if Nathan used his car for business, he'd record the number of miles he traveled each day in order to reimburse himself for the gas used.

I inspected the headrest—it was clean. Gripping the steering wheel, I leaned across to open the passenger's door. My glove stuck to the wheel in spots. Something tacky had either been applied or run across it. When I looked closer at the glove and steering wheel, I could see no visible trace of blood. Sniffing the area, I did detect an underlying odor of polyurethane. It was an odor I was familiar with from not only years of painting but working on home improvement projects. Then I walked around and sat in the passenger's seat.

The upholstery was spotless on that side as well. Nothing suspicious in the glove compartment. I looked up at the ceiling of the car for spatter marks. There were none. "Thank God," I whispered. Satisfied there was nothing important to see up front, I went into the backseat.

The police would do a more thorough job and be indignant that I'd done my own search. But the clock was ticking down each second Nathan had been missing. It was only a waste of valuable time worrying if I was stepping on official toes.

I ran my hands across the back seat and then along the crevice between the seat and the back. My fingers hit something. Something hard. I pulled at whatever it was and came up with a cell phone. Opening the back door, I shouted to Rosie to come see what I'd found.

"That's his phone, all right. I'd recognize that purple case anywhere. We gave it to the boss on his last birthday. Just for laughs, ya know? We were all surprised when he used the thing. Turn it on."

I pressed the on button and then swiped my finger across the screen. The battery had only a 5 percent charge left. I was ready to tap on the message icon when the screen went black. "We'll have to take it back to the office. Nothing we can do out here."

Rosie shook her head slowly. "Somebody musta grabbed the boss. That's the only way he'd ever leave his cell behind."

"Maybe he intentionally stuck it in the seat when he knew he was in trouble. With any luck, there's something on it that will help us find him."

I carefully took out another glove and wrapped it around the phone. A knot was tightening in my stomach. "We still have to check out one more thing."

"What's that?" Rosie asked.

"Open the trunk. Let's see what's in there." I'd found a few bodies in cars throughout my years on the force. But I'd never known any of those poor souls personally. And as Rosie worked on the lock, I wondered if I'd be able to handle seeing Nathan's body in that trunk.

"Done."

My legs shook as she lifted the trunk lid.

A few spots of oil on the light carpet, but nothing else. We both exhaled a loud sigh of relief.

"I never knew the boss was such a clean freak," Rosie said. We both laughed uneasily.

"There was something tacky, like glue, on the steering wheel."

"Huh." She thought a minute. "Maybe he gunked up his hands doin' a job. Sometimes things can get messy, especially in them older homes."

"I suppose," I told her. "I'll ask E.T. about it later. But now, you call the guys and tell them I'm taking the phone to Polly." I looked at my watch. "I want all of you to stay out here until it gets dark. Divide the work any way you want, but one of you should start canvassing the neighborhood while the other two keep looking in the park. And don't let anyone touch this car."

"Don't worry. I'll take care of it."

"Thanks, Rosie." I started to walk to my jeep and then stopped. "Oh, and tell the guys to take pictures of anyone or anything suspicious. Get names and addresses. Be as thorough as they can. I'll come back for them around five."

"Will do," she said.

I still had my latex gloves on as I steered back to the office. Before handing the phone over to Polly, I insisted she put on a pair as well. While she unwrapped the cell, I asked if Nathan recorded his vehicles' miles every day, before and after work.

"We all did that," Polly said. "If the van was being used and we had to pick up some equipment or go to the post office, we got reimbursed at the end of the week."

I told her the mileage number on the car's odometer. "Can you look up the number Nathan noted at the beginning of the day on Friday, calculate the distance between each call he made on Friday, and tell me if the numbers match up?"

"It'll take me a while. But yes, I can do that."

"How long?" I asked anxiously.

"No more than twenty minutes." She started bringing up reports and addresses. I felt helpless, but all I could do was sit and watch.

After twelve minutes, Polly turned to me. "If the boss drove directly to his first call, and the next and the next, there are almost ten miles unaccounted for. But that could have been a lunch break or a stop to get gas, miscellaneous things like that."

"And how far do you think it is between his last call and the park where his car was found?" I asked.

Polly bit her bottom lip. "Less than five miles."

"Seven miles means whatever happened to Nathan happened in that general vicinity."

"What now?" she asked.

"I'm going to visit Chief Bostwick and then check out those three jobs while you see what you can do with that phone."

"Wish me luck," she said as an afterthought.

Chapter Eight

As I drove, I turned on the radio but instantly switched it off. I needed quiet to think.

There could be several explanations for why Nathan's phone was in the car, I reasoned. One: It had just fallen back behind the seat while he was working. A dumb accident. Things like that happened all the time. Two: it could have been knocked out of his hand during a fight or struggle. Road rage, maybe? Had someone chased him off the highway? Assaulted him? Was he lying somewhere, hurt? Three: he'd left it behind on purpose, hoping it would direct police to his location. Four: if someone took him, maybe they'd driven the car to the park and planted the phone to misdirect the search. Maybe . . .

I stopped.

Stay focused, I told myself. Wait until Polly checks the call history in the cell phone. Wait and see if the others come up with something.

But I was never good at waiting. With each member of Nathan's crew assigned a job, I headed for the police station.

I'd been Dean's superior for years. And for all those years, he expressed his displeasure at having an older woman for a boss, making snide remarks and jokes. Toward the end, he got bold and made them right to my face. Since my retirement, however, and his promotion, I think he'd mellowed a bit. The last time I'd seen him, we parted on good terms. And the murder case he was working now would certainly be his main focus, not an old grudge.

It was the big story in town. Customers discussed the demise of poor Mrs. Watson while I'd waited in line at the bakery earlier that morning. Listening to the car radio later, I'd been able to fill in the blanks.

Forty-two-year-old Carolyn Watson had been found, fully clothed, beneath a foot of dirt in the back of George Coleman's old barn. Coleman, however, was recently deceased, and his wife had died at least ten years before he had, which eliminated the couple from any sort of suspect list. The husband, Sid Watson, was a salesman and traveled a lot on company business. Ten-year-old David, their only child, was visiting his grandparents that week. The Watsons supposedly had a good marriage. From what I could gather, Carolyn was well liked, was a member of the Community Lutheran Church, and worked part-time at a boutique. Her body had been found before her husband and son even knew she was missing. In fact, her coworkers thought she was with her family. There were never any reports of domestic violence. The reporter said the police were asking for help in solving the crime; there was a ten-thousand-dollar reward.

Property crimes take up the bulk of the police force's time in Edina. Petty offenses, such as larceny, shoplifting, and vandalism, that don't involve force or the threat of force against a victim keep officers busy. Statistically, Edina, Minnesota, is safer than 73 percent of all US cities. Dean Bostwick may have been the chief for a few years, but that didn't mean he was experienced in all levels of crime. And now I was bringing him a possible kidnapping.

* * *

He was seated behind his desk when Officer DeYoung escorted me into the office. Bostwick glanced up from the papers he seemed to be studying and, realizing who was standing in front of him, leaned back in his chair.

"What are you doing here?" he asked, irritated. "There's no way you could have heard."

I was not going to let that man get to me . . . not today. "I assume you're talking about Carolyn Watson. It's no big secret. Her murder's all over the news."

Confusion flashed across his face. "I know it is. I thought you were here because . . ."

"I'm here to file a missing persons report," I said and sat down across from him.

"You know better than anyone that you can fill out all the paperwork at the BFD." He was referring to the front desk. He thought it made him sound cool to refer to the big front desk that way, but he was the only one with that notion.

"I think Bobby's on duty. You didn't have to come in here and bother me with that. I'm kind of busy with more important things."

"I thought you'd be interested in knowing who's gone missing."

"Okay," he said, crossing his arms across his chest. "I'll bite. Who's gone missing?"

"Nathan Walker."

Now he looked interested. "Sully's old partner?"

"Yes."

"Geez. Are you sure? Walker's one of the good guys. How long has he been gone?"

"No one has seen him since Friday, as far as we know. And don't give me the run around about how he's a grown man and can come and go as he pleases. You know how important it is that we move quickly."

"After you get the paperwork filled out, come back here, and I'll see if I can spare a couple extra men. You know, besides the detectives who'll be in charge and—"

"We found his car out at Bredesen Park about two hours ago. I inspected it inside and out." I waited for the lecture, positive he was going to rant about how I'd compromised evidence. This was the perfect spot in our conversation for him to zing me with a senile joke, asking if I'd forgotten how the police operated. I sat there, ready with a comeback.

"You're a professional," he said. "I'm sure you took the usual precautions."

Fighting to hide my surprise, I studied Bostwick. He'd always been so particular about his appearance, relentlessly striving for that *GQ* look. The guys would tease him about his plastic hair, every strand waxed in place. I swear he got more manicures in a month than I got in a year. But the man in front of me looked rumpled. The two top buttons of his shirt were undone; his suit coat lay in a heap on the chair next to me instead of neatly hung up. And now that I looked closer, I saw how bloodshot his eyes were and that he hadn't shaven that morning.

"Ah . . . thanks," I started. "I guess the Watson case is keeping you busy."

He nodded. "Did you know her? I mean, your family's been in Edina forever, right? You must have bumped into her occasionally."

"No." Then I got why he seemed to be taking the murder so personally. "But you did know her, right?"

He nodded weakly, like it was an effort to lift his head. "She was good friends with my wife. My youngest went to school with Davey. Great kid."

"And Mr. Watson?"

"Sid's a good guy. We're not buddies or anything like that, but he's good people. Never deserved anything like this . . . that's for sure."

"When was she found?" I asked as gently as I could.

"It's been eleven days."

"So why did you say there was no way I could have heard about Carolyn Watson when I walked in? The case has been active for almost two weeks."

He ran all ten fingers through his hair. I could see he was struggling, debating if he should tell me something.

Cautiously, he began, "What the hell, you'll find out anyway."
Then he abruptly stopped.

"Look, Dean, how do you think I lasted so long on the
force? I know how to keep my mouth shut. If there's something you want to get off your chest, you can trust me not to
say a word to anyone."

Then, like yanking a bandage off a wound, he blurted
out, "Another body was found."

I was stunned.

"Clear across town, nowhere close to where Carolyn was
found."

"A female?" I asked.

"No. A male."

My heart stopped. It couldn't be Nathan. Bostwick was
insensitive and irritating, but he wasn't cruel. If he'd found
Nathan, surely he would have told me from the start. When
I mentioned the report I was planning to file, he would have
stopped me. Wouldn't he?

Chapter Nine

"A Caucasian male in his twenties. No ID on him. Looks like he's been there awhile. No visible wounds. Could be natural causes, I guess. But that's not likely. A jogger spotted him off the road about fifty yards back. He was wearing camouflage pants and jacket, which is probably why no one saw him sooner."

"Did it look like there was an attempt to bury him?"

"No. Could have been a hit and run. Poor guy was just left out there."

So Dean Bostwick had a heart—who would have known?

"Well obviously, the two cases are unrelated. At least you know there's not a serial killer running loose out there."

His face went white. "I never thought of that."

"And you won't have to." I stood up. "Well, I better get that report filed." I wasn't going to tell him about finding the cell phone. That happened before Nathan's disappearance became official police business. Besides, Dean had enough on his plate.

He didn't stand up when I did. "Later," was all he said as I walked out the door.

Bostwick's offer to lend me two officers to help look for Nathan seemed to have momentarily been forgotten. And that was how I planned to leave it—for now. With the four members of Nathan's crew and myself, plus the detectives who would be assigned the case, extra men would only get in the way.

*　*　*

I dug in my purse for my phone. "What did you find?" I asked Polly as I sat in the Cherokee. "Please tell me you found something we can use."

"Sorry, Kate. Every number matches up with customers he dealt with. All very professional. Every incoming and outgoing call seems to be about business. Except for you in New Mexico. It's a shame the boss didn't have any kids or grandkids."

"How would that help us find him?" I asked.

"Oh, it wouldn't. I've just been thinking that he was so alone after his wife died."

Now wasn't the time to get melancholy. "What about pictures?"

"You hoping he took a selfie with the kidnapper?" she laughed. "The gallery is pretty much empty except for our last Christmas party, and we took those. Nathan uses this phone almost exclusively for work."

"What about texts?" I really didn't have to ask. Nathan always complained that his fingers were too big for those little keys. But I hoped.

"A few regarding jobs: measurements of living rooms, outside placements of surveillance cameras, estimates. You know, I don't understand why your generation—no offense—is so adverse to technological change. At least once a day, Mr. Walker would complain about his computer or cell. I was forever showing him how to go to a website or—"

"And your generation—no offense—doesn't understand that maybe we don't like the backward steps modern technology brings with it." I tried, believe me I tried, but I couldn't let another twentysomething sweet young thing tell me how the world worked. "Things used to be easier and more efficient. Phone calls didn't get dropped, books didn't need batteries, and business was conducted every day from nine to five without fail, because there weren't any computers to go down."

When she didn't answer, I realized I'd gone too far.

"Sorry, Polly, I didn't mean to go off on you like that."

"We're all upset, Kate. Not to worry. You and me are good."

"Thanks." I opened the top folder on the stack next to me. "I just filed the missing persons report. Have you heard anything from the guys or Rosie?"

"They're still in the park. Where are you now?"

"Sitting in my car, down the street from the police station. I'm going to check out the calls Nathan made on Friday."

"Should I send Brock to meet you? You might need some backup."

"Depending on the situation, I'll introduce myself either as a member of your staff or as an investigator. So if you get a call, vouch for me."

"You can say you're a field manager, something like that."

"Good. And call if you come up with anything on Nathan's phone. Even the tiniest thing could be helpful."

"You didn't say if I should send Brock. We can't have anything happen to you, Kate."

"You're right. Okay, I'll work my way through the three calls. I'll go in the order Nathan went and check in with you after each one. If you don't hear from me in a reasonable amount of time, send Brock. How's that?"

"Better." She sounded relieved. "Each call shouldn't take more than an hour, tops."

I looked at my watch. "It's twelve thirty now. I'm going to grab some lunch and then start at the Larkin house."

"Half an hour to eat, twenty minutes driving time, an hour there—I'll expect your call around three. Be careful, Kate, and please . . . find Mr. Walker."

Chapter Ten

The section of Excelsior Boulevard my GPS had steered me to was still under construction. Bulldozers rumbled; at least a dozen workers, all wearing yellow hard hats, yelled to each other as they pounded or sawed. Pools of mud and gravel made a temporary road through the half-finished neighborhood. Everything was coated in a thick gray dust, and I wondered why anyone would want to move into such a mess. House numbers were written on frames with a black marker. I bumped along, heading for the three finished homes beyond the noisy cloud. And there, standing like a fortress, was number thirty-four.

It was big; I'll say that for it. The fragrance of fresh-cut wood still clung to the Larkin house as I stood in front of the massive double doors. Instead of a bell, a heavy brass knocker would announce my arrival. I lifted it up and let it fall. While I waited for an answer, I took a few steps back to admire the etched glass panes on each side. They must have been ten feet high, both tinted amber. When no one came to the door, I lifted the knocker once more.

I could hear a dog yelping inside, and then a male voice shouted for the animal to shut up. Someone shuffled across a bare floor, and finally, the door was pulled open.

A man in his sixties scowled into the sun. "What do you want?"

"Mr. Larkin?"

He shielded his eyes from the glare and then took a good look at me. "Yes."

My instincts told me that I'd get better results with this man if I assumed a professional persona. "I'm Mrs. Sullivan, the field manager for Walker Securities. I see from our records that Mr. Walker made a call out here last Friday. Is that correct?"

He returned my smile, realizing I wasn't a threat. "Why don't you come in so we can have some peace and quiet?" He stood back, waiting for me to enter.

"Thank you."

"Let me put Fluffy in her room. I'll be right back." Mr. Larkin gathered the white poodle gently into his arms and walked out of the room, leaving me in the foyer.

The floor was white marble; the walls were papered in what appeared to be green silk. A large floral arrangement made up of mums and asters surrounded by orange and green leaves was in the middle of a marble table. It was all very formal and . . . pretentious. This man had a lot of money and wanted everyone to know it the minute they entered his home.

Walking over to the wall to my left, I delighted in seeing work by Molly Hartung, a newer artist I'd been following for years. Her technique of layering fabric and enamel was magical. But in what obviously was intended as a grouping of six, one was missing, ruining the symmetry. A large fin-de-siècle—which meant it depicted a scene set at the close of the nineteenth century—Cezanne landscape in shades of blues and yellows dominated the wall directly across from the door. The piece looked genuine, but I knew it couldn't be since I'd seen the original at the Art Institute in Chicago. Before I could study the crystal pieces on a shelf to my right, Larkin returned.

"All this fancy stuff, and I don't know a Picasso from a piccolo, but it sure cost a lot to insure it all." Obviously, he'd noticed me checking out the room.

"It's all very beautiful." Before I could be specific, Mr. Larkin pointed.

"We can sit in here," he said, walking ahead of me into the living room.

The three pieces of worn furniture looked silly in the spacious area. Mr. Larkin stood and pointed toward a wingback chair. "That's the most comfortable place in here. Be my guest." I expected him to make some sort of apology for the condition of the room, but he didn't. I thought he might explain that work on the house hadn't been completed yet, but he acted as though things were perfectly normal. So I followed his lead and smiled as I walked across the rough wooden floor.

He plumped up a faded pillow on the lumpy couch, then sat down. "So is this a survey of some sort? Everybody and his brother are all about surveys. Can't even get a hamburger without someone handing me a survey."

"No survey. This is just a follow-up visit to make sure the work done by our company was satisfactory." I took out a pen and opened the file. "I see you had four surveillance cameras installed around the perimeter of your house. Is that correct?"

"Initially. Mr. Walker assured me that four would be enough, but I wanted more—that's why I called again. He said they could always come back if I wasn't happy. And I wasn't, so he came out here himself, instead of sending an employee."

"And that's what you discussed on Friday?"

"More cameras, right. There's always someone lurking around all that equipment over there." He motioned toward the construction site. "Those men leave everything out in the open all night and then get upset if something goes missing. And there's so many of 'em! I don't think even the boss knows how many workers are on his crew."

"So you lump those men in the same category as petty criminals?"

"Damn straight. I worked hard for what I have, and just 'cause I'm retired doesn't mean I'm going to let some idiots come along and take it. The first night we were in the house, my car got broken into. And I heard this area is supposed to be upper class." He huffed his disgust.

"Were you the only residents living here at the time?" I asked.

"I know, I know, we should have waited to move in, but my old house sold quicker than we expected. That still doesn't give anyone the right to—"

"Of course not. I'm sure things will settle down once all the construction's done and you have neighbors."

"That's what the cops said."

I glanced over the file to make sure the cameras were the only items Nathan had sold Mr. Larkin. "And you found our personnel to be helpful and easy to work with?"

"Well, that guy with the ponytail, he was kind of weird."

I knew he meant E.T. and nodded. "But he's very good at what he does, wouldn't you agree?"

"Sure."

"You said 'we' several times. Is there a Mrs. Larkin?" There had to be. The foyer obviously reflected a woman's taste, while this room . . . well . . . didn't.

"She couldn't stand all the noise and dirt. She flew to New York on business."

So the husband was retired, and the wife was still working. Which probably meant she was younger. An actual field manager wouldn't be concerned with the marital status of a client or ask the next few questions I considered, but you can get away with almost anything with the right attitude.

"Well, I can't blame her. No woman would want to deal with all that dust out there. This house is certainly going to be a showpiece when she gets done with it. How many rooms are there?"

"Fifteen, I think," he said. "Give or take a bathroom."

"Do they still build attics and basements in newer homes?" And could Nathan be stashed away inside here somewhere?

"Well, not in this model." He pulled at a thread on the pillow. "Is that all you came for, Mrs. Sullivan, or is there something else? Like wanting me to sign up for an additional warranty or service?"

"Nothing else." I closed the file and stood up. "Thank you for your time."

"Tell Mr. Walker hello for me."

"I will."

After Larkin closed the door and I was settled inside the jeep, I called Polly.

"Is everything okay, Kate?"

"Fine. I just finished interviewing Mr. Larkin. I don't think he'd have any motive to grab Nathan. He's the type of man who just wants to be left alone. Would his marital status be mentioned in the files?"

"No, but I can look up his payment record and see if a credit card or check was used. Maybe his wife's name is on one of those. But why?"

"Just checking that he was being honest with me. Thanks."

"Sure. And I've been monitoring the boss's credit-card activity, which is pretty easy, since he only has one AmEx for business and a Visa for his personal use."

I didn't want to know how she'd managed to hack into those systems; I was just glad she'd been able to do it. "Did you find anything?"

"No. He filled up his car Friday morning, over at the Mobil down the street. It's on the way to the Larkin's, so no extra miles accounted for there. That was the last transaction."

"Isn't there a company van?" I asked. "I didn't see it this morning."

"E.T. keeps it at his place when he has an early job the next day."

"Oh. Have you heard from the guys?"

"About ten minutes ago. Still nothing to report. Should I tell them you'll swing by there and bring them back here when you're done?"

"Perfect. We can have a meeting to compare notes. Not too long, though. I have to go see my grandkids."

As much as I adored Cameron and Chloe, I wasn't looking forward to the distraction. And no way would they ever understand that I was too involved with something to see them. By now, Lizzie had told them I was in town, so there was no postponing my visit for a few days. Then there was Tom. Since he was divorced from my daughter, I wasn't sure how I felt about him.

I didn't need any distractions from my search for Nathan, but they were family, so I was just going to have to make it work.

Chapter Eleven

My second stop was also along Excelsior Boulevard, but in an older section, about five miles from the Larkin house. The yellow colonial belonged to the Ordway family. Nathan had made a notation that in addition to their three-year-old son, there was a new baby girl. Mrs. Ordway had contacted Walker Securities wanting a quote for audio and video equipment to be installed throughout the house so she could monitor not only her children but their nanny as well.

The neighborhood was quiet—too early for kids to be home from school. Even though I had their number, I didn't call first. Surprise was the best tool I had at that point. Catching someone off guard could sometimes tell me more about a person than an all-night interrogation ever could.

Before getting out of the jeep, I checked for messages. There was a text from Lizzie saying she had arrived in Baltimore safely, and that was it. Putting my phone in the tote bag with Nathan's Friday files, I turned to open the door and saw a small boy with his nose pressed to the front window of the house.

When I smiled, he waved. *What a cutie.* I waved back and walked toward the front steps. As I was reaching out to ring the bell, the front door was yanked open.

A petite woman, struggling to hold a crying baby, looked up at me. "Can I help you?"

The little boy I'd seen at the window came running over, grabbed onto one of the woman's legs, and started shouting, "Mommy! Mommy! Mommy!"

"Not now, Mikey!"

She had her dirty hair pulled back with a headband, had no makeup on her ruddy complexion, and was wearing an oversized sweat shirt and faded jogging pants. This woman looked like she was balancing on the edge and might go over any second. I'd have to handle her gently . . . motherly.

"Mrs. Ordway?"

Her pale eyes were focused on the baby, not me. "Yes. What do you want?" she asked impatiently. "I'm very busy."

"I'm with Walker Securities—"

"Oh, about the monitors. Your boss promised to call me with an estimate for the job days ago." The more agitated she became, the more the baby fussed.

"That's why I'm here." I smiled warmly. "To apologize for any inconvenience we caused you. Mr. Walker has been . . . ill . . . and wanted me to go over everything with you. Many times a client will change their mind, and we wouldn't want you to be unhappy."

"Couldn't you have done all this over the phone? I don't understand why . . ."

I was running out of excuses to get inside of her house until the baby started screaming. "Mr. Walker made a notation about your baby. He was concerned that the job might disrupt the household and wanted me to advise you of the time involved."

Mikey started yelling, again, "Mommy! Mommy!" trying to be heard over the baby's screams. Feeling sorry for this poor woman and also seeing my chance, I held out my arms.

"My daughter was colicky. Let me give you a break while we talk?"

I thought she might cry. Opening the screen door, she thrust the baby into my arms, grabbed her son's hand, and said, "Come on in."

It felt good to hold the little body, even if she squirmed to be free of me. As I walked into the living room, I tried not to show my surprise at the mess. Hundreds of Lego pieces, stuffed animals of all sizes, and pages ripped from picture books all were strewn across the living room carpet. A playpen had been placed in front of the TV, which was turned to a cartoon show. Cereal crunched beneath my feet. The place smelled like a potent air freshener had been sprayed to cover up the underlying odor of spoiled milk.

"Would you like some coffee?" she asked, in a hurry to get out of the room.

"Thanks," I called after her.

I sat on the edge of a large recliner, rocking the baby.

"That's sister!" Mikey shouted, looking me over. "She Beffany." Coming closer, he leaned over and kissed the baby on the top of her head.

"Are you a good big brother?" I asked.

He nodded.

"Here we go," Mrs. Ordway said, holding two large mugs. She put one down on the table next to me and then took hers and plopped down on a chair draped with a Disney throw.

When Mikey saw the cups, he started to whine. "Me too!"

"No coffee for little boys!"

Doesn't anyone in this house speak below a shout? I wondered.

"You must think I'm terrible, but it's been one of those days. Let me know when you've had enough of her." She motioned toward the baby.

"When I was raising my daughter, I realized one day that somehow she could pick up on my mood. If I went to get her up in the morning and was upset about something, she was a terror all day."

"Well she can sure feel your calm mood. Hopefully she'll go to sleep . . . finally."

I was unable to reach my file with the baby in my arms, but I didn't think I really needed it. "Have you had bad luck with babysitters and nannies? Is that the reason for the monitors?"

"Not really. But you hear all sorts of horrible things on the news every night. My husband, Mark, is a worrier. And a hypochondriac. He seems to get a new phobia every day. Last week, he saw a report online about a sitter that shook a baby to death. That's when he called Mr. Walker. Mark's on the neighborhood watch, checks the FBI's Most Wanted list, always trying to catch a bad guy before he can hurt us. There must be a name for that."

"Paranoia?"

She shrugged while a confused look played across her face. "Whatever it is, he drives me crazy, always so full of anxiety."

"Has he ever been the victim of a crime?" I asked.

"No. That's the crazy part. Neither of us has been robbed or assaulted—no threats, no stalkers . . . nothing."

The baby snored peacefully, and Mrs. Ordway's shoulders relaxed. Mikey sat in front of the TV, sucking his thumb. I decided to be straight with the woman now that she was calm.

"Years ago, when I was on the police force, I met people like your husband," I told her.

"Really?"

"Oh yes. And with the way the world is now, who can blame him? Has he thought about therapy? That might help."

"That's what I tell him." After a sip of her coffee, she smiled. "By the way, I'm Sophie."

"And I'm Katherine."

She stood up and came to take the baby out of my arms. "Let me put her to bed, and then we can talk about the monitors. I'll be right back."

Mikey didn't notice his mother leaving the room, and I had a moment to drink my coffee and double-check the Ordway's file. Even from an outsider's perspective, the amount of equipment they wanted seemed excessive. Was there more going on here than Nathan was told? Was it possible that Mrs. Ordway might be afraid her husband would hurt their children? Or was Mr. Ordway's paranoia the result of some real threat?

I spent an hour with Sophie Ordway. Feigning interest in the period of her home, I convinced her to take me on a tour, from top to bottom. Dust covering the floor and surfaces in the attic had been undisturbed. While no part of any room was immaculate, at least there was no sign she was hiding someone or something from me. I believed every word she uttered and promised to have one of the crew call with an estimate. Ideally, I would have gotten to meet Mark Ordway, but there was too much left to do that day to allow me to stay longer.

Chapter Twelve

The final call Nathan had made on Friday was in Hopkins, one town over. It was a small medical building, housing six eye specialists. But the job was for only one doctor, Easton Tate. The front of the building was lined with reserved parking spaces, so I had to drive around to the side. As I reviewed the file, I noticed several people huddled around a trash can near a back exit door. All of them were obviously on a smoke break, and as a chilly breeze whipped around the corner, they puffed quickly, eager to get back inside.

I tightened my favorite green-and-beige silk scarf around my neck. I'd bought it in Italy years ago, and it had gone on every trip with me since then. Then I zipped up my jacket before making the walk around the large building.

Beneath a glass cover, near the elevator, was a registry. Dr. Tate's office took up three suites on the second floor. After pushing the up button, I stood back to wait . . . and wait. As I started for the stairs, the elevator doors slowly opened. A nurse pushing a woman in a wheelchair started to exit.

"Is there someone to drive you home?" she asked her patient.

"My son should be out front. Maybe he's there now, but I can't see that far." The elderly woman adjusted an oversized green shade that had been attached to her glasses.

I felt invisible as the two of them chatted, unaware they were blocking my entrance into the elevator. Again I thought of making a dash for the stairs. But would I be saving time or wasting it? Minutes and hours were counting down, and I was growing more frustrated. Finally, I got to Dr. Tate's office.

The waiting room was large; there must have been at least thirty chairs lined up along the walls, each of them occupied. A large TV, turned to CNN, was holding most everyone's attention. Those not interested in the news, or unable to see it, talked on their phones (loudly) or to the person next to them. Three women were behind a registration window; none of them wore a uniform of any kind. Two were walking in and out of the enclosed office while one sat right in front of me, managing to avoid eye contact while she pecked away at her keyboard.

I stood in front of that window for a good two minutes, being ignored the entire time. Finally I said, "Excuse me . . ."

Before I could say another word, computer woman held up a finger, signaling me to wait. She did all this without looking me in the eyes once.

An "excuse me" or "just a minute" would have at least shown some respect. Or that she saw me. That arrogant finger wave might be acceptable in this multitasking, busy world, but I hated it. Every time someone points at me to be quiet or wait a minute, assuming their business is far more important than mine, I wanted to break that finger off! Of course, in this instance I knew it had more to do with my stress from Nathan being missing than anything else. This girl was just in danger of paying the price.

Fishing into the tote bag dangling from my arm, I brought out my police ID. Careful to cover the retired stamp across the bottom, I held it up. "I'm here to see Dr. Tate. This is a professional call."

That got her attention. It got everyone's attention—even the man in the corner with a patch over each eye.

"Come around to the door. Susan will let you in. I'll tell the doctor you're here." She said all this without so much as a smile or apologetic nod.

Her rudeness absolved me of offering a thank you. Besides, she'd gotten me angry, and it would take a few minutes to calm down.

Behind the door was a maze of small rooms. Most appeared to be used for examinations, but one was slightly larger than the rest. On the door, under the word "Private," was printed the doctor's name.

"Dr. Tate will be right with you. Have a seat." Susan motioned to two chairs in front of a heavy wooden desk.

It was the kind of desk that looked as though it had been in the family for years and had been moved, with great difficulty, into this office. In the middle was an old-fashioned green blotter; the design carved along the edges of the desk had been worn smooth in spots. A plastic model of an eyeball was propped on top of a bookcase. A large, colorful chart illustrating the optical nerves was centered between two windows.

It had taken years to hone the profiling skills that served me well during my time on the force. But now, trying to mentally draw a picture of someone before we'd even met was more of a game I played with myself. Seeing how close I could come was a challenge.

As I looked around the office, I determined the doctor was in his sixties, maybe older. Everything in that room felt well worn. He'd had his practice for at least thirty years, but somehow the office itself didn't suit the man in my mind.

Spotting certificates on the wall, I walked over to have a closer look. Easton Tate had gotten his degree from the University of Illinois in 2000. That would put him somewhere in his thirties.

As I settled back in my chair, a pale man wearing a white lab coat walked in.

"I'm Dr. Tate. My nurse said you're here on official business?" He smiled as he sat in the chair next to me.

I didn't know if it was his usual custom, sitting so close to his patients. Maybe he thought it made them feel more comfortable. Or maybe he wanted to throw me off guard. Whatever his intention, I moved my chair so that we were face-to-face.

"My name's Katherine Sullivan. I'm investigating the disappearance of Nathan Walker. I believe you met with him last Friday, to talk about additional surveillance—"

"Nate's missing?" His brown eyes opened wide with surprise, looking even larger magnified behind his bifocals.

"Nate? You knew Mr. Walker before Friday?"

"My father was his eye doctor for years. When Dad retired, I took over the practice. And when I needed help, I called Nate."

I took out my notepad and pen. "What kind of help?" I asked.

"This will stay between us, right? I know police don't take the same oath as a priest or psychiatrist, but I need to know everything I tell you won't leave this room."

"I'm retired, Dr. Tate," I admitted sheepishly. "My husband and Nathan were partners on the force. He's almost a part of my family. I had to scare your receptionist into action—that's why I showed my old ID card. It's important that we move quickly on this."

"Was it Gloria?" he asked. "Short blonde hair?" He didn't give me a chance to answer. "I've been getting a lot of complaints about her. Maybe it's time to—"

"I don't want to get anyone fired. I just needed to talk to you. When a person goes missing, time is crucial."

"Of course."

I continued. "And believe me, I have no interest in gossiping about your staff. I came today because you were the last job he had on Friday. No one in his office has seen him since."

He took a deep breath. "Anything for Nate." Then he got up and walked around to sit behind his desk.

"Good," I said, "let's start with the reason for your call. Because from what I could see, every hallway, elevator, and office in this building seems to have a camera attached to it. So why did you feel the need for additional security?"

"I wanted audio surveillance. You see, all the nurses worked with my father. Gloria, the receptionist, started with Dad part-time when she was in high school. That was back at the old office. We've only been here a year. I told Nate that I felt she was stealing my patients' personal information. A couple of my elderly patients told me their identities had been stolen. Insurance companies require we have a photo ID and social security number on file for every patient. Older folks make up the majority of my patient list. They come in here frightened, sometimes in pain and lonely. They'll talk your ear off. And if they know you, they'll tell you all about their family and finances. You'd think that a person who's lived a long life would have wised up, wouldn't you?" He leaned back, making his chair creak.

I nodded. "You sure would."

"I wanted to hire my own staff, but Dad insisted I keep his people. That was part of our agreement when he handed over the practice."

"Let me get this straight," I said. "You wanted Nathan to bug your offices?"

"Well . . . yes. Nate said we'd give it a month, and if nothing showed up, he'd take them out. You see, from the video tapes I reviewed, everything looked like standard procedure. The patient stands in front of the camera; he tells his information. And the nurse types it all into a computer. But I can't see what she's typing. If I could hear the questions she's asking . . . maybe she's going beyond what we need on the insurance forms. It was a place to start."

I made notes as Dr. Tate spoke. "And you met with Nathan at . . ."—I looked at the folder on my lap—"the end of the day on Friday. Around five o'clock?"

"It was more like five thirty. I had to make sure the patients were gone. I even told the girls to leave at four, just to make sure we'd be alone."

"And he was in good spirits?" I asked. "Nothing was bothering him?"

"Same old Nate. Big smile—cheerful."

"How long do you think your visit lasted?"

"Oh, I'd say we discussed the job for about an hour."

"Did you walk to the parking lot together?" I asked. "You know, leave the office at the same time?"

"No. I had paperwork to finish up. Nate left before me. I asked if he had plans for the weekend, though, before he took off."

"Did he?"

"No. So I told him I was going to our lake house Saturday morning and he should come up. But you know how he is since Terry's been gone. He'd rather be alone, I guess."

"And that was the last time you saw him?" I asked, folding my note pad.

"Yep." He stared down at his desk. Then struck with an idea, he looked at me. "Have you thought that maybe he got into an accident on the way home from here?"

"We found his car this morning, out at Bredesen Park. There was no sign of him, and the car's in perfect shape. Not even a ding. Maybe we could call your father and ask if he—"

"Dad and Mom are on a cruise, have been out of the country for ten days. As far as I know, they haven't seen Nate since our Fourth of July barbecue."

"And where are your folks cruising?" I asked, planning to give Polly the name of the ship to check out the doctor's story. The smallest detail could unravel a mystery.

* * *

When there was nothing more to ask, I thanked Dr. Tate and left his office.

As I walked to my jeep, I couldn't stop wondering why not one page of Nathan's notes was marked confidential. If this particular job was so secret, wouldn't that make it unusual and out of the ordinary? And yet no one in Nathan's office had told me the special circumstances. Were they even aware of the situation? I'd have to remember to ask E.T. if he'd handled similar cases.

Chapter Thirteen

I pulled out my phone in the elevator and checked in with Polly. As I walked to the parking lot, I told her that I'd just finished with the last of Nathan's Friday calls. She said E.T., Brock, and Rosie were still questioning people around the park area.

"Would you tell them I'll pick them up in about an hour, depending on traffic? They can meet me by Nathan's car."

"Rosie said two cops came out to go over the vehicle. When they're done, they'll haul it to the impound lot to examine it more thoroughly."

"Good. Sounds like Bostwick's on top of things."

"Anything else?" she asked.

"When I get back to the office, we'll all sit down to compare notes."

"Okay then, see ya soon. And Kate . . . ?"

"Yes?"

"Don't get discouraged. We'll find him."

"I was going to tell you the same thing."

* * *

I could see two people smoking outside the building as I approached the jeep. And I suddenly remembered something a friend had told me years before about her first day on a new job.

The smokers in the building were allowed fifteen-minute breaks every three hours, not to mention lunchtime. Thinking she'd found a quiet spot, she walked upstairs to the roof and was surprised to see a group of ten others who jokingly welcomed her into their exclusive club. Gathering at the same times every day, week after week, the members became friends, and as they smoked, they gossiped. They talked about office personnel, from the CEO to the janitor. They talked about their own spouses and personal problems. The tiniest tidbit could be fuel for hours of conversation. Children's school grades were analyzed; vacation plans were reviewed. They even knew the times the UPS truck arrived and the mail was delivered. It was like a real-life soap opera, she told me once. The Smoker's Club knew everybody's business in every department; nothing got past them.

With this thought in mind, I walked over to the two women.

The alcove they stood in kept out the cold but also held in the smoke. As I got closer, my eyes started to sting.

"Excuse me, my name's Katherine Sullivan. I'm investigating the disappearance of—"

"For real?" A large woman huddling beneath a puffer coat asked. "Like on TV?"

"Yes, just like that." If this was the way to get them to talk to me, I'd play the roles of Jim Rockford and Magnum PI if I had to.

"I'm Cee, and that's MaryJo," a small black woman said. "I'm a sucker for all those crime shows. So who's gone missin'?"

"His name's Nathan Walker. He owns a surveillance company and was on a call out here Friday. He came to see Dr. Tate. He didn't leave the office until six o'clock. I don't suppose you girls work that late?"

"I do," Cee said. "I work for Dr. Crawford on the first floor. Fridays he's here til nine."

"What's your Mr. Walker look like?" MaryJo asked.

"He's African American, six feet tall, around one ninety, and he . . . well he . . . looks like Denzel." There was no need for a last name. Everyone knew who the actor was just at the mention of his first name.

Both women appeared starstruck.

"Oh my, yes, I do remember seeing that man coming into the building as I was leaving for the day. Monday morning, Cee and I talked about him. We don't get many gorgeous hunks of chocolate in here," MaryJo said. Then to Cee, "Remember how you said if you were a few years older, you'd go and—"

"Girlfriend, I was lyin'. That man was ageless. I'd go out with him now, then, or in twenty years." She smiled to herself at the memory.

"And this is the person who went missing?" MaryJo asked.

I was getting hopeful that these two could give me some solid information. "Yes. No one's seen him since Friday. So, please, tell me everything you can remember."

"Like I said," MaryJo began, "I was going home when Mr. Walker was coming in. He smiled at me. I remember thinking how he was so handsome. That's all I know."

I turned toward Cee. "And you were where when you saw him?"

"Right here, all alone. It was around six forty-five and colder than my ex-husband's heart. I remember thinking that if I didn't kick this vile habit"—she held up her cigarette—"real soon that I was gonna freeze to death. That's when I saw Mr. Walker. He was going to his car, I guess. This lot's lit up real good, but there are some dark spots. We complain about it. It isn't safe for us women who have to work late, not to mention that there have been cars broken into. And if someone was screamin' for help out there, they might not get heard. There's always commotion what with visitors and doctors, car alarms, and such. The noise can get deafening."

"What do you mean you 'guess' it was his car?" I asked, trying to get her back on track.

"Well, a man was standing by a little car, like he was waiting for someone. They talked awhile—Mr. Walker and that man. I couldn't tell if they were friendly or not, but there was no shouting or anything like that going on."

"Did Mr. Walker look happy to see this person? Did everything seem normal?"

"Honey," she said, "we both know that normal's just a setting on the washin' machine."

I laughed and had to agree with her.

Cee continued. "So your friend talked to this guy awhile, and then they got into a bigger car—it was either green or black—and drove away. That's all she wrote. Sorry."

"Can you describe the other man?" I asked, praying that she could.

"Like I said, it was dark, and the cars were in a corner over there. But I could make out that the guy was about the same size as your man and he was wearing this raggedy old jacket. I remember that for sure."

"Why?"

"Because my ex used to have a jacket like that. Thankfully he only wore it when he went hunting. After he moved out, the first thing I did was burn that old thing."

MaryJo laughed. "Amen to that."

"Can you be more specific?" I asked. "Exactly what did this jacket look like?"

"Green, black—dark like that—with a hood. You know, camouflage, same as the army men wear."

"What do you think of Dr. Tate?" I asked. "Is he a good guy?"

"Never heard anything bad about him. It's that nurse of his no one can stand."

"Gloria?" I asked.

"Around here we call her Godzilla," Cee told me.

It looked like I got all I was going to from them, so I wrapped things up. "You two have been great. Let me give you my number. Please call if you remember anything." We programmed my cell number into their phones.

After thanking them again, I hurried to my jeep.

Nathan always said there was no such thing as a coincidence in a police investigation, that every bit of information meant something. And I always disagreed with him. The universe, inside our head and outside in the world, is constantly bombarding us with facts and memories, opinions and garbage. There's just too darn much of the stuff for it all to have significance.

Lots of men own camouflage jackets, I reasoned. Women, too. The military look is always in style. Cee could be wrong, though. She admitted that it was difficult to see certain areas of the parking lot. The fact that the body Bostwick told me about was wearing a camouflage hoodie could have no connection at all to Nathan. But just in case . . . it wouldn't hurt to check it out.

Chapter Fourteen

Brock and E.T. were waiting for me when I pulled around the corner. Rosie rode back to the office on her bike. Nathan's car was wrapped with yellow police tape. When E.T. started to get into the back seat, I hurried around and asked him to drive so I could call Bostwick.

The police chief sounded more tired than irritated when he recognized my voice. I asked if there was any news regarding the identity of the man they'd found earlier.

"Why are you asking?" he asked. "This has nothing to do with Walker. And especially nothing to do with you. I shouldn't have told you anything about it this morning."

"There might be a connection, Chief." I hoped that by addressing him that way, he'd know I was offering my respect. If only he could drop that macho act, we might be able to work together . . . at least long enough to find Nathan.

I briefed him on what I'd done all day, ending with my interview with Cee and MaryJo. Then I topped it all off with the sighting of Camo Guy.

"Come on," I pleaded, "it could be a lead, if not for your case, then for mine."

"Look, Sullivan, right now I'm focused on finding out who killed Carolyn Watson. I haven't gotten a decent night's sleep since she was found, and I don't intend to let up until I get her killer. The John Doe in the morgue is probably just a transient who happened to be in the wrong place at the wrong time. I've assigned two of my men to work that case. Come on, we've both seen our share of hit and runs."

"Yes, we have . . ."

"And I've just released an official statement asking the public for help identifying the man. Standard procedure in a case like this—you know the drill. There's nothing more I can do for that guy."

A small part of me felt sorry for Dean, but a larger part wanted to tell him that he was too personally involved to be handling the Watson case. But instead of offering encouragement or lecturing him about the importance of remaining professional, I just thanked him for his time and hung up.

Closure—the Holy Grail of cures. Prescribed by therapists, talk show hosts, and support groups daily, it's an elusive, invisible entity that we're all looking for but rarely find. Truth is, no one's life is tied up with neat little bows. We're all tangled in a lot of ragged loose ends. And the longer we live, the more knotted they get until we have to either cut them loose or just stop moving forward.

Dean needed to solve Carolyn's murder for her family and also for himself. He needed answers. He needed closure. But being a police chief meant there would be other crimes to solve that would lead to more questions, most of which would forever go unanswered. And Rosie, E.T., Brock, and Polly needed closure. But I needed it the most. Nathan wasn't just a boss I saw five days a week between nine and five. He wasn't a casual acquaintance. He was my best friend. And at my age, there wouldn't be many more of those.

*   *   *

By six o'clock, the five of us were all back in the office. We gathered around the front desk. I started off with what I'd learned from Cee and MaryJo. Then I continued, reporting my visit and later conversation with Bostwick.

"That Camo Guy has to be the bastard who took the boss!" Brock shouted. "And now he's dead? Is that what happened?"

"We don't know it's the same man. These could be two separate incidents. Calm down, Brock," I said.

"Katie's right." Rosie reached out to pat Brock's hand. "You're not any good if you go psycho on us."

Brock nodded. "It's just that I'm so . . . so . . . scared for the boss."

I tried to reassure him. "We all are. But we can't find Nathan unless we calm down and work together." Then I turned to Polly. "Did you find anything else on the phone or computer?"

"At seven thirty-two, Friday night, there were several numbers dialed on the boss's phone. Each call lasted less than ten seconds, so at first, I assumed they were just butt dials. Nathan keeps his phone in his back pocket sometimes and that happens."

"No way would the boss ever get into some strange guy's car . . ." Rosie began.

"Unless that creep was holdin' a gun on him," Brock finished.

Polly nodded excitedly. "And there was probably a struggle, the phone kept dialing while they wrestled, and somehow it got jammed in the backseat. We could call all the numbers to see if anyone heard anything, but you know how people are with those kinds of calls. They laugh and hang up."

"It's all my fault." E.T. bowed his head, looking embarrassed. "I should have been with him. I should have been there."

I had to save everyone from their imaginations. "Look, the only fact we have now is that Nathan was seen last Friday getting into a green or black car with a man in a dark jacket. That's it. No one saw a struggle or a gun; he wasn't even forced into the car as far as the witness could see. There could be dozens of explanations."

When they all agreed with me, I knew it was because my theory was much safer than theirs.

"Rosie, what have you got?" I asked.

"Nothin'. Not one single thing. I stood around while the forensic team went over the car. I asked so many damn questions that I thought for sure they were gonna haul me in for obstructing an investigation or somethin' like that. But all they kept sayin' was they couldn't tell me anything. After they left, I combed every inch of that park again until it was dark."

I looked at Brock and E.T. "Did you find anyone who saw something on Friday or maybe during the weekend?"

"No," E.T. said. "Most people in that neighborhood worked on Friday. And Saturday and Sunday, it rained, so most of them were inside."

"So now what?" Brock asked.

"Tomorrow I'll go to the coroner's office and see if they found out anything about the hit and run. While I do that, I want all of you to search your files and memories. There have to be some clients who weren't happy with your installations. Or maybe someone had words with Nathan? Go back as far as you can."

Rosie scooched her chair closer to the desk. "You know, the boss musta made some enemies from his time on the force. Suppose he was responsible for sendin' some lowlife to the joint, and for years and years, that con's been planning his revenge. Finally he gets out, and when he does, he comes for the boss."

"You're reading my mind," I told Rosie. "Revenge is one of the leading motives behind most—" I stopped myself before I said "murders."

"Grudges don't have expiration dates," E.T. said. "I've learned that the hard way."

E.T. was what my mother would have called "an odd duck." Of the four members of Nathan's crew, I knew him the least.

"There was something tacky on Nathan's steering wheel," I told E.T. "It smelled like glue or paint. Do you ever use anything like that on a job?"

"Oh sure. There have been some challenging situations. Remember last year, Polly? That woman over in the apartments on Cedar?"

Polly shook her head and rolled her eyes. "I think she was paranoid with a touch of OCD."

"What happened?" I asked them.

E.T. folded his hands on top of the desk. "She swore the rental agent was coming into her apartment while she was at work and moving things around. Not stealing them—just moving things to mess with her. She wanted a few cameras installed but gave strict instructions that we couldn't make any holes in the wall. Finally the boss had to use some industrial strength glue that dried clear."

At least that might have explained why the steering wheel of Nathan's car seemed sticky.

"You learn more than you'd ever want to about people when you go where they live," I said.

"Too much," E.T. said.

After a moment, Rosie spoke up. "So are you coming in early tomorrow?"

I didn't get a chance to answer because my phone started ringing. Looking down at the number, I saw it was Tom, my ex-son-in-law.

"Tom! I'm so sorry I didn't call. It's been a crazy day . . ."

"Lizzie told me about Nathan. I'm so sorry, Kate. And believe me, I wouldn't bother you, but Cam and Chloe are here, and they won't eat dinner or go to bed until they see you."

I felt a flash of resentment that I'd have to put my search for Nathan on hold for a few hours and switch into grandmother mode.

After the resentment passed, guilt took over.

"I'm just finishing up a meeting. I can be there in half an hour. If that's too late for the kids to eat, I can—"

"Not to worry. You know where I live now? I assume Lizzie gave you the address."

"Yes, she did."

"Then we'll see you. Hope you like sweet and sour chicken. I ordered from the place on the corner."

"Love it. I'll see you soon."

Brock started to get up. "We'll all be here at eight tomorrow morning," he said.

"Then so will I."

Polly came around to me. "Thanks for everything, Kate." She gave me a quick hug.

"Yeah," Rosie said. "Thanks. I don't know what we'd do without you."

"Just count me as a member of the crew, okay?"

"Sure," Brock said. "And when we find him, the boss can give you a nickname like he done us."

"I can hardly wait."

Chapter Fifteen

Thomas Farina was charming and handsome. He studied under some of the best doctors in Europe and finally got his medical degree at Harvard. By the time he married my daughter, he was a prominent surgeon. Their wedding was written up in all the society pages; they were the picture-perfect couple. Sully said Tom looked exactly like the groom on top of the wedding cake—plastic and shiny. He shrugged off his son-in-law's superior attitude, never taking offense at his condescending remarks. As long as Lizzie was happy, that's all that mattered.

I, on the other hand, knew right from the start that Tom wasn't the right man for Lizzie. I tried, ever so gently, to point out little things that would sooner or later become major issues. But she was blinded by love. And being my only child, I didn't want to ruin our relationship, so I learned to shut my mouth and smile . . . a lot.

When Tom gave up his practice and joined Doctors Without Borders, I still kept silent. Lizzie needed support while she was working full time as an attorney and raising two children. I did what I could to help, but I came to think of Tom's working in foreign countries as more of an escape than an altruistic act. When everything finally came to a head and divorce papers were drawn up, I still kept my mouth shut, but I couldn't help but be relieved.

I drove into Tom's complex expecting to see nondescript apartments crammed together on small parcels of land. But as I passed a fountain, populated by baby ducks, I was impressed. Large oak trees bent over the private drive that wound between brick townhouses. Yellow and red mums trailed along either side of the road. Ornate wrought-iron lampposts held white globes that lit the way. I passed tennis courts, a swimming pool, and a clubhouse before finding his front door and parking in a spot marked "Visitor." As I got out of the jeep, I could see Chloe through a large bay window. I started up the steps. Before I could knock, the door was jerked open.

"Grandma!" Chloe shouted. "Daddy, Grandma's here!" Then she threw herself at me and hugged with all her might.

Chloe was thirteen and at that uncomfortable age when she was unsure how she felt about anything. And that uncertainty manifested itself in moods ranging from nobody-loves-me depression to Taylor-Swift's-new-album-came-out-today euphoria.

"Hey, Chloe Girl." I hugged her back and kissed the top of her head. Soon enough she'd be just as tall or taller than me, and I wouldn't be able to bury my nose in that soft red hair. The choppy layers that had been there on my last visit had grown out and now fell down to her shoulders.

"Let your poor grandmother come inside," Tom told her, smiling at me.

Walking across the threshold was like wandering into a magazine spread. Surely Tom must have hired a professional decorator. It was beautiful. Every detail was done to perfection, all in masculine browns and beiges with touches of burgundy. As I took it all in, I scanned the room for my grandson, Cam.

"Wow! Tom, this is gorgeous."

He smiled broadly. "I'm so glad you like it. I was worried you'd think I was forcing the kids to stay in some dirty hovel."

"Well, it's wonderful."

Chloe ran into the kitchen. I could hear her whisper to her brother, "Cam, Grandma's here. Come say hi."

Slowly Cam walked into the room, keeping his distance. But I was used to his reticence and never took it to heart. Asperger's syndrome made social interaction difficult for him. I just had to respect his space and give him a few moments to adjust to me again.

"Hi, Grammy," he finally said.

"Well, you look handsome as ever. And I see you still have the Mohawk."

Cam was a year older than his sister, a B student and exceptionally creative. I took all the credit for his artistic soul . . . but kept that to myself. Some of my happiest times have been sitting alongside him, each of us painting, sharing our thoughts and secrets.

"We've been waiting for you so we can eat," he said.

"Sorry, but I'm glad you did. I'm so hungry I could eat a . . . plate of frogs."

He laughed. "Gross, Grammy."

As his mood lightened, he walked toward me for a hug.

"Chloe," Tom called, "is the table all set?"

"Yep."

"Right this way." Tom motioned for me to follow him.

To the right of the living room was a formal dining area. The walls were painted a rich taupe, hung with pictures from Tom's travels, all framed in gold. A large table was positioned beneath a chandelier that appeared to be made of teak. There were four places set with elegant dishes and linen napkins. Sensing Tom's happiness at pleasing me, I realized that while he was wrong for Lizzie as a life mate, that didn't mean he wasn't still a good person. And as he was still Cam and Chloe's father, I owed it to him to give him a second chance.

We all took our places, and Chloe started by passing a large bowl of white rice. Cam sat across from me, next to his father.

"So how long are you home for this time?" I asked. I was still aware of his questionable history.

"Dad's staying longer," Cam answered before his father had a chance to speak. "He says he wants to know us better."

I looked from Cam to Chloe. "That's great. Isn't it?"

"I wanted the chance to be with the kids more. In a few years, they won't have time for me. You know how it is, Kate . . . ahh . . . Mom."

I nodded. "When Lizzie was Chloe's age, all of a sudden she wanted to spend her time with friends, not Sully and me.

But by this age, you've taught them all the basics. Now your job is to just stand on the sideline and shout advice."

"I'll have to work on the standing back part," Tom said, grinning.

Cam scooped up a large spoonful of rice and carefully emptied it onto his plate. "That's for sure. Dad still thinks I'm a little kid. He's always trying to tell me how to do things I learned years ago."

"I just haven't been around you a lot recently," his father told him.

If Tom blamed the divorce or my daughter for his situation, he was smart enough not to complain in front of his children.

"So, Chloe"—I turned toward her—"are you still friends with Jennifer?"

Chloe nodded enthusiastically. "Jen's so cool. Every morning we send each other our OOTDs and—"

"Your what?"

"All the girls do it now," Cam grumbled. "They take a selfie before they go anywhere. Like they need all this approval. As if anyone cares what their Outfit Of The Day is. Stupid, huh?"

"I think it sounds like fun," I said. And I meant it.

Every time I ranted about recorded messages instead of real people on the other end of a phone, or how every computer had a built-in obsolete factor, or there being thousands of TV stations and nothing to watch, I knew I was standing on a senior soapbox. But if I were Chloe's age, I'd be the champion texter or queen of the selfies.

"See!" Chloe gloated. "It's not stupid." She stuck out her tongue at Cam.

Tom seemed to be enjoying himself, watching his kids.

We passed around the chicken. Tom had brewed a pot of tea and placed a matching porcelain teacup by our plate. The atmosphere in the room was light, and that night, neither of the children seemed to want to hurry off. They chattered about school and Thanksgiving vacation, when Tom would be taking them to the Bahamas. Their happiness filled the dark hole in the pit of my stomach . . . for a while. By the time we were done with dinner, it was almost nine.

"You guys can watch one hour of TV and then it's bedtime."

They didn't argue with their father.

"I'll come in to say goodnight before I leave," I told them.

"Will you come back tomorrow?" Chloe asked.

"For sure."

"TTFN," she said after kissing my cheek.

Tom leaned in to translate, but there was no need. I knew a "ta-ta for now" when I heard it. So I replied with text speak of my own, just as a reminder to never underestimate her dear old grandmother.

"SYL," I said and waited.

Chloe stopped dead in her tracks, looking confused. "What?"

"See you later."

After she left, Cam walked over to stand by my chair. "I hope you find Mr. Walker. He's an awesome dude." A quick hug and he was off.

Surprised, I turned to Tom. "I didn't think you'd tell them the reason I'm in town."

"I didn't. But you know Cameron. He might not show it, but he catches every little thing that goes on. A very wise soul resides inside that boy of mine. Sometimes I feel like I'm the kid, and he's the father." Tom got up to clear the table.

I pushed back my chair and stood to help. At that moment, it seemed important that I let Tom know how I felt about him. "I'm very proud of you, Tom, for moving home to be closer to the kids and be a bigger part of their lives."

"Thanks. That means a lot to me." He glanced up at the clock. "We have a few minutes before the kids go to bed. Let's adjourn to the living room. You can tell me all about how bored you are now that you're retired."

"I noticed how awkward it was for you at dinner. Not knowing what to call me after the divorce. Please, whatever makes you feel comfortable is okay by me."

"I guess I'll have to feel my way along. This is all so new and strange."

"For both of us," I assured him. "But it'll be fine."

Chapter Sixteen

Having a one-on-one conversation with Tom, just being myself, not Lizzie's mother, was easy. I'd forgotten that he'd known Nathan for years and was genuinely interested in what we'd done so far to find him. He'd also read about the deaths of Carolyn Watson and John Doe.

"I know the whole team at the morgue if there's anything I can do to help."

"Barbara Nylander's one of my dearest friends," I told him.

"Of course, I should have known you'd be better connected than I am. Madame Coroner is quite a character, isn't she?"

"She's great. I'm gonna plant myself in her office bright and early tomorrow and see what she's found out about our hit and run."

"I was watching the news earlier. There's a composite sketch of him on every channel. Hopefully someone will come forward with information, especially if there's a reward offered."

"A reward usually shakes all the nuts out of the trees. The phones go crazy. Every potential lead has to be checked out, and that takes manpower and time. If we don't ID the man within the next week or so, then a reward would help. But not now."

"You're probably right. It's a shame though. No one should be left alongside the road like a dog."

"No, they shouldn't."

The kids started calling from their rooms before we could continue.

"Do you think you might have time to go to the movies tomorrow?" he asked. "I know we're cutting into your investigation, but Chloe wants to see some coming-of-age flick. I thought two hours for that, then a quick burger afterward. Three hours tops."

"Call me and I'll try to meet you in front of the theater. If that doesn't work out, I'll drop by before I go home."

"Great."

* * *

After parking in Lizzie's driveway, I rested my forehead on the steering wheel for a minute. The day had finally caught up to me, and I was exhausted. Now if only I could get my brain to sync up with my body, I might be able to get a good night's sleep.

In the house, as I undressed, I visualized my family's first television. It was a big old thing, set inside a blond wooden cabinet with a wire antenna on top. There was no twenty-four-hour broadcasting back then; the stations just shut down for the night. But if you turned your TV on after hours, you'd hear static beneath gray and black lines flickering across the screen. Looking back, I see now that I was using the lines to meditate, the static, my first form of white noise, to block everything out. As I got older and my problems got serious and complicated, I'd conjure up that image to help me clear my mind.

I fell back onto the pillow, my mind's eye watching the television, my ears filled with static. *Relax*, I told myself. *Sleep. Relax . . . sleep . . . relax . . .*

When I woke up, I was lying in the same position I'd started in eight hours before. My television therapy had worked, and I felt almost like myself again. After a warm shower and a few minutes fussing with hair and makeup, I pulled on my favorite black jeans. Then I buttoned up a green blouse and grabbed my scarf. Thank goodness for those worn-in boots I'd brought. I could walk miles in them, or run if necessary. I picked up my twenty-fifth anniversary present from Sully—a gold Cartier watch. As I fastened it around my wrist, I thought of him. He would have done anything, and for as long as he had to, to find Nathan. I couldn't let either of them down.

I went into the kitchen and made a pot of coffee while checking the weather on my phone. Today was supposed to be mild, which meant I'd only need the black cardigan. Looking through the cabinets, I finally found a package of biscotti and took out two, which I ate leaning over the kitchen sink. The small TV on the counter was begging to be turned on, but I resisted. I needed just a few more minutes before starting up my investigation again. I'd listen to the news on the way to Nathan's office.

* * *

The four of them were gathered around the front desk, a tint of fear at the corners of each smile. If they needed a cheerleader today, that's what I'd be. Anything to keep up morale.

"I got the donuts," Brock said, proud of himself. "And there's coffee."

"Thanks." I sat. "Any news to report?"

They took turns saying, "No."

I turned to E.T. "I didn't get the chance to ask you about the job at Dr. Tate's office. I looked all through Nathan's notes, and there isn't a mention of the doctor wanting to have his office bugged, to check up on his staff. Have you done things like that before?"

His eyes looked even sadder today. "I don't know what you're talking about. Honestly. I knew the boss and Tate were friends and that the doc wanted to talk about amping up security in his office, but I just figured there had been some robberies . . . you know . . . drugs. That happens a lot in medical buildings. But he never said a word about putting in audio equipment."

"Maybe the deal was just between Tate and the boss. The doc coulda figured that if his people knew what he was doin', they'd just cool it for a while," Rosie said.

"Or get around the mikes somehow," Polly added.

"I agree with Rosie," I told them. "Knowing the doctor would be aware of what they were saying would have been a very effective incentive to keep everything aboveboard."

"True," E.T. said. "What if the boss didn't know what Tate wanted before he got there? And afterward, he didn't have time to write up notes because of that . . . man."

"Didn't you say a woman outside the office building told you Nathan and this Camo Guy got into a dark car?" Polly asked. "Mr. Walker's car is dark. Don't you think maybe we should focus on this guy and stop wasting time talking about Dr. Tate?" She looked irritated, twisting a large ring on her index finger.

"Look, we're all frustrated. But we can't just make assumptions, hoping something will pan out. Until we come up with concrete evidence, we have to consider everyone's a suspect."

"I know. It's just that I . . . I can't stand this." Polly started to cry. Rosie hugged her, and Brock went to grab a box of tissues from a nearby desk.

I wanted to join her and have a good, long cry. To hell with what any of them thought of me. But as I resisted the urge to mother Polly, my eyes met E.T.'s. He looked so lost and helpless. "We're going to find him," I said in a steady voice.

Brock sat back down; Rosie released Polly so she could dab at her eyes. I remained stiff in my chair, remembering a line from Kipling, something about keeping your head while those around you are losing theirs.

Polly finally calmed down and blew her nose. "Sorry, I'm fine now."

Brock looked at E.T. "We're all good, ain't we, Katherine?"

"Yes, we are. Now come on, we have a busy day ahead. Polly, I want you to go through the files, go as far back as you can. Look for any complaints or jobs that went sour. Disgruntled customers . . . things like that."

Before she could answer, I turned to E.T. "Do you have any jobs lined up today?"

"Two. One at a private residence, and the other's a jewelry store."

"You take care of those," I told him. "When you're finished, come back here and help Polly. Maybe something will jump out at you. A name, a location, anything out of the ordinary."

He nodded.

"What should I do, Katie?" Rosie asked. "I need to be doin' somethin', you know?"

"Nathan once told me that you're . . . connected?"

"Yeah," she said, looking puzzled. "So?"

"Are any of your contacts working on the inside—"

"You mean are any of 'em snitches?"

"That's exactly what I mean." I'd had my own list of informants when I was on the force—every cop did. But that was years ago. By now most of them were probably dead or in jail.

"A few. Why?" she asked.

"Find out if any of them have heard about a kidnapping."

"Why haven't we gotten a ransom note by now?" Polly asked.

"With some guys, it ain't about the money," Brock told her. "Sometimes it's more personal. Like what E.T. said about revenge."

"I'll do what I can." Rosie wrote on the paper in front of her.

"And Brock," I started, "I didn't forget about you."

"How could you?" He grinned.

"I want you to come with me today."

"Doin' what?"

"The only thing I know for sure is there'll be a whole lot of sitting around and waiting."

"I do both those things real good."

Chapter Seventeen

I wasn't sure why I'd brought Brock with me. Maybe it was because the last time I'd been in town, Nathan insisted Brock come along on a trip I'd made to Minneapolis. During the ride back and forth, throughout lunch and several stops, we'd gotten to know each other. Maybe having Nathan's "muscle man" beside me made me feel stronger. Or maybe I just needed a friend that day.

We were about five miles from the office when my phone rang.

"Want me to get it?" Brock asked.

"Thanks."

"It's Polly. She says to tell you that you left the Waterton file behind."

"Who's that?"

Brock pushed the speaker button and held the phone between us. "Tell her, Pol."

"Kate, remember the man we told you about when you first got here? The old guy with the walker who gave everyone such a hard time?"

It took a second, but I remembered. "Sure. I'll pick it up—"

"No need. I thought I'd save you some time and called him. A hospice worker answered. Mr. Waterton died yesterday . . . natural causes. Looks like we can cross his name off our list."

"Some people make the world a whole lot better when they check out," Brock said.

"Amen," Polly agreed.

After disconnecting, Brock turned to watch the scenery flashing by on his side of the jeep. I hated the small talk people felt obligated to use as filler when too much quiet made them uncomfortable. I used to be one of those people until I realized the value of silence. Brock seemed perfectly content to sit quietly until we came to one of those stoplights that seem to last forever.

"So are we goin' to the coroner's office now?"

I nodded. "I'm hoping they found out the identity of that hit and run. But it's probably too early to know anything."

"I keep wonderin'," he said, still looking out his window, "what kinda heartless creep would just leave someone by the side of the road like that? Have you noticed how people seem to be gettin' meaner? Everyone's either hollerin' about politics or jobs or even a kid's baseball game. All the time, there's these stories about parents goin' berserk. Scary, ain't it?"

"Scary times breed scary people, I guess."

"In a crazy way, I should be glad for all of it. Scary times means more work for guys like me."

"I never thought about it that way."

When I pulled up in front of the morgue, Brock asked if he could wait for me in the car. He explained that the odors in any medical facility stirred up bad memories. It was obvious he didn't want to elaborate, and so we left it at that. But the muscle-bound man with the sensitive heart continued to surprise me.

*   *   *

I thought of Barbara Nylander as my mentor even though she was younger by a few years and had never worked on the force. I'd learned how a professional woman, working in a male-dominated profession, handles her team. She was direct, honest, and funny without even trying to get a laugh. Shortly after meeting, we'd formed our exclusive admiration society of two.

She was standing at an examination table, wearing her standard uniform: dark slacks, sensible shoes, and white lab coat with a colorful T-shirt underneath. Barbara claimed she hated politics, that she kept her personal opinions at home. But the graphics splashed across her T-shirts begged to differ. That day she was wearing a black one with large white letters across her chest that read: "Shy Women Never Make History."

I came up behind her as she reached up to lower the bright lamp hanging overhead.

"Hey, girl," I said, touching her shoulder gently, hoping not to startle her.

Turning, she grinned. "Well, lookie who's here! I knew you'd turn up when I heard about Nate. But now that Katherine

Sullivan's on the case, Nathan Walker will be back faster than you can say, 'Welcome home party!'"

"Hold the applause until I find him."

"And so far . . . no good?" She frowned.

"Afraid not. Can you take a break? I need to talk."

"I don't think Mr. Kerrigan here will mind." She nodded toward the corpse. "Do you, Charlie?"

"I'll wait in your office."

"Be there in a minute, darlin'."

Against the wall, opposite her desk, was a large coffeepot. And next to the pot was the space reserved for a cake or cookies. Her husband, John, was a baker and brought home what was left at the end of the day. I always thought my ideal man would be either a baker or an artist . . . until I met Sully. That man couldn't draw a straight line, and the only thing he ever made in the kitchen was a mess.

I poured myself a cup and took a cookie. I was into my second bite when Barbara came through the door.

"How y'all holdin' up, Katie?" She patted my shoulder as she walked past me to fill up her mug. "I'm talkin' about you, personally, darlin'. I expect hearing that he'd gone missing was a real shock to your system."

"You expect right. But I'm trying to hold it together for Nathan's crew."

She walked around to sit behind her desk, one hand holding a coffee mug labeled "Dallas" and the other clutching two cookies and a napkin.

After she was settled in her chair, she asked, "So when did y'all get into town?"

"Day before yesterday, and I haven't stopped running since. I've questioned all the clients he visited on Friday. And I hadn't gotten anywhere until a witness told me she saw Nathan get into the car with a man Friday night. And that's the last anyone saw of him. I'm scared, Barb. We both know that the longer this goes on the worse—"

"Stop it, now. Getting yourself all worked up won't help anyone. You know that . . . right?"

"Yes."

"Now tell me what I can do. This Texas girl knows you came by for more than a friendly smile and her baked goods."

Her humor came so naturally, and I felt better. "The man who was last seen with Nathan was wearing a camouflage jacket. Dean Bostwick told me there was a hit and run reported, and the man was wearing the same kind of printed jacket. I was hoping, and I know this is expecting a lot, but I was hoping that maybe you'd found out the identity of the man. He would have been sent here for an autopsy sometime yesterday."

"Well today's you're lucky day, girl. I know who he is. In fact, you've met him."

"What? How could I—"

"Charlie . . . Charles Kerrigan. The man out there on the table."

Chapter Eighteen

Whether it was surprise or shock that played across my face, Barbara got a kick out of my expression.

"Now I know how you idolize me, darlin', but I wasn't the one that figured out who John Doe really was. That sketch the news was showing brought in his girlfriend. She went to the police, and after they took her statement, they escorted her here to make a positive identification."

"When was this?"

"Late, a little after midnight. I wasn't here. My assistant, Max, left me his notes. But Dean won't be making an official announcement until they can notify Charlie's parents, children—you know, living relatives. And he's waiting for me to tell him the actual cause of death. Standard procedure." Then she laughed to herself. "But you probably know all of this better than I do."

"I did put in a lot of hours trying to ID victims. So do you think Charlie was a typical hit and run?"

"Nothing typical about it. More like a hit and backed over and ran over again. This was no accident; I can tell you that for sure. Whoever the driver was wanted to make sure the poor guy was good an' dead. But just because he was wearing the same kind of jacket as the man with Nathan doesn't mean he's connected in any way."

"Well, you know what they say about coincidences . . ." I couldn't help rolling my eyes.

"Oh, horse doody. People see what they want to see. Like that woman in Mexico who saw Jesus in a tortilla. 'Member her? Our brain is geared up to make familiar images out of scrambled eggs. Logic is what leads the cops to a killer . . . or kidnapper. Gather enough hard-core evidence, and you have a direct path to the bad guy."

"You're preaching to the choir. But for now, it's all I've got."

Barbara chewed on a cookie as she reached for her notes. "Maybe something in here will help you. Max requested the police file before he left for the day. Very thorough young man." She lowered the reading glasses tucked in the short hair above her forehead. "Let's have a look-see. Hmm. Charles Kerrigan served a year for assaulting his wife. He was released three months ago. From the look of the tattoos on his hands and arms, I'd say he's been in and out of trouble his whole life. First there was juvie, then jail for carjacking, lewd and lascivious behavior, and selling drugs. He's got records in Indiana, Michigan, and Wisconsin."

"And his girlfriend lives here in Edina?" I asked.

"I called Max this morning to go over his notes. As adorable as that boy is, his handwriting's atrocious! He went on and on about how surprised he was when Charlie's girlfriend walked in. Come to find out he'd gone to high school with her. She was one of those popular cheerleader types that all the fellas had a crush on. And if that wasn't enough, her daddy's loaded. Max just couldn't get over a girl like that hookin' up with someone like Charlie."

"What was her name?" I asked.

"Ashley Knight."

I thought a minute. "Doesn't ring a bell."

"No surprise there. Our kids were out of school and on their own when her people moved here. Lizzie wouldn't have known Ashley. But I bet you've seen those cheesy ads on TV. Her daddy's wearin' a suit of armor, chargin' up on a white horse. Then he looks into the camera and, ever so dramatically, says, 'Do you need rescuing?' He goes on an' on about his construction company having a spotless record an' call his eight-hundred number if you need a hero." She leaned back in her chair and laughed. "Really makes the most of the Knight name."

"Nope, I've never seen them. But then, I zone out when a commercial comes on."

"It's good for a laugh." The more she thought about it, the funnier it got. "When that horse gets spooked and starts backing up, that fella looks so scared. And that crazy helmet of his goes crooked on his head . . ."

Her laughter was contagious, and I couldn't help myself. Soon we were both trying to catch our breath, dabbing tears away with napkins.

"Come on now." I tried sounding serious. "Back to Ashley. Do you know anything else about her?"

"Spoilsport." Barbara wrinkled up her nose when she realized I didn't want to play anymore. "Well, she told Max she met Charles at a bar, and there was this instant connection—brought on by booze, no doubt—and within a week, he moved in with her. She's the one who got Charlie his job, workin' construction with one of her daddy's crews."

"Aside from broken bones and internal injuries, did you find anything that the cops can use?"

"Blue paint. Pieces of it were embedded at the point of the first impact. The vehicle must have been low to the ground because he sustained a lot of injuries from the waist down. I'd say it was a sports car. Oh, and there was something sticky on the fingers of his right hand. Smelled like varnish or paint, which would be reasonable considering the work he was doing. But I won't be sure until we test it."

"The witness I spoke to said a man was standing by a sports car that night. She couldn't be sure of the exact color, but it was dark."

"And you think that guy was Charlie?" Barbara asked seriously.

"If he owned a car, there'll be a record at the DMV. I gotta go, Barb. Thanks for everything." As I started to get up, Barbara came around the desk and hugged me.

"You're gonna find Nate, don't worry. An' when you do, I'll have John whip up a big ole cake."

Chapter Nineteen

"You okay, Katherine?" Brock asked as I settled back into the jeep. "I was gettin' worried."

"I'm fine."

"Good. Where to now?"

"Would you call Polly and have her check the DMV records for a license and plates issued to a Charles Kerrigan? First check locally, and if nothing turns up, try Wisconsin, Michigan, or Indiana. I need to know what kind of car he owned."

"Is that the dead guy?"

"Yes. If the man in the parking lot that night was Charlie, either he had to have driven himself there to meet Nathan or a second person drove him. That stranger could be the one who ran him over. But I'm hoping the blue sports car the coroner mentioned is connected to Charlie Kerrigan somehow."

Brock just listened as I talked myself through a logical scenario. When I finished, he picked up the phone and called Polly. He repeated my instructions verbatim. After he was done, he asked, "What about that girl of his? She'd know what kinda car the guy drove."

Why hadn't I asked Barbara for Ashley Knight's address? "I don't know where she lives," I had to admit.

"Hold up," Brock said and picked up my phone. After a few minutes on Google, he proudly announced that Ms. Knight lived 5.3 miles from where we were.

*   *   *

Brock started to get out of the jeep after I parked in front of Ashley's house.

I reached across the seat to stop him. "You can wait—"

"No way, Katherine. You don't know what kinda stuff this woman is involved in or who her friends are. This could be dangerous. No arguments! I'm goin' in with ya."

As always, Brock made a lot of sense. "You're right."

I could tell he was a little disappointed that I agreed so easily. He probably had half a dozen more arguments ready to fire at me if I resisted his plan.

The house was large, boxy, and painted white. Plain and simple with no decorative shrubs, no flowers, not even a welcome mat. No-frills-functional is how I referred to such unfriendly dwellings. The very sight of it made my creative self want to cry.

There was no doorbell, and as I started to raise my hand, Brock banged on the front door with his fist.

"That'll get her attention." He grinned.

The woman who answered the door was somewhere in her thirties. It was obvious this cheerleader had shouted her last hurrah. She was short, round, and wearing what we used to call a muumuu but now is referred to as a caftan, making it sound much more glamorous. The one Ashley wore had a dark spot on the front. She probably figured that the large elephant design would cover up any food that had missed its way to her mouth.

"Look, I'm really busy and not in the mood to buy a vacuum cleaner or whatever the hell you're selling."

She started to shut the door, but Brock stuck his foot in front of it before she could manage a good slam.

"Ms. Knight, I'm here about the death of your boyfriend, Charles Kerrigan. I assure you I'm not selling anything. Do you have a few minutes to talk?"

Both of her chins dropped. "Oh." Tears welled up in her swollen eyes. "Sorry. Sorry I was so mean. Ever since I saw that sketch on TV . . . Well you can imagine how I felt . . . I'm sure that if it was your boyfriend . . . and seeing him laid out at the morgue . . . I've never seen anything like that . . . never . . . Well, maybe on CSI . . ."

She had to be stopped or her frantic rambling would have gone on forever. "I'm so sorry for your loss and know what a difficult time this must be for you. But if you could give us just a few minutes—we'll try to make it quick." It was an automatic response, one I'd delivered too many times to grief-stricken relatives during my time on the force. It also served as a way to separate myself from getting personally involved in a case. But when the words came out of my mouth so easily, after years as a civilian, I was surprised.

"Well . . ." She thought it over a moment. And while she did that, her tears dried up. "Sure."

I assumed from her mood change that she thought Brock and I were police detectives. And I'd explain exactly who we were . . . later. But first I needed to find out more about Charles Kerrigan.

She backed up a few steps, holding the door open. I was half way into the house when a loud noise stopped all three of us in our tracks.

A gunshot.

Then another.

Brock shouted, "Get inside and stay down!" to Ashley. Then, grabbing me to his chest, he threw us both over the threshold onto the floor and kicked the door closed with his foot.

The three of us lay frozen for a few minutes, afraid to move, waiting for what was to come next.

"Are you guys okay?" Brock whispered.

We mumbled that we were fine.

Our labored breathing was the only sound filling the room during a silence that seemed to last for hours.

Then came a loud screech. Tires racing against the asphalt out front.

It was obvious whoever it was had given up and driven away. But still the three of us remained sprawled out on the floor.

Finally, Ashley made the first move. "I knew that jerk was up to something!" she said as she sat up. "All day, driving by, looking at my house . . . stalking me. But I never thought somebody would try to kill me!"

Brock got on his knees. Pulling a gun from the holster inside his jacket, he crawled over to the front window. Cautiously he lifted a corner of the curtain to check the front yard.

I held my breath and could see Ashley doing the same.

"They're gone," Brock said as he turned to face us.

I sat up and looked at Ashley. "So you know for sure it was a man? Any idea who it was?"

"No. I couldn't get a good look. The windows were tinted. But I do know they were driving a blue car . . . I can tell you that for sure . . . a Ferrari . . . I think, but I really don't know anything about cars . . . just that it's one of those little things that makes a lot of noise . . ."

Slowly we all stood up, each of us checking ourselves and each other for any sign of a wound. Luckily the bullets hadn't hit their target—whoever that might be.

Ashley fussed with her hair a moment then calmly said, "Well, I need a drink; how about you two?"

In the ten minutes I'd known this woman, I'd seen her roller coaster through a range of emotions that any actress would envy. From angry to sad, genial back to angry, stopping at charming . . . at least for the moment. But the one emotion I hadn't seen her exhibit was fear. She'd just been shot at. Yet Ashley seemed oblivious to the danger. Even Brock, a man used to physical confrontation, needed a moment to reboot. And I could feel my heart racing. But Ms. Knight was fine.

Brock shot me a confused look as he sat on the edge of an overstuffed chair. Then shrugging, he told our hostess, "I guess I could drink somethin'."

"Nobody's having a drink," I said sternly. "We have to call nine-one-one first, and it's better that none of us have alcohol on our breath."

"You want I should do it?" Brock asked.

I shook my head. "No, I want Ashley to call."

"Why should I call the cops? You think this is my first time? What do you think drove me to drink? I been shot at by crazy ex-boyfriends, jealous girlfriends, my father's insane ex-partner. There was this one time, when I was a kid, we had to hide out for a month at a Super Eight in St. Paul from my nanny's husband, who escaped from jail."

"Humor me. Act like it's the first time and just explain what happened so they'll send a patrol car."

"By then I'll really need a drink," Ashley complained.

* * *

It took the better part of an hour for a patrol car to come, take our statements, call for technicians to pry bullets from the wall of the house, and then leave. They told Ashley she might be hearing from detectives later on. Once they drove away, that was Ashley's cue to go for the drinks.

"She's one cool cookie, ain't she?" Brock whispered as she left the room.

"I was thinking the same thing. Considering those bullets must have been meant for her."

Brock thought about my theory. "Or you, on account of your snoopin' around, lookin' for the boss."

Ashley came back into the room pushing a brass cart. Bottles crowded together on the bottom clanked as she moved it across the carpeting. Stopping in front of us, she picked up a glass from the top shelf and asked, "What'll you have?"

Chapter Twenty

Ashley smiled as though we were at a tea party. No trace of fear on her face. No perspiration, no twitching around her mouth. Either this girl was accustomed to violence or there was something a little off here.

"Whatever ya got is fine," Brock told her as he put his gun away. "Bourbon . . . gin . . . whatever. But just a shot—I'm workin'."

Ashley put down the large glass and picked up a smaller one. "You got it."

While she poured, I asked, "So Charlie didn't own a blue sports car? Or have a friend who owned one?"

"Charlie was a bum. A charming, good-looking bum, but a bum all the same. And he didn't own anything, especially not a sports car." She laughed. "He fooled me at first. Handsome men are real good at tricks, and Charles Kerrigan had a suitcase full."

Handing the shot glass to Brock, she stepped back to her minibar. "What's your pleasure, Ms. Sullivan?"

"Just a splash of vodka would be great."

"I've got Absolut and . . ."

I had to wonder if she was an alcoholic but reserved my opinion until I saw what she was going to drink. "That's fine, thanks."

After grabbing the vodka bottle, she stopped and looked at me. "You said something about being here because of Charlie, right?"

I nodded.

"But the cops said it was a hit and run. After I identified his body, I thought that was it. So . . . I don't understand . . . what do you want, exactly?"

"I'm looking for my friend, Nathan Walker. He's been missing since last Friday. A witness I spoke to said she saw a man standing by a sports car, wearing a camouflage jacket in the parking lot outside the building she works in. This man approached Nathan. They spoke for a few minutes and then got into Nathan's car and drove away."

"And you think that man was Charlie? There must be a hundred guys in this town alone that looked like him. And a thousand more who have that same kind of ugly jacket."

"You're right. But then I heard there was a hit and run yesterday, and the victim was also wearing a camouflage jacket. I thought maybe it was a place to start. So this morning, I visited the coroner." I didn't tell her what was in Barbara's report. Holding back information would allow me to figure out how much of the truth I was going to get from Ms. Knight.

She stared wide-eyed, then handed me my drink in a crystal glass. "Why do I get the feeling that you've done this before? You're not some ordinary lady off the street, are you?"

"She used to be the chief of police here," Brock said. "And no way is she ordinary." He held up his glass to toast me.

"For real? That's so cool. A real life police chief, huh?" She reached for a large tumbler and filled it halfway with gin.

Yep, this lady was a serious drinker.

"Do you know why Charlie would have been alone on that stretch of highway?" I asked.

"Sure do. We had a fight and I . . . well . . . I threw him out of my car."

"You what?" I asked, shocked.

"Oh, I slowed down. I couldn't have been going more than ten miles an hour. Besides, for the last fifteen minutes, he kept shouting to stop, that he wanted to get out. So . . . I let him out."

"You musta been really mad to do somethin' like that," Brock said.

"I've never been so infuriated! I swear I was seeing red." She finished her drink and poured another. "After all I did for him? Letting him move in with me, never asking for a penny to help out with bills . . . or food . . . every time we'd go out, I paid for the whole thing . . . He never offered . . . felt entitled. And then I find out he's doing drugs. Taking the money I gave him for gas or food—anything he wanted—and spending it all on drugs. No way, José!"

I gave her a minute to calm down. Brock looked uncomfortable, swirling alcohol around in his glass, afraid to make eye contact with the irate woman.

When I thought the time was right, I asked, "What kind of car do you drive, Ms. Knight?"

"That ugly blue pickup out front. Daddy bought it for me, insists that we only drive American vehicles. Why? Does this have something to do with the car that hit Charlie?"

No, I reminded myself, I wasn't there investigating the death of Charles Kerrigan. I only wanted information that would help me find out if he'd been involved in a kidnapping or . . . murder.

"I'm not sure," I lied and hurried on to my next question. "Was he working?" Of course, I knew he was working, and for whom. But I still felt the need to test her further.

"I got him a job at my father's company. He had some experience. Said he'd worked in the machine shop in prison once . . . But he lied all the time. To think I believed a single word that came out of his mouth . . ."

"I understand your father owns Knight Construction?"

"Ya mean that guy in all them crazy ads is your old man?" Brock asked, amused.

Ashley looked insulted. "They're not crazy . . . they're . . . artistic. I wrote and directed all of them."

"I've heard they're very . . . memorable." I tried soothing her ruffled feathers. "And so appropriate with a name like Knight." I flashed Brock a stern look, warning him to be nice.

"Oh, yeah, memorable," he agreed.

She took a big gulp of booze. "Thanks."

"I imagine Knight Construction has all sorts of projects going on around town?"

"Across the entire state and even a few in North and South Dakota." She was obviously proud of her father.

"Where was Charlie working?" I asked. "Do you know the exact location?"

She nodded. "There's a big subdivision going up on Excelsior Boulevard. At least three of the homes are finished. People are already living in them. The plan is to create an area featuring modern design but surrounded with elegance and old-world charm. They're even going to have their own little grocery store and gift shop. A planned community like they've done in Florida . . . but of course we don't have an ocean here . . . we have lakes . . . lots and lots of lakes . . ."

She was talking about the site where Mr. Larkin, the first client I'd interviewed, lived. While Ashley rambled on and Brock seemed entertained, I replayed my drive past bulldozers and work crews yesterday and then remembered the trailer. It was as large as a railroad car and on the side was painted the helmeted head of a knight. Of course it meant nothing to me then, but I'd obviously stored the image deep down in my memory bank.

We finished our drinks and stood to leave. Ashley seemed disappointed that our meeting was over.

"I'm afraid I didn't help much . . . you know, with finding your friend. If you need anything else, I'll be here . . . I'm always here . . ."

I was going to ask if it ever crossed her mind that the police would be stopping by to question her about Charlie.

If she admitted to throwing him out of a moving vehicle, it wasn't much of a stretch to figure she ran him over. She might not have made the initial hit, but she could have been responsible for the fatal last few. Love that turns to hate is a common motive for murder. Throw in a scorned woman—an alcoholic, unbalanced woman—and you've got your number-one suspect.

Chapter
Twenty-One

The construction site was busier and louder than the first time I'd been there. The white van had been joined with another smaller one. I let Brock take the lead. Experience had taught me that I wouldn't be taken seriously by any member of the construction crew. They took orders from men, worked with men, and while on the job, expressed their opinions of women by leering and shouting suggestive remarks. It wasn't fair and I didn't like it. But I was also very aware that I was an uninvited creature on their turf. An alien who didn't understand or speak their language.

But everyone paid attention and understood when Brock asked where we could find the foreman.

We were pointed toward a man in his forties, holding a clipboard. Obviously angry, he waved his arms, shouting at one of his crew. But with all the noise, I couldn't make out a word.

After explaining that we wanted to talk to him about Charles Kerrigan, the head honcho escorted us into the trailer where he'd set up a temporary office. He took off his hardhat, then closed the door.

"Ahh, that's better," he said. "Have a seat."

There were several folding chairs scattered around the room. Brock dragged two over to the table that served as a desk.

"Now what exactly is it you want to know about Charlie?" he asked, making eye contact with Brock.

I leaned forward. "My name's Katherine Sullivan, and this is—"

At first he seemed surprised when I spoke, like he hadn't seen me sitting there. But then he took a good look. "You were the police chief in Edina, right?"

"Yes."

"I'm Ray DeYoung. My brother worked with you for years. Said you were fair and decent, an all right broad—pardon my French."

It was my turn to study his face. "Jim was one of my best men. And now that I take a good look at you, I see the resemblance around the mouth and nose."

"I'm Brock." The big guy must have been feeling left out.

"Nice to meet both of you," Ray said. "Can I offer you something? The coffee's cold, but I've got soda or water."

Brock shook his head. "Nothin' for me, thanks."

"We're good," I told him. "I understand that Mr. Knight personally hired Charles Kerrigan." I went on to explain about how Nathan was missing and how our investigation had led us to this trailer.

Ray leaned back and whistled. "All I can tell you is the guy was a bona fide, grade-A loser. 'Course I'm sorry he's dead and all, but those kind usually come to a bad end. I've seen dozens just like him."

"What do you mean, 'those kind'? Did he make trouble for you?" I asked.

"I wouldn't call it trouble, really. Just little stuff here and there, but it all added up. One day he'd come in late; the next he wouldn't show up at all. Then I'd have to send him home for being drunk. His girlfriend would sit out there, waiting for him. With all this heavy equipment, it was dangerous. She was a distraction. But I couldn't say a word because of her being Mr. Knight's daughter."

"Did he have any friends? Guys he hung out with?"

"The men out there didn't take to him much. But there was a woman, a real beauty. She'd come around sometimes."

"She have a name?" Brock asked.

"His girlfriend didn't say anything about Charlie cheating on her, but it's a possibility," I said. "I guess that was the other woman?"

"I doubt it. Didn't look like any kind of a romance going on between them," Ray said.

"Why did you think that?"

"As you found out for yourselves, it's almost impossible to hear much out there. But you can tell from a smile or look if there's some heat. Know what I mean? I never saw them even come close to touching. No lovebird stuff. He always seemed very respectful toward her."

"An' you never heard him call her nothin'?" Brock asked.

"He called her Mrs. something. She looked a few years older than Kerrigan. I never could get a handle on what was going on there."

"Would you happen to know what kind of a car she drove?" I asked.

"Man, would I ever! It was a shiny new blue Porsche. Beautiful machine. When she'd drive up in that car, the guys weren't paying attention to the beautiful blonde behind the wheel. No, they were drooling over that Porsche."

"Blonde and beautiful—that's something to go on, I guess." But the odds weren't too good. Minnesota was overflowing with blondes. "And each time she came here, he'd get in the car, and they'd leave together?"

"No, they'd just talk. Both of the times I saw her, she'd drive off by herself over to that house." He pointed. "Number thirty-four. Just figured the old coot who lives there was her father."

The door suddenly opened, and a man wearing a hard hat stuck his head in. "We need you out here, boss."

Ray rolled his eyes and said, "It's always something. I'll be right back. Make yourself comfortable." With that, he left.

Brock got up to look out the window, and I stood to stretch my legs. From that position, I could see a canvas leaning against the wall behind the desk. My curiosity got the best of me, and I had to go take a better look.

Carefully, I picked it up and turned it around. It was a Molly Hartung piece, the same size as the ones in the Larkin house. If this was the missing one in the series, why did

Ray DeYoung have it here, in a dirty trailer? Did he know its value? Had he stolen it?

"He's comin' back," Brock said.

Quickly, I set the painting back down where it had been, facing the wall.

"Sorry about that," Ray said, walking back to his desk. "Do you have any more questions for me?"

"No. You've been great, thanks. If I need anything else, I'll be back. Say hi to Jim for me."

"Will do."

Chapter Twenty-Two

"What was with that painting you was lookin' at?" Brock asked.

"I'm not sure, but I know it doesn't belong in a construction trailer. In fact, I think it matches a set on Larkin's wall. But that'll have to wait for later. Right now, I have to digest everything Ray told us."

Brock and I got back in the car. As we drove, I wondered if it was possible that Larkin had a daughter. But my gut told me the blonde was his wife, and the blue Porsche belonged to one of them. As I pulled up in front of the house, the irony that I was back where I'd started wasn't lost on me. And the thought that I might have missed something crucial on my first visit was upsetting.

There was no sign of a car anywhere in the driveway. But it could have been parked behind one of the four metal doors attached to a garage next to the house.

"I thought you checked this guy out yesterday," Brock said.

"It was the first stop I made." I could hear my defensive tone. "Want me to talk to him?"

"No, I just need you there . . . in case . . ."

Brock's expression turned serious. "Gotcha."

"But first I want to check something out before we go in." I picked up my phone and dialed Polly. When I asked if she'd tracked down a credit card or evidence of a joint checking account for Mr. Larkin, Polly started to recite the statistics.

Larkin did indeed have a wife. Her full name was Diana Marie Larkin née Shaw. She was born in 1975, making her at least twenty years younger than her husband. Born and raised in Portland, Oregon, and graduated from Harvard with a business degree. She was founder and owner of the Beautiful Lady Cosmetic Company with two locations—one in New York and the other in Miami. For two consecutive years, her business had been listed in *Forbes* as one of the top companies run by a woman.

"She could buy and sell her husband five times over," Polly concluded her report.

I was stunned. "So she didn't marry him for money."

"Then it had to be for love . . . I guess." I could imagine Polly smirking when she said that. "You've seen him. Is Mr. Larkin handsome? Or charismatic? Does he have some sexy vibe that oozes off of him?"

"None of the above."

"Okay then," she said. "Keep us posted. Rosie's climbing the walls, and E.T. just walked in. This waiting, not knowing anything, is driving us all crazy."

"Hang in there. I'll check in later."

As soon as I tucked the phone into my purse, Brock wanted to know what the call was all about.

"Looks like the guy's on the level," he said after hearing my explanation. "About his wife at least. That don't mean he ain't lyin' about other stuff, though."

"Keep focused, Brock. We're not here to accuse Mr. Larkin of anything. His wife might have been having an affair with Charlie Kerrigan, and we certainly don't want to be the ones to tell him. He'd never talk to us if we spilled the beans. There's still a possibility that the blonde was his daughter or friend. We're here to find out about that Porsche—that's all. So try not to look . . . intimidating. Keep your attitude light . . . Maybe you shouldn't come with me. If he is hiding something, I don't want to spook him."

"Didn't you tell us that when he first moved into this place, his car got broken into?"

"Yes."

"So I'll play like I'm from the neighborhood watch or some fancy private security company and wanna ask a few questions. You're with me on account of it was you who called me . . . about his car." He smiled, proud of his ingenuity.

I had to admit it was a good plan. But I only hoped that Brock would be as good at improvisation as he was with his muscles.

We got out of the jeep and walked toward the house.

Brock whistled. "This place looks like a castle. Right outta some fairytale."

"It's big, all right. Remember, let me do the talking. And if he asks you any questions, keep your answers short."

"I ain't gonna blow it, Katherine."

When Brock saw the large brass knocker attached to the front door, he looked to me for permission to use it. And when I nodded, he acted as though he'd won the grand prize.

Hearing our voices, Fluffy started to bark frantically while at the same time clawing the wood on his side, desperate to escape whatever was in the house with him.

Brock lifted the knocker with both hands and dramatically let it drop.

The weight of it pushed the door open.

"Well, look at that," Brock said, puzzled. "It ain't even locked. What do you make of that?"

Fluffy came racing out and licked my shoes. I bent down to pet him. "Either someone was in a hurry to leave and forgot to lock this poor animal up or a stranger broke in and is still in there."

"Maybe the Larkin guy's layin' on the floor, hurt. You know, a heart attack, somethin' like that? An' he can't get to his phone."

I picked up the dog. "Just be careful," I said, walking over the threshold.

Brock followed, closing the door behind him.

"Mr. Larkin!" I shouted. "Are you okay?"

Brock rushed ahead of me, his gun drawn. "Mr. Larkin, you in here?"

Everything looked the same as it had yesterday. Nothing was missing or damaged. We walked into the living room. Still the same tacky furniture. Peeking around the corner, I could see a small gate had been set up across the doorway of a bathroom. Carefully, I bent down to put Fluffy on the other side, where he'd be out of the way and safe.

As I was straightening up, the hammering started. A rapid beating, coming from a room upstairs. At the same time, we heard the back door slam.

"Someone's goin' out the back!" Brock shouted. "Did you hear that poundin'?"

"Go after them. I'll check on the pounding."

He didn't try to stop me when I headed for the stairs.

There were rooms on either side of the long hallway, and as I walked, the pounding stopped. I stood frozen for a minute, waiting to decide which direction to go next.

As Brock pounded up the stairs, the noise started up again. Out of breath, he said, "He got away."

"Did you see who it was?"

"Some old dude with gray hair jumped into a car."

I pointed down the hall to the last room on the left. "That pounding is coming from there." Together, we rushed down the hall.

I grabbed for the knob and twisted. The door was locked, but the beating continued. *Bang-bang-bang-bang! Bang-bang-bang-bang!*

"Stand back!" Brock commanded, taking charge.

Heaving his weight against the door, he rammed it several times with his shoulder before the lock gave way.

There was Nathan, lying on an old mattress, his wrists and ankles bound together with shiny gray duct tape. A white cloth had been stuffed into his mouth and then covered with tape also. There was no furniture in the room; the lack of carpeting had allowed us to hear his shoes beating against the bare floor. His eyes darted around in his head. He was obviously afraid whoever had done this to him was still in the house. Holding up his hands, he shook them, signaling me to hurry and cut him free.

I fell to my knees and tore at the tape covering his mouth. Brock put his gun away and worked on the bindings.

"Kathy! You're here? Thank God."

I hugged him, tears streaming down my face. "Don't worry, Nathan. You're safe now."

"We gotcha, boss." The big guy was crying too.

Chapter Twenty-Three

"You want I should call the cops, boss? Are ya hurt? Geez, you look like hell. D'ya need an ambulance?" Looking at me, he asked, "What should we do?"

"I'm fine, I'm fine. No ambulance! Maybe Kathy can notify the police that I've been found, but that can wait until tomorrow. I'm not up to an interrogation right now. I just want to get out of here."

"Are you sure you're okay? Do you know who did this? What's going on? Was it Larkin?" I tried to stop asking questions, tried giving us all a moment to calm down, but my concerns wouldn't stop pushing their way out of my mouth. "I really think we should go straight to the police."

"Are you gonna drive me home, or do I have to walk?" he insisted, obviously embarrassed.

At this point, I decided to do whatever would make him happy. He was right—reports could wait until tomorrow. The important thing now was to get Nathan home, safe and sound.

Brock gently gripped Nathan under the arms and lifted him up to his feet. "Can you walk okay, boss?"

"Give me a minute." His legs wobbled, reminding me of a foal, fresh from its mother, trying to stand and take a few steps. I stood closer in case he fell. But he didn't.

"Is there anyone in the house?" I asked.

"I'm pretty sure they left. But they'll be back."

It was a strain not to ask who "they" were, but I managed to keep quiet.

"Can ya make it, boss?"

"Sure, just stay close . . . in case."

Brock held his gun, leading the way through the hall and down the stairs. Nathan followed. And I brought up the rear, ready to catch my wobbly friend if he stumbled.

Once we were outside, I raced around to open the doors of the jeep. Brock helped Nathan into the passenger's seat and buckled him in. Then the big guy crawled into the back while I took my position in the driver's seat and started the ignition. I couldn't help scrutinizing my shaky passenger. No visible cuts or bruises, and his eyes were clear and focused; he was aware of his surroundings. *Thank God*, I kept thinking, *Nathan was alive and well*. I only hoped that his ordeal hadn't affected him emotionally.

He insisted we take him back to the office. More than anything, he wanted to assure his crew that he was okay and they didn't have to worry anymore. We had a thirty-minute drive ahead of us, and for the first third of the trip, all we could do was smile at each other. Then we laughed our relief. When his shaking subsided, Nathan started talking. He spoke slowly, deliberately, trying to make sense of the last six days. I was hungry for details and wanted him to hurry it along. But I just stared ahead at the highway and let him tell his story at his own pace.

*   *   *

"I had four appointments scheduled last Friday," he started, "a typical workload for the end of the week. After a drive-thru breakfast, I arrived at the office around eight thirty. The minute I walked in the door, Polly started in on me about the mountain of paperwork on my desk. I spent about two hours paying bills, ordering equipment, satisfied I'd reduced that mountain to a molehill.

"The eleven o'clock appointment got cancelled, so I bumped Larkin up an hour, to the top of the list, hoping maybe that demanding jerk would think he was getting preferential treatment and be more pleasant. It was ten thirty when I headed out to Excelsior Boulevard."

He went on to explain that Everett Larkin raged on about damage to his car the first time he'd called Walker Securities. Polly tried but, after a few minutes, realized nothing she could say would calm the man down. So she handed the phone off to Rosie. She listened and nodded and listened some more. Realizing nothing she could say would appease him, she passed the call over to Nathan.

"I've learned how to handle people, never making them aware that they're being handled."

"I know that," I said with feeling.

He ignored the comment and went on. "I sympathized with Larkin, giving the man my full attention. When the anger had fizzled out, I made some suggestions about what could be done, securitywise. I sent E.T. over the next day to assess the area and estimate what the job would cost. There wasn't any need for me to go out to the house. Truth was, I didn't want to go. Besides, E.T. is the calm member of the crew—he meditates twice a day."

"I'm not sure I knew that about him," I said.

"Hey, there's still a lot I don't know about him. He keeps to himself. Anyway, a few days later, E.T. drove out to Excelsior Boulevard for a second time and installed four security cameras and a monitoring system. The work had taken the entire morning. And as far as everyone concerned thought, we were done with the job, and with Everett Larkin."

"Not the case?" I asked.

"Oh, no. Three days later, he called, insisting four cameras were not enough. Claimed E.T. was incompetent, that the acre of land surrounding the house certainly needed more equipment, and if something happened to his property or him and his wife, he'd sue the pants off of Walker Securities. So I made an appointment, again, for the next day—Friday. That was the first time I met the man face-to-face.

"He was older than he'd sounded on the phone. Old and irritated. I wasn't sure if Larkin was angry by nature or if the unexpected change in our appointment time had interrupted something he was doing."

"So what happened?"

"Inside, muddy boot prints were all over the shiny marble floor of the foyer. I laughed to myself, thinking about the chewing out Larkin was going to get from his wife. The prints led into a large living room, across the beige carpeting, and stopped in front of a white sofa where a young man sat. When he saw me, he hesitated a second, unsure what to do. Then, like a frightened animal, he scurried out of sight, into another part of the house.

"But that short minute had been just long enough for me to see the dark hair hanging in the stranger's eyes and dirty white socks bagging around his ankles. Raggedy, that's the impression I got from that guy in the ripped pants and dirty jacket."

"What did Larkin have to say about him?"

"The weirdest part was that Larkin acted as if he hadn't even seen the man on the sofa. He never offered an explanation for the dirt, or the stranger.

"The old man led me upstairs to a small office where E.T. had installed the camera monitors. The whole time, Larkin pointed and complained about blind spots, saying he could have done a better job himself. Then he insisted we go out to walk the perimeter of the house and lawn."

"Still no sign of the other man?" I asked.

"Not then. There was no sense in arguing about it. If the old guy wanted more equipment, I was happy to oblige. After all, my job was to sell surveillance, not talk a customer out of making additional purchases. So I wrote up another work order."

Then he headed for the Ordway house, his next appointment. He explained how that woman was glad to see him. She was overjoyed he'd come early. The job took a little over an hour, which left plenty of time for an early dinner before going to the eye clinic in Hopkins.

"I'd known Easton since he was a little dude and always looked forward to catching up on the family news. Tate Senior traveled a lot, and we'd lose touch now and then. We talked about the problems Easton was having with his staff. I took notes, laying out the options he had. By the time I left, it was getting dark.

"I had trouble remembering where the car was parked. But that was just my age acting up. I wandered around for a few minutes, not wanting to push the alarm button on my key because of it being a hospital zone. But I finally spotted my faithful Nissan. Then someone called to me."

I didn't interrupt him, because I felt we were getting to the nitty-gritty of his kidnapping.

"Standing there was that man I'd seen at the Larkin house. Only this time, he looked cleaner and was wearing a hunter's jacket. I kept a good distance between us but couldn't help noticing that Porsche of his. All shined up like that, no way could it belong to that fella.

"He was polite enough, but I couldn't help wondering how he knew where the Nissan had been parked. The guy said that Mr. Larkin wanted to see me on account of he felt ashamed for being so rude and wondered if I could have dinner with him.

"I didn't buy a word of it. Nothing about the invitation or this guy felt right. So I refused but did it in a polite way. I assured the man there was no need for an apology. As far as I was concerned, Larkin and I were cool.

"But the guy wouldn't take no for an answer. He went on about the old man being a sick dude, and it would only take a minute for me to ease his mind. He smiled a lot, talking about how he did part-time work for Larkin and how his employer wasn't all that bad.

"The corner of the parking lot where we were standing was dark. I didn't want to offend the kid but wasn't about to change my mind. Finally I made up a story about having to meet some friends.

"But the kid persisted, practically begged. I finally had enough and turned to get into my car. That's when I felt the gun on my back.

"'Look, I tried being nice,' he said, 'but I got orders to bring you back to the house, and that's exactly what I'm going to do.'

"Before I knew what was happening, the guy grabbed my keys, shoved me inside the Nissan, and ordered me to drive to Excelsior Boulevard."

Chapter
Twenty-Four

Nathan stopped abruptly when I pulled up in front of his office.

"Are you sure you're okay?" I asked, patting his shoulder. "Don't you think we should go to the hospital, just to get you checked—"

"No hospital. I'm fine. Just dirty and hungry." He smiled weakly. "Come on, I have to show my crew that I'm alive and well, don't I?"

"You should go in first, boss," Brock told him. "Act like nothin' happened and it's a regular day. It'll drive 'em crazy."

Nathan laughed. "You've all been through enough already. Especially sending out an SOS for Kathy." He leaned over closer to me and said, "I'm so sorry about all of this."

"You would have done the same for me."

"In a heartbeat."

I got out of the jeep and ran around to help Nathan, but he was almost to the office door by the time I got to him. Brock and I brought up the rear as he walked inside. It took a second before his presence registered, and then I heard a loud squeal followed by a stampede as Rosie, E.T., and Polly came running toward us.

Polly got there first. Unable to do anything but hug Nathan, she started to laugh uncontrollably. E.T. was next. All smiles, he patted his boss on the back. "I knew it, I knew it. I sent out prayers to the universe, and it took over." And Rosie—tough, strong Rosie—cried like a baby.

I was surprised, but I guess I shouldn't have been, when Brock joined in, grabbing everyone closer in a group hug. It was wonderful seeing them all so happy, at the same time, in the same place. And I knew enough to enjoy the moment because, in a few minutes, anger would set in when Nathan finished his story. Plans would be made to find whoever had kidnapped and held him for almost a week. I also knew I wouldn't be going back to Taos until we were all satisfied that the guilty party was behind bars.

Rosie looked over at me. "Come on, Katie. Get yourself over here."

I started toward the group when my phone rang. It was Tom.

"I have to get this," I told them. "I'll be right back."

Walking into Nathan's office, I pulled out a chair and took the call.

"Hey . . . Mom . . . I wanted to remind you about the movies tonight. We'll meet you over at the IMAX on Southdale around five . . ."

"We found Nathan today!" I blurted, unable to hold back my excitement. "I'm at the office with him now."

"That's great news! The kids will be happy to hear he's okay. Cam was especially upset. You know how he gets."

"Well, tell him Nathan's fine."

"Did you get the guys who kidnapped him?"

"No. That comes next."

"Well, after the day you've had, I don't suppose you feel like going to a theater filled with screaming kids and watching a movie about zoo animals."

"Not really." Guilt tried to edge its way in, but I shut it down quickly. Cam and Chloe were perfectly fine with their father.

"Lizzie told me you and Nathan had grown . . . close the past few years." Tom was as subtle as a two-ton weight.

"He's been a very good friend."

"Sure."

"Okay then, tell the kids I'll see them tomorrow. Promise."

"I'll explain the situation. They'll understand."

"Thanks, Tom. Give them both my love."

"Wait! Is Nathan okay . . . physically?"

"He seems to be."

"If you want me to come over there and examine him, I'd be happy to."

"I might take you up on that. He hates hospitals, and I have a feeling we won't be able to get him to one."

"You have my number. Feel free to call anytime . . . Kate." He was still unsure about what to call me and seemed to be trying out a few choices before deciding on one that fit.

"That's very kind of you."

"Anytime. Now go celebrate with your friends, and we'll see you tomorrow."

Everyone seemed calmer when I returned.

Rosie held up a bottle of champagne. "I had this stashed away for when we found the boss. I poured you a glass—well, a paper cup full. Come on, Katie, put your feet up and have some."

"That sounds great."

"When you're rested, you can tell us what happened. You probably don't want to talk about it now," E.T. said to Nathan.

"The boss started tellin' us everything on the drive over," Brock said.

"I know you all have a lot of questions. And you can ask Brock or Kathy for a recap. I think I can just make it the rest of the way, and then I have to get home. I need a shower and a good night's sleep."

"We'll take what we can get," Rosie said.

"Just tell us as much as you can," Polly told him. "It's been so awful not knowing what happened to you. I just read that every forty seconds, a person goes missing. That can't be right, but there it was—"

"Is there any food back there?" Nathan motioned to the break room. "I'll take anything."

"Let me check, boss." Brock hurried to have a look.

We all sat, eagerly waiting for him to return so we could hear the rest of Nathan's story.

Brock returned with an armful of plastic containers, paper bags, plastic silverware, and an orange plate. Spreading it all out on the desk in front of him, he started going through the potluck.

"Looks like some pizza."

"That was my lunch today," Rosie said. "Pepperoni. It's still good."

"I can go get you a hamburger if you like," I offered. "I can be there and back in ten minutes."

"This is fine," Nathan said. "Sit still." He ignored everything else and unwrapped the pizza.

The five of us sat there staring as he ate. I didn't realize we were doing that until he stopped chewing and laughed. "Give me a minute to digest."

After a few sips of water, Nathan leaned back and picked up his story right where he'd left off during the ride over.

Chapter Twenty-Five

"I couldn't believe that it was the same man I'd seen in Larkin's house a few hours earlier. But there he was, bigger than life, in the parking lot of the medical building, waiting for me. He said Larkin wanted to see me. When I made an excuse, refusing to go back to the house, the guy pulled a gun and shoved me into the Nissan."

We were all sitting there, hanging on his every word.

"We struggled. My only thought was to get the gun away from that idiot. So while the man kept trying to push me into the back seat, I stiffened my legs to hold the car door open. If I was going to get out of this, it had to be now. While we wrestled for the weapon, the phone in my front pocket beeped. Hearing the familiar sound reminded me of other times the keypad had been hit unintentionally. It was crazy, but I hoped a connection would be made and the person on the other end would figure out something was wrong. I shouted, I grunted, but no one heard me."

"Yeah," Brock said, "we thought those were butt dials."

"The stranger was bigger, younger, and finally won the battle. He ordered me to get into the driver's seat, made me fasten my seat belt, then tightened the bindings. The guy climbed into the backseat and held the gun to my head, demanding I drive to the Larkin house."

"Did you go right back to the house?" Polly asked, anxiously.

"Yes. The old man was waiting outside for us. When he saw the gun in his man's hand, he knew instantly that their plan hadn't gone the way he'd intended. Walking over to my car, he banged on the hood, shouting like a maniac at the man he called Charlie. Ranting at him for making such a mess of such a simple plan."

"Thieves falling out," E.T. said, even though they weren't really thieves.

"Shh," Polly said, because she was still eager to hear Nathan's story and didn't want him to be interrupted.

Nathan went on to say that Larkin opened the car door, unleashing his frustration on him while he was still bound to the driver's seat. Struggling to keep his voice down, Larkin went on about their schedule. If only Nathan would have stuck to their original appointment and come an hour later, everything would have been fine. None of this would have been necessary. It was all Nathan's fault, he complained to Charlie. And now there was nothing left to do but take drastic measures.

"Larkin ordered Charlie to get out of the car and release me," Nathan went on. "But the confused kid couldn't handle the gun and take care of the seat belt at the same time, so he shoved the weapon into his pocket."

"There it was, just sticking out of the jacket pocket. An easy grab. I started to reach for it. But all of a sudden, Larkin was holding a Taser on me, threatening to use it if he had to. Anger overtook calm, and he started in on Charlie again. I thought the old guy was going to hit the kid. And so did the kid, because he flinched.

"It was dark; there were no streetlights installed in front of the house yet, and it was obvious that Larkin and Charlie had never done anything like this before and were frustrated. All those circumstances came together just long enough to give me a chance to quickly shove my phone deep into the backseat."

"Good thinking," Rosie said.

"I thought so. If someone found it, I reasoned, they'd know I was in trouble. Besides, the device would be the first thing Larkin would take away from me anyway. But the instant it left my hand, I regretted what I'd done. The battery needed charging, and now I was left with no way to call for help."

"You made a split-second decision," E.T. said.

"I suppose. So when Larkin's temper finally ran out, he started for the house, shouting to Charlie to bring me. Charlie drew his gun and did as he was told."

Inside the house, Nathan noticed everything was different about the living room. No more thick carpeting, and the white furniture had been replaced with thrift shop rejects. And while he demanded to know what was going on, Larkin just stood there smiling. Suddenly polite and calm, he reassured Nathan that no one was going to hurt him. They simply needed a day or so to complete a project. No more questions allowed.

"But Charlie didn't agree," Nathan went on, "and urged his boss to just shoot me, be done with it. And now it was Charlie's turn to rant at Larkin. Surprisingly, the old man stood there and took it.

"The two of them began grilling me. What exactly had I seen or heard earlier? Did I recognize Charlie? They knew I was an ex-cop, and that had them worried."

"So what'd you tell 'em?" Brock asked.

"I explained that I saw muddy foot prints across the floor and that's all. I didn't hear a thing. But I kept the details about the carpet and furniture to myself. Larkin didn't believe me. But at that point, he wasn't willing to hurt me.

"Charlie was told to escort me to my room. The one on the second floor, in the rear of the house. It had been made ready.

"I took one last try, telling Larkin that I had people who would miss me. And those people would call the police if I didn't show up for my meetings. If the two of them just let me walk away now, things would go easier for both of them. After all, I hadn't been hurt. Why not stop while they were ahead and let me get in my car and ride away? But even as I was trying to be convincing, I didn't believe my own words."

"And neither did they, I bet," Polly said.

"And when neither man wanted to make a deal or listen to another word," Nathan said, "I wasn't that surprised.

"But their sudden attack did surprise me. It just took a slight nod from Larkin, and Charlie pulled back and knocked me to the floor. Before I knew what was happening, I was being dragged up the stairs."

Nathan told us that a mattress, covered with worn blankets, was centered on the floor of a small room. The walls hadn't been painted yet but had a coat of white primer on them. There was no furniture, no lamps. The two windows were covered over with white curtains to keep up the outward appearance of the house.

"Charlie aimed his gun at my chest while Larkin wrapped me in duct tape. Around and around, tighter and tighter. It took two rolls before he was satisfied there was no way I could get loose. Pushing me back off my feet and onto the mattress, Larkin added extra tape, securing me to the bed and floor. It was all so sloppy and yet very effective. I couldn't move a muscle.

"Throughout the next five days, the men took turns checking on me. I would be jerked up into a sitting position and fed. Twice a day, the tape was cut off from my waist down to allow for a five-minute bathroom break. But my chest and arms were always tightly bound. Each time the breaks were over, I was wrapped up again with fresh tape or heavy rope. The rest of the time—morning, noon, and night—I was forced to lie flat on my back and stare at the ceiling . . . and wonder what was going to happen to me."

He stopped, and it got very silent in the room.

Chapter Twenty-Six

Nathan leaned back, exhausted. We waited for him to continue his story, but he seemed distracted and gulped down more water.

Rosie took advantage of the pause. "So how did you guys get inside?" she asked, looking from Brock to me.

"We just walked in," I told her. "The door was unlocked."

"Someone was sure in a hurry to get outta there," Brock added.

"Or maybe they wanted to make it easy for whoever showed up to get into the house," Nathan said. "All I know is that Charlie just stopped showing up a few days ago. I never saw him again. And when Larkin didn't bring me food last night or today, I figured he was taking care of that project they mentioned."

He might as well know now, I thought. *Get everything out so there are no surprises left.* "Charlie's dead." I hadn't meant to be so blunt and wished I'd delivered the news a bit more gently.

It was as if an invisible club hit Nathan square in the face the way he jerked back. Stunned—no, shocked was a better description. We all sat watching him, afraid what would come next.

"You okay, boss?" Brock asked timidly.

E.T. rolled his chair close to Nathan. "That's good news, right? Now that creep can't hurt you again or make any more threats."

I remembered what Nathan had told me about E.T. before I met him. How he thought his employee was quite an enigma. A pacifist who would do whatever was necessary to stop a bad guy but refused to kill a mosquito or ant. He'd been trained in martial arts but would much rather talk his way out of a dangerous situation than have to fight. And yet, as I watched him reassure Nathan, I knew he'd probably be the one crew member who would go the furthest to protect their boss.

"So what happened to Charlie?" Nathan finally asked.

I explained what I'd found out from Bostwick and then later from Barbara. "The car that hit him was a blue sports car, so I think it's a safe bet the car belonged to Larkin," I explained.

Nathan sat forward and nodded. "Well, Charlie was standing next to it in the parking lot that first night. But he had to drive me back to the house in my car. It would have been too dangerous in that little thing with me fighting to get away or him trying to hold me down."

"And one of them had to come back to get the Porsche after they got you in the house," Polly said. "I bet it's parked in Mr. Larkin's garage. That should be easy to check out."

Rosie joined in, eager to play detective. "So all we gotta do is see if the paint on Charlie matches up with the paint on the car. Then bingo! The cops grab Larkin for murder and kidnappin'. That dude'll never see daylight again."

"Kidnapping, maybe, but there's no way to prove he was driving the car that ran down Charlie," Nathan said. "By the way"—he looked at me—"where's my car?"

"I found it over at Bredesen Park, on Wednesday," E.T. explained. "The cops impounded it. They have to go over it for evidence . . . you know."

The pieces were fitting together nicely. "The steering wheel was tacky with varnish from the job Charlie was working on," I said. "So he had to be the one who drove it out there." That effectively did away with any questions about glue.

"Anybody hungry besides me?" Brock asked, distracting us.

Tension can do crazy things to your body. You can look relaxed on the outside but be frustrated and scared to death on the inside. The knots in my stomach had been tightening ever since I heard Nathan was missing. Nothing had been easy or steady for days. But now that he was sitting in front of me, alive and well, I could feel the muscles in my neck loosening. I could also hear my stomach growling. "Now that you mention it, I'm starving."

"Sorry, guys," Nathan said. "I just want to go home and sleep in my own bed, in my own house."

I expected a big discussion over who would drive him home, but there was none. The crew just looked at me.

"Katie, you should take the boss home." There was a look that passed between Rosie and Polly. I could see they had already discussed the possibility of this situation happening.

Polly smiled. "Yeah, Kate, you take him. We'll handle the stuff here and lock up." Then she pointed to Nathan. "And don't expect any of us to show up before noon tomorrow."

"Yeah," Brock said, "if we was to charge you for all the hours we put in this week, you'd go bankrupt."

"In that case, I'll have to think of a way to thank all of you with something other than money," he said. "Money's so . . . so impersonal. Right, Kathy?"

I nodded. "I think a nice turkey. Thanksgiving's coming. Everyone likes turkey." It was mean of us, and I tried to keep a straight face. "Or maybe a gift card at the grocery store would be better. That way they can get what they like."

Nathan got up and started walking to the door. "I'll come up with something real nice."

"Turkey?" Brock looked at the others, confused. "I was just makin' a joke."

Chapter Twenty-Seven

It felt good when Nathan didn't resist my help getting into the jeep. But I reminded myself not to push the nurse routine too far. He was a proud man and would be humiliated if he thought I saw him as weak. I'd have to tread softly and, as Teddy Roosevelt advised, keep a big stick at the ready . . . just until Larkin was locked up.

"We have to call and report that you've been found," I said.

"Maybe we could hold off until tomorrow? I'll call it in early. You know there'll be reporters outside my door all night if I do it now. I won't get any sleep. And the neighbors won't be too happy."

"But the longer you wait, the more time Larkin has to get away. We know that man's a kidnapper, and he might have even killed Charlie."

"I know, I know."

"Would you rather I call?"

"No . . . I'll do it . . . later tonight."

"Sometimes doing the right thing sucks, doesn't it?"

A smile flashed across his face but then immediately dissolved. "Kathy"—he touched my arm—"how can I ever thank you for coming all this way—"

"Shush. Let's not mention it again. Deal?"

"Deal."

"Good. Now each of us gets the rest of the night and some of the morning to pull ourselves together. Then tomorrow, let's say around noon, I'll pick you up for lunch, and we'll drive to the station to have a sit-down with Bostwick."

Nathan stretched and deflated into his seat.

Before I could say another word, he was snoring.

* * *

The next morning, I watched a game show while getting dressed. The frenzied audience carried on like they had just witnessed the Second Coming. I couldn't remember ever being excited about anything enough to scream and shout like they were. Before I could change the channel, a red-and-blue banner filled the screen, announcing "Breaking News." And there they were—reporters lined up in front of Nathan's house. As I walked toward my phone, it started to ring.

"Told you so," was all he said.

"Duck out the back, and I'll pick you up on the corner," I told him. "I'll be there in fifteen minutes."

"Make it ten. And don't go telling me about speed limits. Just hurry."

"I'm so sorry."

"You're buyin' breakfast."

I raced around the house, managing to get myself together in five minutes. By the time I picked up Nathan, it was 9:30. How naïve of me to think things would be calmer today.

"It should be quiet out at the diner," he said. "The breakfast crowd has come and gone. It's way too early for lunch. And don't forget—"

"I know—I'm buying."

* * *

The Twelfth Street Diner had been an Edina tradition since I was a kid. Benny Angelo, the original owner, had long since retired to Florida. A young couple from Connecticut ran it now and, thankfully, hadn't updated the decor inside or out. The only thing they'd given into was installing Wi-Fi for their customers. But I would have been okay without it.

"Smells good in here," Nathan said as we were shown to a table. "Always does."

"Comforting . . . like home." I looked over the menu, but there was really no need. Except for the daily special, it was always the same. I could recite each item and category by the time I started high school.

After the waitress brought our coffee, I ordered, then sat back and studied Nathan while he told the woman what he wanted. His hands shook slightly as he spoke, pointing out the breakfast he wanted. Was he aware of the tremor? His eyes flitted around the large room, watching, waiting. He was guarded and uncomfortable, which made me feel the same way.

Starting a conversation while we waited for our order was awkward. *Why should that be?* I wondered. I'd known the man sitting across from me for decades. But he was different. He must have sensed my discomfort and started first.

"So how have you been? I bet Lizzie and the grandbabies were glad to see you."

Was it frustration I felt or sadness? Nathan knew how I was; we talked often. I wrestled with my emotions. Should I force the issue? Make him talk about something he obviously didn't want to deal with yet? Or should I just play along and act as though things went back to normal—magically, overnight—and his life hadn't been at risk for days?

"Lizzie's at a convention, and the kids are with Tom," I managed to say.

Nathan nodded and tried on a smile. "How long is he in town for this time?"

That burning feeling behind my eyes signaled tears of frustration were coming. Oh, how I hated them. Women over the age of forty came off as weak and silly when they cried. No doubt there were people who thought it touching, but my experience showed that the reaction they usually got was negative. So I blinked to hold those stupid tears at bay and waited a beat until I was sure my voice wouldn't crack.

When I was ready, I said, "What the hell are you doing, Nathan? You were a prisoner for days. Bound and gagged, unsure if you were going to be murdered or released. There had to be moments when you wondered if you'd get out of there alive. And now we're supposed to act as though none of it happened?"

His head dropped, and he stared at the table.

I'd jumped in the deep end, and now I had to swim my heart out. "Talk to me. Tell me what you went through in that room. You can tell me anything." I held back a few tears. "Nathan, we've been through so much together. Nobody knew the hell we suffered after Sully's death. And here we are again, trying to deal with another crazy situation. So start talking, 'cause it's either me or a therapist. You have to get it all out, or it'll break you."

He nodded, still looking at the table. This was going to be tougher than I thought.

"Of course you were afraid—anyone would have been. But I need to know what's going on with you now. I care about you, Nathan. Please . . ."

"Okay." He looked into my eyes. "I'll tell you what happened in that room. I had to face the fact that I'm all alone, Kathy. Funny, but that was the hardest thing I've ever had to admit to myself."

I started to say something, but he stopped me.

"You wanted me to talk, woman. So that means you have to sit back and listen."

I nodded.

"We've both interviewed people after they've escaped a deadly situation. Robbery, gunfire, a car accident, and a whole lot worse. Some say they knew, no doubt about it, that they were gonna be fine. Others tell you they made peace with their Maker and gave in, sure they were gonna die that day. But you see, Kathy, I've always known I'd be okay. Every day, going out on the job, when Terry would fuss at me. The times I'd overhear her tell her friends how scared she was that maybe one day she'd end up a widow. I brushed all of it off. Because I knew I wouldn't end up that way. Of course, when I'm old . . . real old," his eyes brightened when he smiled, "like when I'm a hundred . . . I'll pass on in a simple, ordinary fashion. But until then, I'll always be okay."

The waitress came back carrying four plates of food. She laid out eggs, toast, bacon, hash browns, and pancakes. Sensing the mood at our table, she didn't say a word and left.

Nathan picked up a piece of toast and spread grape jelly on it.

"So you're upset that you're alive? I don't understand."

"Lying on that dirty floor for all those hours, there was nothing to do but think. Then think some more. I have no children, no wife, my sister died years ago, and I don't really know my nephews."

"Come on, you know, or should at your age, that family isn't always defined by blood. Brock would do anything for you—no questions asked. Polly's like a daughter, always trying to please and be helpful. Rosie"—I had to laugh—"she's a dynamo. You hired her knowing she had a record and helped her start over with a new life. Her loyalty is indelible. And E.T., well, he's your eccentric brother. Every one of them loves and respects you."

"And what about you?"

I could feel my face getting warm. Trying to delay the moment while I thought of just the right words, I picked up a piece of bacon and shoved it into my mouth. Then I chewed . . . slowly.

But Nathan was going to wait me out. While I chewed, he calmly ate his eggs.

I finished the bacon, and still he waited.

"When I heard you were missing, I couldn't get out here fast enough. The thought of my life without you in it is unacceptable. We have a mutual respect for each other; you know that. I consider you my best friend, my confidante. I adore you, Nathan."

He seemed happy with my words. "Do you think that maybe . . . someday . . . we could be more? Come on Kathy, you must have thought about you and me that way."

If I was forcing him to be truthful, I had to return the favor. So I admitted, "I have. More times than I can count. But our timing always seems to be off."

Nathan laughed. "Like now. Life-and-death situations can sure put a damper on romance."

"Romance? That sounds nice. I haven't had any romance in my life for a long time. Maybe you could come visit me for a trauma-free weekend."

"Sounds good. That's exactly what I need right now. Something to look forward to."

And just like that, the wedge between us dissolved, and we were able to be ourselves again.

Chapter
Twenty-Eight

We enjoyed breakfast at a leisurely pace, as well as our time alone. After the food was gone, we ordered more coffee.

Nathan looked at his watch. "When I called last night, I left a message for Bostwick. I told him we'd come in to see him this afternoon. But first, I guess we should get to the office and check that my crew's okay. Now that I'm back, it'll be business as usual."

"Are you sure you don't want to stop by the hospital for a quick exam? You're famous now. I'm sure there won't be any waiting for Mr. Celebrity."

He scoffed at the idea that he'd get special treatment. "I'm sore around my wrists where the tape rubbed. But if I had to be kidnapped, I'd pick those two. Get this: One day, Larkin comes in with a whole chicken dinner. Mashed potatoes, slaw, biscuits—the works. He'd even put it on china plates. After he pulled the tape off my mouth and arms, he set me up. And while I'm eating, he held a gun on me but kept apologizing over and over."

"Could you hear me when I came to the house on Wednesday?" I asked.

"You were there?" He looked surprised.

"I retraced all the calls you made on Friday. Larkin was the first stop I made."

"No, I never heard a sound. But I was all the way upstairs, on the other side of the house."

"But you heard when Brock and I came back. That's why you banged your feet against the floor, right?"

"I heard voices and knew they didn't belong to Larkin or Charlie. I just hoped I'd attract some attention."

"Did you overhear anything between those two?" I asked. "Or a woman's voice? When I visited with Mr. Larkin, he told me his wife was out of town on business."

"No, I don't think so. The house was pretty quiet most of the time. Except for that construction work going on. Seems it started as soon as the sun came up and lasted until dark."

"Did you know that Charlie was one of the on-site workers? He got the job because his girlfriend was the construction company owner's daughter."

"I suppose we could go talk to the foreman. Maybe he—"

"Brock and I questioned him. That's what led us to the Larkin house."

"So what did he have to say about poor ole Charlie?"

"Not much, really. He had a record. None of his coworkers liked him much. I suppose they resented him because of his pull with the boss. But there was a blonde who came around. She drove a blue Porsche, and one time, the foreman saw her drive right up to Larkin's house. He figured she was his daughter because of the age difference. But from what

Polly found out, Mrs. Larkin is much younger than her husband and has blonde hair."

"Well, you know what I always say about coincidence." Nathan grinned. "And I also know that you've never agreed."

"Maybe I'm starting to come around," I said sheepishly. "I'm not saying that I agree with you about everything being fraught with meaningful signs. But here's something else I saw yesterday." I went on to tell him about the painting I found in Ray DeYoung's trailer and how it matched a set in the Larkin house where one was missing.

Nathan leaned back and folded his arms across his chest, looking satisfied with himself. "Well, well, Mrs. Sullivan. Score a point for me. Now that's got to be more than coincidence. Why don't we go and ask him? But first I've got to go see my people."

* * *

The crew looked annoyed when they saw us walk through the door.

"The phone's been ringin' off the hook," Rosie called from her desk.

"And we're jammed with e-mails," Polly added.

Brock joined in. "I had to chase away a whole gang of lookie loos standin' in front of the office. They were blockin' traffic out there, an' the other store owners were mad."

"Looks like you're living your fifteen minutes of fame, boss," E.T. told Nathan. "Enjoy it while you can. It might even be good for business."

"Maybe if you give a statement to the press," I advised, "everyone will leave you alone."

Rosie walked over to where we stood. "Your story has a happy ending, ya know? People can't get enough of good news. Me included, boss. They just want to see that you're okay."

I could tell he was embarrassed. After all, as far as he was concerned, he'd never been in any real danger. He hadn't been beaten or tortured. And the only pain he'd suffered was from the duct tape.

"You're a survivor, no matter what happened to you in there," I whispered.

"How's everyone in here?" he asked.

They nodded and said they were all good.

"Well, it's not as if what we do here is life-and-death important. And today's Friday, right?" He looked around to check with the others. Everyone nodded. "Okay, all of you take the rest of the day off. Have a nice long weekend. Polly, would you call and cancel today's appointments before you go?"

"There's only one. I'll reschedule for sometime next week."

"Great. Then you can switch the phones over and leave. I'll talk to the press and get everyone calmed down."

"But first I think we should go to the station and tell Bostwick everything that's happened, in person," I said.

Nathan considered my plan for a minute. "Sounds good. Any questions?"

A unified "No" filled the room.

"Then I'll see everyone on Monday. And thanks again. Thanks for everything."

Brock spoke for the group. "What can we say? We love ya, boss."

Chapter Twenty-Nine

"I'm sure Bostwick will want to deliver your statement to the press," I said as we drove to the police station.

"That egomaniac?" Nathan laughed. "He lives for his moments in the spotlight. And this is good for public relations, especially if he hasn't gotten closer to finding whoever killed that woman a few weeks ago."

"Did I tell you Carolyn Watson was a family friend of his? Dean's son went to school with her son. Their wives were pretty close, too. I left there with the impression that finding her killer is his top priority right now. Charlie got handed off to his detectives, and you . . . well . . . he let me take the lead finding you. I mean, your case got assigned, but I don't know what they did to find you."

"Well, they didn't—you did," Nathan said. I hoped Nathan didn't feel slighted. But instead, he seemed happy that his crew and I had been left alone long enough to track him down.

"Do you think there's a connection between Mrs. Watson's murder and Charlie's . . . accident?" he asked.

"Well, the blue sports car seems to be the common denominator connecting Charlie to Larkin and Larkin to you. I think if we can find that car, it'll answer some questions."

Nathan thought a moment. "I don't mean to sound callous, and believe me, I'm sorry that poor woman was murdered, but my main concern is seeing that Larkin gets put in jail for kidnapping. It's too bad Charlie had to go that way, but he was involved in some shady business. And the bad guys, more times than not, come to a bad end. Besides, it's not our job to find out who killed either of them."

"But . . ." I started, "maybe along the way . . . while we're looking for Mr. Larkin . . . maybe we'll find something that . . . might help the police . . ."

"You never give up, do you, Kathy?"

"Do you?"

* * *

When we walked into the station on West Fiftieth Street, the guys hurried to gather around Nathan. They patted his back, excited to see him alive and well. Far too often a missing person's case either goes unsolved or has a grim outcome.

"Geez, it's great to see you!" Officer DeYoung said, grinning.

"Really great!" a new recruit agreed.

"So how ya doin', man?" one of the old timers asked. "Ya okay?"

"I'm fine," Nathan assured them. "Don't I look fine?"

"If you mean, do you look like the same old crotchety dude, then the answer's yes," DeYoung joked. "Definitely yes."

"You had us real worried," a cop in the back of the room said.

"You all sound like a bunch of mother hens," Nathan told them. "Peckin' around, trying to find something to fuss about."

"Your crew must have been worried if they had to bring in the big guns," DeYoung kidded, nodding toward me.

"Hey," I tried to look indignant. "I've lost five pounds in the last week. I resent the word 'big.'"

"Small, medium, or large, if it wasn't for Kathy—"

"Kathy?" one of the guys kidded. "So it's Kathy now, is it?"

The old timer joined in. "Back in the day, Chief Sullivan would have written you up for insubordination for being so . . . familiar. But now that you're both retired, I guess—"

"Hey, hey!" Dean Bostwick had obviously heard the commotion and came out of his office, rushing toward the front desk. "What's going on out here?" When he saw Nathan and me standing there, he stopped in his tracks.

"Sorry we disturbed you, Chief," Nathan said.

"Walker! Glad to have you back in one piece." In spite of the fact that kidnapping is a capital offense and Nathan was an ex-cop, his case still took a back seat to two murders, as far as Chief Bostwick was concerned. The chief had a habit of making his own rules.

"Life is good, Chief."

Bostwick looked around at his men. "Now if all you ladies are done out here, I suggest you get back to work while I talk with Mr. Walker . . . in private."

Slowly, each man walked back to his desk, high fiving and mumbling a good-bye to Nathan.

I followed the two men down the hall to Bostwick's office, even though the chief hadn't acknowledged my presence. I was the only person who could recount the story of how Brock and I had found Nathan. Sooner or later, he'd be forced to deal with me. The last time I'd spoken with him, things had been cordial between us. I'd even thought our relationship might take on a new dimension. But maybe his pride had been bruised a bit. And maybe it was time for Police Chief Dean Bostwick to get over himself.

After we were seated, Dean closed the door. Removing his suit jacket and hanging it up, he then walked around his desk and sat.

"Well, Katherine, it looks like you did it again. What is that now? Two for two? You're on a winning streak."

His words came out as complimentary, but his attitude betrayed him. I could see that familiar look in his eyes. He resented me. Maybe he thought I was meddling; maybe he thought I was trying to show him up. But none of that mattered. Nathan was home, alive and well.

"I don't know about a winning streak. All I wanted to do was find my friend."

Bostwick nodded, pursing his lips while I spoke.

Nathan leaned forward. "We need your help Dean. The reporters are gonna keep buggin' me if you don't make a statement. An official statement—you know, like you've done before."

Dean's expression changed from indignant to self-important. All of a sudden he was the star quarterback instead of the third string.

Following Nathan's lead, I said, "Maybe you could arrange to go on air during the evening news." Maybe? I knew he could make one call and interrupt regularly scheduled programming any time he wanted.

He made us wait, just a few minutes. Just to hold the power tighter to his chest. "I'll need all the facts. And of course, I'll have to credit my department with doing some of the work."

"Your forensic team went over Nathan's car. It's in the impound lot now. And the county coroner was the one who put me on the right track to find Nathan."

"She did?" It was obvious the chief had been letting reports pile up on his desk. "How?"

It took a good hour to go over the details with him. From my interview with the smokers outside Dr. Tate's office to my meeting with Barbara. From the identification of Charles Kerrigan to meeting with his girlfriend and getting shot at by someone in a blue car. All of which led Brock and me to Larkin's house. I even told him about the painting in the trailer on the construction site.

Periodically he'd look up from taking notes to ask a question, but I did most of the talking while Nathan sat smiling and nodding.

"And as far as you knew," he asked Nathan, "this Larkin character was just a customer? The two of you never had words? There was no confrontation of any sort?"

"All he said was that I'd interrupted a project he was working on. He never explained what the project was or how long it would take to finish whatever the hell he was doing. But it had to be something illegal." Nathan went on to explain about seeing Charlie Kerrigan for the first time.

"Obviously the two of them were working together. Where was the wife during all this?" Bostwick asked.

"Supposedly out of town on business," I said. "At least that's what he told me."

Bostwick wrote on his pad. "I'll have my men find out her exact whereabouts. She could be behind all this."

"Or dead," Nathan said calmly.

Chapter Thirty

A press conference was to be held in front of the police station at five o'clock that same day. When Nathan asked me to be there with him, I agreed, thinking he needed some moral support. Otherwise, there was no need for me to stay.

The day had started off cool and windy. When we walked out of the diner after breakfast, dark clouds had started to move in, hanging overhead, threatening to open up and dump the rain at any moment. As a podium was being set up and folding chairs positioned around it, a cold drizzle began.

Now, I'm not a vain woman. And after all that had happened during the past few days, I felt silly even thinking about my hair. But as I watched female reporters huddling under umbrellas, their makeup and hair people buzzing around, I felt that I should at least try . . . just a little.

So I found a quiet corner in the lobby of the police station, behind heavy glass doors, where I could do a quick touch-up and still keep my eyes on the activity out front. When I was satisfied there was no more magic my comb and lipstick could work, I decided to take the next few minutes to call Tom.

Feeling like the worst grandparent ever created, I explained about the conference, telling him I wouldn't have much time to visit with Chloe and Cam that evening.

"Don't worry. In fact, this actually works out better for me," he said. "Tomorrow there's a symposium in Duluth I wanted to check out. But when Lizzie said she was going out of town, I figured there was no way. You'd be doing me a huge favor if you could spend tomorrow with the kids."

"Perfect. How about I come by later and ask them what they'd like to do? Maybe they could stay over Saturday night, and I'll bring them back Sunday afternoon? That way you don't have to hurry home."

"You're a real lifesaver . . . Kate. Thanks."

"Glad I could help out, Tom. I'll drop by after dinner."

"See you then."

I had just ended my call when I heard shouting. One of the voices was Nathan on the other side of the door. "They're ready, Kathy!"

*　*　*

A man adjusted the microphone. An American flag stood on one side of the podium, the Minnesota state flag on the other. Nathan was told to sit in the front row and pulled me next to him.

"Are you okay?" I whispered.

"Fine. I just want this whole thing to be over with."

"Come on, you're the happy ending everyone hoped for."

Nathan nodded. "I suppose."

I reached over and squeezed his hand. "All you gotta do is go up there and be your charming self."

The wind died down a bit, and the rain stopped as if an off switch had been flipped. Introductions were made by a public relations person whom I didn't recognize. She was a strong-looking woman, tall, wearing a red dress. Her short brunette hair fell back in place effortlessly each time a breeze passed by. Unlike mine, which was now a tangled mess.

Dean walked out to applause. He'd changed clothes since our meeting and was now immaculate in a gray pinstripe suit, white shirt, and burgundy tie with a matching pocket square. He gave the initial impression that he was totally responsible for bringing Nathan back safely. But as he laid out all the information and details, I had to admit he spoke eloquently. When he was finished basking in his own glory, Dean pointed to the guest of honor and invited him up.

The conference had occurred so quickly that Nathan hadn't had a chance to go home and change. But as long as I'd known him, he'd never given his clothes much thought. So I was surprised that before leaving his seat, he asked me if he looked okay.

Nathan always looked great. A white T-shirt beneath his brown leather jacket, the faded jeans, it all worked.

"You look fine."

While he recounted the events of last Friday, some reporters took notes, some held up microphones or recording devices. Cameramen moved through the crowd, trying for the best angles. Nathan seemed nervous at first, but once he got going, he appeared calm. Bostwick stood by silently, nodding at the appropriate moments. And when his story was almost finished, Nathan pointed to me.

"Some of you may not recognize her, but it was our own former police chief, Katherine Sullivan, who found me and brought me home. Stand up, Kathy."

These were the awkward moments I dreaded. Unprepared, I stood and smiled. Should I wave? Should I turn around so everyone can see the uncomfortable lady in the front row?

Bostwick managed a smile and led the applause. "I had the opportunity to work with Mrs. Sullivan when I first came on the force," he said, leaning into the mike, forcing Nathan to take a few steps back. "It was during that time I learned how to be a leader . . ."

I sat down as Dean went on about himself and his men, giving the impression that they had worked tirelessly, never taking a minute off, until they found Nathan.

Questions and answers volleyed back and forth for the last fifteen minutes. When everyone was satisfied they had enough words to fill columns or air time, it was over. And in less than twenty minutes, the podium and chairs were hustled off, leaving the area looking as if nothing had even taken place there.

"I think that went well, don't you?" Dean asked.

I couldn't resist a jab. "It went off just like I thought it would," I told him.

"Yeah, it was good." He smiled an artificially whitened grin, and I had to wonder if he was choosing to ignore my comment or if he was thicker than I thought and hadn't picked up on my sarcasm.

"So we're done now, right?" Nathan finally asked. "You'll write up all the reports; you have my statement. You know as much as Kathy and I do about this Larkin idiot. No more interviews—you don't need me for anything else?"

Dean rolled his eyes skyward, thinking. "Probably . . . but there might be something I forgot, so stay close."

We said our good-byes and had just gotten into my jeep when the storm that had been taunting us all day finally struck.

"I'll have to see about getting my car back," Nathan said as I drove through the downpour. "I can always use the company van, I guess. Just until things get back to normal." He looked out the window, peacefully watching the rain. "I'm hungry, how about you?"

"Is there something you missed while you were . . . away? Some food you've been craving?"

"A big juicy steak. I think there's a couple in my freezer. Care to join me?"

"Sure. But I can't stay long," I told him. "Gotta get over to Tom's and see the kids."

"I'll have you fed and on your way by seven . . . give or take a few minutes."

Chapter Thirty-One

Nathan was true to his word, and I was on my way to Tom's place by 7:15. The rain had let up, but the wetness each car kicked up as it passed forced me to switch on the wipers. I felt chilled and longed to be back in Taos with the sun on my face and a glass of wine in my hand.

So much had happened in the last three days that it was hard to organize the events in some kind of logical order. I'd been so single-minded, concentrating so fully on finding Nathan, that now that he was safe, I was unsure what should come next. The police were organizing to hunt down Everett Larkin. I could leave that to them, no problem. Barbara was doing a complete autopsy on the body of Charles Kerrigan, which would determine the cause of death. If foul play was suspected, it would be up to the police chief to decide his next course of action. But whether it had been intentional or accidental, it was official police business now. Which left me out of the picture completely and with free time on my hands, since my plane ticket home wouldn't be good for another week.

I could always change my departure date and leave sooner.

But there wasn't any reason to rush back to New Mexico. Another few days would give me time to catch up with Lizzie's news. She was always so excited to tell me every detail after a trip. And there was usually a funny story about someone she'd met that we'd laugh about for weeks. The kids were at that age where they were changing daily. Not their appearance so much, but their ideas and ambitions. I should spend more time with them before they headed off to college. Then I could go home happy that I'd accomplished what I came to do . . . and more.

But a part of me knew I was fooling myself. The part that had been a cop for so many years knew all too well I'd go crazy at home. Every minute I'd be checking e-mails and texts, calling Nathan for updates. I'd make everyone miserable. And that cop in me managed to convince my retired self that it would be very inconsiderate to just go home and leave so many loose ends hanging.

Hadn't Nathan said he wanted to see Larkin behind bars? And I'd have to stay in Edina a few days, just to make sure my friend was fully recovered. He might not have visible scars from his ordeal, but there could be emotional ones. I often thought of the three officers I'd known who suffered breakdowns after being on the job too long. I didn't want anything like that to happen to Nathan.

In the end, both parts of me agreed: it was my duty to stay in town awhile longer.

* * *

Tom answered the door as I was raising my hand to knock a second time. I got the impression he'd been standing there with his hand on the knob, waiting.

"I've been watching so you wouldn't have to stand outside in the rain." He smiled. "Come on in. Let me take your jacket. You must be cold and wet."

It felt so nice being taken care of. "Luckily the rain stopped, but I am cold. Thanks."

"There's one of Lizzie's old sweaters in here," he said as he opened the closet door. "She keeps forgetting to pick it up."

I recognized it immediately as the one I'd bought her three Christmases ago. As I pulled it on, I could smell the vanilla oil she wore and missed her.

"I wanted to get to you before the kids did. There's a small war going on."

"A war?"

"Chloe wants to go to the mall tomorrow."

"On Saturday?"

"I know! Grown-up brains, like ours, know it's the worst place to be, especially on the weekend. But to Chloe and her friends, it's nirvana."

"Friends?"

He walked me to a chair. "She's going to try to talk you into taking her and two girlfriends to the mall. She has a whole speech prepared about how responsible they are, how safe the mall is with security and all; she really thinks you'll buy it."

It was hard not to laugh out loud, so I just smirked. "I guess she forgot I raised a daughter."

"I know. But far be it for me to tell her anything. I'm just a dumb old dad."

"What about Cam? What does he want to do?"

"He just grumbles that he resents being forced to leave the house and how we should realize he's old enough to be left alone."

"Maybe I can come up with something that will make everyone happy."

"Good luck with that one, Kate."

We walked back to what looked like a combination office and family room. Chloe was spread out on a couch, talking on her phone, and Cam was sitting in front of the TV, totally engrossed.

"Hey, you two," I said.

Chloe looked up. "I gotta go," she told the person on the other end. "My grandma's here."

Cam picked up the remote and turned the TV off without looking at me.

Tom walked over to his desk and settled into a soft leather chair. When I was comfortable on the end of the couch, Chloe cuddled up beside me, and I put my arm around her. I knew she was getting ready to turn on the charm, but it didn't matter what her motive was—a hug from either of them was always delicious.

"We have the whole day tomorrow," I started, "and I've been thinking about what we can do."

Chloe put her phone aside, signaling she was about to say something important. "I've been thinking about it too, Grandma."

I had to play the all-seeing, all-knowing grandmother card, and before she had a chance, I started. "At your age, I'm sure you'd like to go to the mall. And maybe bring along some friends? I know that's exactly what your mother loved to do on the weekends."

Tom cringed. I guess he thought I hadn't heard a word he'd said in the living room.

Chloe looked like she was going to burst, she was so excited.

"But things aren't like they were back when your mother was a little girl," I told her.

The poor kid went from ecstatic to morose in a second.

"But . . . Grandma . . . all my friends are really responsible. Mom lets us go by ourselves all the time."

"No, she doesn't," Cam said, unable to ignore her exaggeration.

"But I thought you wanted to spend time with me," I said. As she continued to look at me with those big puppy-dog eyes of hers, I opened mine wider. "You can be with your girlfriends any old time."

Tom got it when he heard my tone. "Yeah, you don't get to see your grandmother that often," he said.

Chloe knew she was outnumbered. "I can see Grandma after. We'll have dinner and the whole night to be together." Nuzzling closer to me, she said, "I can tell you all the things I did . . . we'll have lots to talk about . . ."

"I'll come along with you, then. That way I can meet your friends, and we can all go shopping together. It'll be great—"

"Sometimes Jennifer's sister takes us," Chloe interrupted. "She's seventeen."

"Well . . ." I acted as though I had to think about it. "What do you think, Dad?"

"It's up to you, Grandma."

"I'll have to meet your friends, especially Jennifer's sister. And I'll pick everyone up. Then we'll arrange a place and time to meet up to go home."

"I guess so. Can I go to my room now and call Jen?" she asked.

"Go." Tom waved her on.

The three of us were left behind.

"Cam, I have a friend who works at MIA."

The mention of the Minneapolis Institute of Art got his attention. "It's really crowded there sometimes," he said as he turned around to face me. I could see anxiety creeping across his face at the very thought of being pushed around by a crowd of strangers.

"Well, I told my friend all about my grandson the artist. She said anytime I wanted, she'd take us on a private tour. No lines, no crowds—we'd get special treatment and see the exhibits by ourselves. Do you think you'd like that?"

"Maybe." He bent his knees, bringing his legs up to his chest, then locked his arms around them and rocked. "Can I decide tomorrow?"

"Sure. How about you ride with me when I drop the girls off? Then it's only about fifteen minutes to the museum. If you're not up to it, we can just go home. Whatever you want to do is fine with me. But I really think you'd enjoy seeing Van Gogh's Olive Trees series. Last time I was here, you seemed to be leaning toward a more modern style with your art. Remember when we went to paint in front of the Buckhorn Mansion? Your approach to a simple landscape really impressed me."

Cam stopped rocking and got to his feet. "Really, Grammy? *I* impressed *you*?" Slowly, he walked to the couch and sat next to me.

"You always have, sweetheart. You're a very talented boy."

"Thanks," he said as he hugged me.

Chapter Thirty-Two

Saturday was another dreary day, but since I'd planned on spending it inside, the weather didn't matter that much. I picked up the kids at ten, which gave Tom plenty of time to get to Duluth for his conference. Chloe seemed happy as she gave me directions to Jennifer's house, but when I insisted on going in with her, I could see a pout coming on.

Jennifer's mother welcomed us inside; Cam stayed out in the jeep. We discussed my plans for the day, and while we waited for big sister, Mom punched her number into my phone. "Just in case."

Mandy was a cute, fresh-faced seventeen-year-old. Her long blonde hair was pulled back in a ponytail, and I got the distinct impression she was a cheerleader and maybe even the prom queen. Her black leggings were tucked into high black boots. A heavy red cardigan hung open, and while we talked, her mother reached over to button it up, telling her daughter that it was chilly outside.

Jennifer and Chloe chattered away, keeping their voices low. I'm sure they thought I was unable to have a conversation with Jen's mom and, at the same time, be aware they were talking about some boys they were supposed to meet up with.

The second girlfriend, Lena, lived down the street. After giving me directions, Mom ended by assuring me that all four were responsible, good kids. But—just in case—she'd be home all day if I needed help. I knew better than most that even the best kids do stupid things and get into trouble. That's why, before leaving home, I'd called the head of security at the mall, a nice woman I'd gone through the academy with. Just in case.

* * *

I used to think that retirement would give me so much freedom. No more watching the clock, no more traveling during rush hours. I could go to the movies while the worker bees sat at desks. The grocery store would be a pleasure instead of an ordeal. Weekends would be spent painting, not doing laundry or cleaning the house, which for years had to be done on my off days. Life was going to pass leisurely by. But I never took into consideration that my friends and family were still punching clocks, busy Monday through Friday, nine to five. And if I wanted to spend time with them, I had to work around their schedules. So when I sat in traffic outside of the mall, slowly edging my way up toward an entrance to drop the kids off, I was probably more frustrated than those around me who just took this as part of their normal weekend routine.

Mandy assured me that she'd take good care of her three charges, and before I could say anything, she slammed the door and ran off after them.

Cam seemed relieved when the giggling trio was gone. "Girls are so noisy."

I agreed but didn't have to let him know. "So how do you feel about going to the museum?"

"Can we have lunch in the café? Mom was going to take me there, but by the time she gets home from work, they're closed."

"Sure, Cam."

Our conversation flowed easier the more he relaxed. While he told me about school and the new video games he loved, I could tell his Asperger's hadn't prevented him from enjoying his life.

As I steered down Third Avenue, toward the front of the museum, I began hunting for a parking spot. Round and round, up and down, there wasn't an empty space anywhere. Starting, stopping for people, bicycles, strollers, and other cars, my determination was quickly drying up. I had to finally admit defeat and called Nora, who directed us to the employee's parking lot.

I'd met Nora Rayburn at a watercolor class I took right after Sully died. She had just gotten her masters in European art and was looking to unwind and relax while I, on the other hand, was hoping to find my style, my medium. We bonded over shopping.

After class one night, Nora asked if I wanted to go with her to an art supply store that had just opened. Aside from the fact that I needed some paint, I wanted to get to know this interesting woman better and agreed to go.

It was bigger and more glorious than that three-story candy shop in New York. Such colors! And brushes, paper in every weight and size. I wanted to buy everything in sight. While we oohed and ahhed, pushed our little cart up and down the aisles, we laughed and told each other our artistic visions. How pretentious we must have seemed to real artists. But it was one of the best nights. And since that time, Nora and I became fast friends. When she got the job as executive director at MIA, I threw her a wonderful party, right on the main floor of that art supply store.

Nora met us at the employee's entrance. After we hugged hello, she looked at my grandson.

"And this must be the handsome and talented Cameron."

I'd explained beforehand about Cam's shyness, and she respected his space by not bending to hug him.

After we got inside and shed our jackets, Nora led us to the café. "While we're eating, I can tell you about some of the things I have planned. How would that be?"

Nora had five kids, which made her the pro when it came to handling children.

"Do they have hamburgers?" Cam asked as seriously as if he were solving a math problem.

"Great ones," Nora told him.

"And as thanks for taking care of us, this will be my treat," I said.

"Then I'll have fries . . . and dessert. How about you, Cam?"

When he laughed, I knew everything would be fine.

* * *

We were given a private tour of the Impressionist gallery. Through my education, I was very familiar with the works of Van Gogh and Matisse, but Cam was eager to see works done by Pissarro.

"Did you know, Grammy, that Pissarro painted this way because it gave him freedom of thought? That's how I feel when I do my art. I can think anything I want. It doesn't matter what everyone else thinks."

Nora smiled. "Pissarro was the one who said that Impressionism was a kind of emancipation from tradition."

"I'm still trying to learn from this kid." I nodded toward my grandson. "My landscapes and portraits need more . . ."

"Not more of anything, Grammy, less. You think too hard. It probably comes because of being a cop."

"You don't miss a thing, do you?"

He smiled, proud of himself.

Chapter Thirty-Three

While we were browsing the gift shop, my phone vibrated. For a moment, I thought about ignoring the call. The number was unfamiliar, and I didn't want Cam to think I was ignoring him. But then I worried that something might have happened to Chloe or Lizzie and answered.

"Kate? It's E.T."

I walked to a quiet corner. "Is something wrong with Nathan? Is he okay?"

"He's fine . . . fine. You don't have to worry about that guy. In fact, I'm sitting in my car, outside his house right now."

"If he's okay, then why are you there?"

"He called about needing the company van until he got his car back from the cops. When I pulled up to his house, I saw a blue Porsche parked down the block. My first instinct was to tell the boss, of course. But when he answered the door, I could tell I woke him up. Mind you, this was in the afternoon. Even though he won't admit it, I think he's a bit shaken after all he went through this week. So I thought I'd wait and see if the car was still there when we came outside, and I'd tell him then."

"And was it?"

"No."

"So you didn't mention it to Nathan at all?"

"Since you're so close to him, I thought it best that I call you first. You know, just until the boss is himself again. And there are hundreds of Porsches in the city . . ."

I was confused. "So you haven't been home? I don't understand."

"We talked awhile. I had to wait for the boss to get dressed. Then he drove me home. As soon as he was out of sight, I got into my car and circled back to his house. I drove around the neighborhood, looking for that car, but it's not here."

"And he doesn't know you're out there now?"

"No. The van's parked in front, so he's obviously inside."

"Did you get a look at the driver? Was it a man or woman?"

"It wasn't Mr. Larkin, that's for sure. It was a woman—a blonde woman. But again, there are dozens—no, thousands—of blondes in this state."

"How many times did you go to the Larkin house?"

"Once to estimate the job. Twice to actually do the work. Three times total."

"And you never once, in all those times, saw Mrs. Larkin?"

"Nope."

"We have to go back to that house," I said. "Maybe we can catch one of them and find out who owns that car." I looked over at Cam, who was happily roaming the book section of the gift shop. "But I can't do it today."

"Then I will."

"Okay . . . but keep me posted. And E.T. . . . ?"

"Yes?"

"Please be careful. I don't want to have to come looking for you."

"I'll be fine."

*   *   *

The rest of Saturday went smoothly. But all the while, I kept my phone close, expecting to hear from E.T. but hoping I wouldn't. I picked the girls up around four. They giggled in the back seat while Cam looked over the Monet art book I'd bought him. By five o'clock, I'd made my drop-off at Jennifer's, and Chloe, Cam, and I were home.

Lizzie was due back on Monday. Tom called that he was home, and if I would bring the kids back tomorrow afternoon, he'd take us all out to lunch. He stressed that they both had homework to finish up, and it would take time for Cam to readjust to his schedule there.

I looked around the kitchen to see what I could put together for dinner. Between searching the refrigerator and opening and closing cabinets, I kept checking my phone.

I ended up salvaging three potatoes and using them in a batter to make potato pancakes. In the freezer were some sausages. And on the bottom shelf of the refrigerator, way in the back, was a carton of sour cream one week shy of its expiration date.

When Chloe saw I'd put the phone by my place at the table, she couldn't contain herself. "Remember the last time you were here, Grandma? You took away my cell 'cause I was using it at the table? You wouldn't give it back to me until you left. Remember that?"

"I do."

"So how come you get to have yours at the table?"

"I might be getting an important call," I told her. "But I'm not using it, see? It's not even in my hand."

"Give Grammy a break, Chloe," Cam told her. "We hardly ever get to see her, so lighten up, will you?"

Then he smiled at me. "Great pancakes." Scooping a blob of sour cream onto his plate, he put his head down and continued eating.

Chloe gave in gracefully and dropped the subject.

"So tell me what you did at the mall. I saw you had a few bags. What did you buy?"

That was all the opening she needed. And she was off.

Jennifer wanted to go to Old Navy, but Mandy wanted to go to Addiction, and since Mandy was the boss, the three of them had to go to her stores first. It wasn't fair, but oh well. Lena liked all those designer stores—Kate Spade, Michael Kors, places like that. But her father's the CEO of some big company, and she has her own credit card, so she gets to buy whatever she wants. Did I think Lizzie would give her a credit card of her own when she turned sixteen? Please could I ask? There was this awesome sweater she had to have. She'd show it to me later. Finally Mandy took them to Old Navy, where Chloe found a pair of sequined sneakers that were fab. Jennifer wanted to go to Torrid. And they stopped for a snack at Johnny Rockets.

I sensed their last stop was where the girls had arranged to meet up with the boys. It was in her hesitation to tell me every morsel they ate. It was in the little smile on her face.

"When I used to go to the mall—yes, they had malls in the olden days—the best part was the boys. We'd check out the guys while we drank Cherry Cokes and ate fries." Geez, I sounded like Sandra Dee mooning over Frankie Avalon. "Do girls still do that?" I knew the answer, but I wanted to hear her rendition.

"I don't know. Maybe."

Cam always looks as though he's not paying attention, but he doesn't miss a thing. "You talk about that Erik guy all the time—the one in your English class."

When Chloe blushed, I knew Cam had struck a nerve. And far be it for me to instigate a fight between them. So I turned toward Cam.

"Did you have a good time at MIA?"

"It was cool. Thanks, Grammy." For the rest of the meal, Cam gave a blow-by-blow description of our day to his sister.

My grandson operated on two speeds: slow and fast. He either talked very little or incessantly. I enjoyed both.

When the pancakes were gone, I went to scoop out some rocky road ice cream I'd seen in the freezer. While she got the bowls, Chloe reminded me to keep Cam's portion on the small side. He didn't need sugar before bed. So as to not make him feel left out, I gave us all one scoop.

After the dishes were cleared away, the counters wiped down, and the kids off in the other room to watch TV, I couldn't stand it anymore and called E.T.

Chapter Thirty-Four

E.T. explained to me he had driven out to the Larkin house to nose around. The inside was dark, not a single light shone through one of the many windows. There was no sign of the Porsche either. He tried getting into the garage, but it was locked tight.

"You went to Chief Bostwick, didn't you? You told him that Larkin was the one behind the kidnapping, right?" he asked.

"Yes. Nathan and I went together and spoke to him."

"Well, it didn't appear the cops had been there. We have to do something, Kate. If the authorities are too busy trying to catch whoever murdered the Watson woman, then we'll have to bring Larkin to them."

As he went on to map out a plan, I was reminded again how responsible E.T. felt for letting Nathan go out to the job alone that day. My reason for staying in Edina had now become twofold: to get Nathan's confidence back and to free E.T. from his guilt.

"If you can, stake out the house overnight—"

"I was planning on doing that even if you told me not to. This just makes it easier knowing you approve."

"I do." There was no need to tell him to be careful. E.T. could take care of himself.

"What about tomorrow?"

"Why don't you come to my house around two in the afternoon? The address is—"

"I know where you live," he said. "I'll be there."

I didn't have a chance to say anything else. He hung up. But at least he sounded happy to be doing something useful. And I sure could relate to that.

* * *

Sunday, around noon, Cam, Chloe, and I met Tom at The Original Pancake House on Seventieth Street. There was a line (there's always a line), but the wait was short, and we were seated by 12:30. While Chloe studied the menu, changing her mind half a dozen times, Cam didn't even look at it. He always ordered the same thing: Belgian waffles with strawberries and whipped cream on top. After Tom and I had decided, he gave the waitress our order. While we waited, he asked me how Nathan was doing.

"I'm not sure. He says he's fine. He wasn't hurt. He wants to brush the whole thing off."

"You'll have to watch him. And before you go back to Taos, tell his people to keep their eyes out for any unusual behavior. He could be suffering from post-traumatic stress disorder. You know, PTSD?"

I nodded. I'd heard about all the vets returning from war. It was heartbreaking how they suffered. But Nathan? My Nathan?

"You know, Nathan was a cop for years. He saw a lot in that time. And he was with Sully when he died. If he's prone to PTSD, wouldn't it have come out then?"

"Was he ever taken hostage? Held at gunpoint? Was his life threatened before that day with Sully?"

I had to think a minute. But when I came up with the answer, it surprised me. "No. Never once."

"Well Nathan has been through a terrifying and dangerous ordeal. That can trigger an anxiety disorder. But not to worry, it can be treated with therapy combined with medication. He just needs to regain a sense of control over his life again."

"Could be he's a little anxious now, which would be normal, and needs some time to regroup." I didn't want to think about something being wrong with Nathan. Of course I knew denial wouldn't fix anything. But at that moment, I just wanted to eat my lunch.

When our food arrived, I was more than happy for the distraction.

For the next hour, all I thought about was watching Tom interact with his children. When Lizzie's name would come up, he'd talk about her with kind words and a smile on his face. It eased my mind that there was no animosity between them, at least none that the kids or I could detect. He even mentioned the possibility of taking them on a vacation to New Mexico, maybe next year. Our relationship had moved to an entirely different level this visit. And the truth was, I'd love to have him be a part of my new life.

As we stood by Tom's car, hugging good-byes, I assured Chloe and Cam that I'd be at the house with them a few more days. They seemed happy with that and got into the backseat and buckled up.

"Well, Kate," Tom said without second-guessing himself about how to address me. "I'm really glad we had some time to ourselves this visit. And I'm especially glad that you don't . . . hate me."

I patted his cheek. "Come on, Tom, we've both been around long enough to know divorce is a two-sided thing. I don't blame either of you. I'm just a little sad about it. But you both have to do what's best for your family."

Relief spread across his face. "No one could have had a better mother-in-law."

"Hey, you talk like she's dead and gone. I'm right in front of you—same person—different name, that's all."

He kissed my cheek and got into the driver's seat. As I stood there, waving good-bye, I was proud of Tom, Lizzie, and myself for getting through their divorce and coming out the other side with our humanity intact.

Chapter Thirty-Five

E.T. arrived a little before two o'clock. When I opened the door, he stood there, dazed and disheveled.

"You look awful," I blurted out as he came inside.

"And you, Katherine Sullivan, are a very blunt and direct woman."

"Have you eaten?" I asked, leading the way to the kitchen.

"That's all I've been doing. There isn't much else to do sitting in a car for hours, except listen to the radio . . . and eat."

"Well, how about something to drink, then?"

"Herbal tea would be nice."

"This is my daughter's house . . . let me have a look . . ."

"Your daughter Elizabeth, right?"

"Right."

Next to the coffee was a wooden box with a variety of teas inside. I brought it out, set it in front of him, and went to boil some water.

"You know, tea is full of antioxidants," he said.

I got out two cups. Tea sounded nice, and I decided to join him.

He held up a packet of lemon zest and pushed the box over to me so I could make my choice. I picked orange spice.

"Are you sure you don't want something with that? I think we have cookies . . ."

"Stop mothering me, Kate. I'm fine. And I'll be better once we decide what our next plan of action will be."

"Okay, okay, let's talk. First we have to agree that Nathan will be informed of our plans. It's important he feel in charge of his life, especially now."

"Ahh, you're worried about PTSD," he nodded and, while he did so, brushed back some hair that had fallen in his face. "Sure. No problem."

"And our investigation can't interfere with his business. Or your job. You all have to make a living."

"Agreed. Anything else?"

I took a moment, then said, "I think that's it."

We had moved to the living room, and E.T. scooted back into the couch pillow. He held his cup with both hands as if warming himself. "We need a picture of Larkin's wife," he said. "Then we'll go back to the foreman of the construction crew and find out exactly who that woman was."

"And once we track her down, she might lead us to her husband. Good. Hopefully we can catch her off guard."

"And I keep thinking about Kerrigan's girlfriend. Brock couldn't get over how calm she was after someone took a shot at her. Any ordinary person would have been shaken—would still be."

"I've been thinking about her, too," I said. "Maybe I should go back and have a visit with her."

"That would be great. She'll respond better to you than she would to a stranger. So I'll see if Polly can find some kind of photo of the wife from a driver's license ID or newspaper article and then head out to the site while you—"

"Will construction be going on out there on Sunday?" I asked.

"I didn't think of that."

"I know you don't relish the idea of staking out the Larkin house for another day, but it may be all you can do for now."

He nodded and, at the same time, checked his military watch. "It's two forty-three now. How about we rendezvous back here at six o'clock?"

"I'll see you then. Hopefully we'll each have something to report."

*   *   *

The only thing different about Ashley Knight's neighborhood since the last time I'd been there were the children. The beautiful weather had brought them out in droves. Five boys kicked a soccer ball in the middle of the street while half a dozen smaller ones shouted and screamed from the grass. Two girls turned a rope while a tall friend jumped and chanted. Farther down the block, men were working on a car that had been parked in the driveway. Before I could even get to Ashley's door, she ran outside shouting to the kids to keep it down; she was trying to sleep. When she saw me, she managed a smile.

"Never move into a house without checking the neighborhood first. I should have listened to all my single friends, but no, I knew better. And now look. It's like a flippin' school yard around here. Next time—"

"Ms. Knight," I managed to say, hoping she'd stop a minute to let me continue.

"I know, I know, you want to talk to me about Charlie." She rolled her eyes. "Good ole, dearly departed Charles. Right?"

Between the noise and her prattling on, all I could do was nod.

"We better go inside." But before she started back up the steps, she couldn't help shouting one more warning. "And all you kids, stay off my lawn!"

None of them hesitated a second. Obviously they were immune to her threats.

I wondered just how many muumuus Ashley had in her closet. This day she was wearing a black one with large white-and-pink Hawaiian flowers printed on it. Her hair was pulled up in a bun on the top of her head. She reminded me of Bloody Mary in *South Pacific*.

She sat down and pointed to a chair for me. "I knew you'd be back." This time she wasn't offering a drink; this time there were no niceties. Maybe Bostwick's men had been there since my last visit. Or a reporter or two. She was probably tired of telling her story again and again. But I was there to get a sense of her emotional state since the shooting and decided the best way to do that was to tap into my motherly side.

"I was worried about you, Ashley. Our last visit was so . . . so . . . traumatic. Are you okay?"

She relaxed a bit. "Oh, I was shaken up. It's not every day someone pulls a gun on me. You know, it wasn't at all like they show on TV or in the movies. Hey, if only there was some menacing music playing in the background, like a warning that a bad guy was coming. Wouldn't that be something? I've had a few nightmares . . . but I'm okay. When the cops were here, I told them everything. But you know, I don't think they'll do much about it. How can they? All I could give them was a description of the car—"

"Oh, so the detectives came later?" I asked. "The patrolmen did say they'd be stopping by. So you told them everything, right?"

"Well . . ." As she thought up an excuse, I could almost hear that voice in her head replaying what we'd told her. Reminding her that she'd have to explain why she threw her boyfriend—her now dead boyfriend—out of a moving car. ". . . not exactly. I was going to, believe me. I was ready to call when two detectives just showed up. They were full of questions, squinting at me with their beady policemen eyes. Always so suspicious, you know?"

I wondered how she knew so much about being questioned by the police.

"I told them everything I knew. But they kept asking and asking. How stupid do they think I am? They can ask the same question a hundred different ways, and the answer will always come out the same. They think they can trick me. But I'm not going to tell them . . ."

She'd slipped up, and she knew it.

"It must feel very threatening," I said in a soothing voice. "Oh sure, Charlie made you angry sometimes; what couple doesn't argue now and then? But I'm sure you loved him very much." Then I sat back and waited for her to start up again.

"You're right . . . so very right. Charlie was my soul mate. Did I tell you we met in rehab? Both of us were so vulnerable and scared back then. He understood me. He loved me . . . in his own way. I miss him." She took a moment of silence to think about her departed lover. When she looked at me again, she smiled. "Funny, you said you've been thinking about me. I've been wondering about you. Did you ever find your friend? The one you were looking for when you came here the first time?"

"I did. A man who lives in one of the houses at that new construction site where Charlie worked was holding Nathan. It's a small world, isn't it? Did Charlie ever mention a Mr. or Mrs. Larkin?"

She was preparing to lie to me but changed her mind. It was in her posture, her eyes, the way her foot shook. "Yes. He did odd jobs for Mr. Larkin sometimes. It was fast money and a lot of it."

"I assume the jobs were illegal, and I don't want you to incriminate yourself, so I won't ask."

"I appreciate that, Mrs. Sullivan. But I feel I can trust you."

"And you haven't told any of this to the police?"

She shrugged. "They didn't ask. Always so full of themselves, aren't they?"

I thought of Bostwick and had to agree.

"They asked if he worked at the construction site, and I said he did. End of story."

"I found out it was Charlie who forced Nathan into the car and brought him to Larkin's house. Maybe working for that man was giving your boyfriend some bouts of guilt? It happens all the time. Decent guys get caught up in illegal activities, and it does a real number on their psyche. A lot of times it becomes more than they can handle. Sooner or later, they have to tell someone—"

"And that's how they get caught," Ashley said. "Charlie spilled his guts to me when he was high. You think I'm bad? You wouldn't believe how that guy could talk."

"Well, nothing can hurt him now," I told her. "And maybe whatever he told you can help Nathan. I'm sure there are others out there who Larkin's hurt. I bet he was the one who hired the person who shot at you."

Her eyes widened. "To shut me up! He had to cover his tracks. He had to know sooner or later Charlie would talk. Why, that lousy bastard."

"Those kinds of men never leave witnesses behind."

"Wanna drink?" she suddenly asked.

Chapter Thirty-Six

I had Ashley relaxed and talking and didn't want to interrupt our conversation with her drink routine. "No thanks, it's a little too early for me."

"You're right; it's too early. I can wait until later. So where were we?"

"Did Charlie tell you anything about a plan Mr. Larkin had to kidnap Nathan Walker? Nathan had installed surveillance cameras around the house. Maybe he mentioned Walker Securities?"

"I remember him telling me about this rich chick in a big house, near the site, who kept bothering him. That was the first time I heard the name Larkin. The husband didn't want him to do anything until later. It was the wife who approached him first."

"Mrs. Larkin? Do you know what she looks like? Did you ever meet her?"

"One time. She'd flirt with the guys out there. Thought she was all that, know what I mean? She was one of those AMWs."

"A what?" I had to ask.

"Actress, Model, Whatever. You see them all the time. Pretty in an artificial way. Fake nails, fake eyelashes, fake blonde hair . . . money can buy a whole lot of pretty."

I felt sorry for Ashley. She must have been so jealous of Mrs. Larkin. "Did you think they were having an affair?"

Her jaw clenched; her hands tightened into fists. She couldn't contain her anger and stood up. First she walked to the door, then back to the large TV mounted on the wall and stared into the black screen as though it was a mirror. As she walked back to the couch, she said, "I sure did. And I told him so. Oh, he denied it of course. He always did. But I kept at him, hounded him, until he finally convinced me that she loved her husband and only wanted Charlie to do a job. She offered to pay him ten thousand dollars. How could he refuse?"

"What did she want him to do?"

"Make the mistress back off."

So Mr. Larkin had a mistress. A beautiful, young wife wasn't enough for him. Maybe he got bored being in that big house alone while she was out in the world running a business. Or maybe he was one of those people who needed constant attention, always having to be in the spotlight.

"How far was he supposed to go?"

"In the beginning, it was all kinds of vague. So Charlie suggested starting off with a phone call, threatening to tell the lover's husband everything. Mrs. Larkin didn't want to do it. Her number could be traced. Her voice could give her away. She had a hundred reasons why Charlie had to do it."

"Why did she pick him in the first place?" I wondered aloud.

"Come on, Mrs. Sullivan," Ashley scoffed. "People can spot a wreck like Charlie a mile off. You see this pathetic guy and you know he'll do just about anything for a few bucks. She knew she could use him."

"How many calls did he make?"

"Just two. The first time seemed to scare her a little. But the second one made her really mad. She told him that if he bothered her again, she'd call the police. When he reminded her about how much her husband and kid would be hurt, she said she didn't care, that she wouldn't be bullied or blackmailed."

"And Charlie reported all this to Mrs. Larkin?"

"Yep, he sure did. That's when she refused to give him any of the money she promised. Not a cent. She claimed he hadn't done the job she'd hired him to do. That really set Charlie off. He told her he should get something. He'd put his neck out there, threatened the woman. But that woman refused to be reasonable. They went back and forth like that for a few days, each of them making demands, getting madder, until they came up with a new . . . arrangement. Twelve thousand if Charlie would go out to that woman's house and . . . you know . . . scare her . . . get in her face."

"Were there any parameters set? Any limits to how far he should go?"

"If there were, he never told me. All I know is, he drove out to where that woman lived. He said he watched her a few days, trying to get familiar with her routine. But with kids coming and going and a husband in and out, it was difficult. Charlie's brain got damaged with all the drugs he did, and he was getting desperate for the money to buy more. Real stupid, I know. And Daddy was threatening to cut me off because I was living with a bum that didn't even show up for work half the time. So I helped him . . . kind of."

"What did you do?"

"I took notes. Charlie would ride out to her house and park down the street. He'd call and tell me what was happening. I'd record the time and date. We did that for a week."

I knew criminals were stupid, but these two took the cake.

"When we knew for sure the husband would be gone and the kids were at school, Charlie forced his way inside. That woman wasn't so smart then."

I got the sense that in some sick way, Ashley was proud of her man. "And he beat her?"

"Charlie was a lot of things, Mrs. Sullivan, but he wasn't violent. He'd yell and shout, but he never touched me. When he got close to that woman, he just wanted to scare her. But she stood up to him. Even when he showed her the gun, she wouldn't back down."

"So he shot her?"

"No, he never used his gun. He just couldn't pull the trigger."

"If he didn't hit her or shoot her, what did he do?"

"He told me he was going to push her around a little, just until she got it through her head that he meant business. That's all he was going to do, I swear. But then she grabbed a knife off the counter and came at him. She was screaming like a lunatic, waving the blade, jabbing at him. He grabbed for it a couple of times and cut his hand. All the while he's trying to calm her down. Charlie didn't want to kill her, Mrs. Sullivan. You have to believe me."

To get the rest of the story, I told her I believed her. But the two people in that kitchen that day were the only ones who knew the complete truth. And they were both dead.

She seemed calmer and continued. "They wrestled around like that awhile. Charlie said they trashed the kitchen. She got him in the shoulder once. When he saw the wound, he got crazy. And real strong. He told me he'd never felt that way before. Not even when he was high. The stronger he got, the weaker and more tired she got until he was on top of her on the floor. By then he'd had enough. All he wanted was for it to be over. So he stabbed her. Once. In the stomach."

"Were you there?" I had a feeling Ashley was more involved in this than she was letting on.

"No! I was here. Alone."

"But Charlie must have called you after realizing that woman was dead. He must have been scared, trying to figure out what his next step would be."

"He was going out of his mind. So I had to talk him through it. And since he didn't want my prints or DNA on anything, he had to do it himself."

Accessory to a crime, aiding and abetting, the DA could come up with a list a mile long to bring Ashley Knight to trial. While I sat there listening to her story, it was difficult not to fall back into police-chief mode. But first I had to hear the ending.

"How did you talk him through it?"

"I told him to wipe everything down. He'd thought enough to wear gloves." She smiled like a mother bragging about her child's report card.

There was still his blood, DNA, and hair left behind. But I didn't bring up those pesky details.

"Then he ran and got a sheet, wrapped her up, and loaded her body into his truck—well, my truck. He said he knew a place outside the city limits and drove out there."

I had a sinking feeling in my stomach when I asked, "Do you know the name of this woman?"

"Carolyn Watson. I thought you knew that when you first came out here. You can imagine how surprised—no, relieved—I was when you never mentioned her. Neither you nor the police thought that Charlie was connected to Mrs. Watson. Don't you think that's strange?"

She was sincere when she asked me. And I hoped my confusion didn't show when I answered. "Well . . . not really. My only concern was for Nathan. First to find him and now to bring him some answers."

"I imagine he needs closure. I know I certainly do. With someone like Charlie, everything was always so simple. All the answers were there, no questions. But I've been debating about if I should call the police and tell them who killed Mrs. Watson so they can stop running around town. But then I'd be in trouble. And that wouldn't bring back Charlie or that poor woman. What good would it do anyone to put me in jail? And a trial costs the state so much money."

She seemed harmless enough, sitting there, trying to reconcile her actions. But I'd witnessed too many seemingly calm, confused people just snap. I half expected her to rush across the room at me as she slowly realized she had incriminated herself and that I was the only person who knew about her part in Carolyn's murder. Smiling, I reviewed self-defense moves I'd learned so many years ago, hoping I wasn't too old or out of practice to use any of them. The front door wasn't locked, and I could certainly outrun her to the back door. If there was one.

"So what do you think I should do?" she asked me. "It's not as if I killed anyone. I wasn't even there. Right?"

"As far as I can see, you're an innocent bystander," I lied. "My daughter's a lawyer. She's fair, and I could talk to her about possibly representing you."

"I'll have to think about that." Ashley stood up again. "Well, now I really need a drink. Sure you won't change your mind?"

"Maybe another time."

When she rushed toward me, every muscle tightened.

"You've been great, Mrs. Sullivan. Thanks for listening to me. I'll stay in touch."

I stood up and started for the door, unable to believe she was going to just let me walk out.

"Wait! You can't leave yet!"

I turned.

"Do you have one of your daughter's cards?"

I fished around in my purse and came up with one that Lizzie had given me when she moved into her new office. "Here you go."

She read every word on it while I watched, still wondering what to make of the woman in front of me.

"Do you think you could wait until tomorrow before you call the cops on me? Or maybe Tuesday? I promise I won't skip town. Where would I go?"

Since we were on good terms, I had to ask about the money Charlie supposedly got for killing Carolyn Watson. "Did he at least get the twelve thousand dollars Mrs. Larkin promised? And if he did, is there any left for you?"

"He said he got it, but I never saw one dollar. Maybe that fool hid it here somewhere. Who knows? Daddy's not speaking to me, even though Charlie's gone. So you can see, I don't have anywhere to go. I can't even try to make a run for it. That truck of mine can barely make it around the block. Besides, it'll probably be taken in as evidence, since it's the one Charlie put her in to drive out to the Coleman Farm."

Chapter Thirty-Seven

As I drove home, I dialed Bostwick to fill him in on the new development in his murder case. His phone rang six times. I was preparing to leave a message when he abruptly answered, obviously irritated.

"It's my day off, for Pete's sake, Sullivan. What can be so important that you have to call when I'm out with my family? Anything you have to say can wait until tomorrow—in my office."

"I wouldn't call if it wasn't important, Dean."

"You got two minutes." He sighed heavily for emphasis.

"I went to see Ashley Knight today. She told me that her boyfriend, Charles Kerrigan, killed Carolyn Watson."

He must have needed a moment to digest what I'd just said or his phone had gone out. "Are you still there?"

"Look. I don't know why you'd go to that Knight woman's house, and I don't want to know . . . until tomorrow when you'll tell me in my office." He disconnected. Clearly, he would take some convincing.

Even I still couldn't believe Ashley Knight's demeanor. Since she came from a wealthy family, I assumed she'd been educated at some of the top schools. And yet . . . she didn't seem to have a clue how the real world worked. I'd seen people like her in movies and on TV but never met one live and in person.

Actually, there was this sweet girl I remembered who just walked into the station one day. She'd robbed two men at gunpoint and wanted to confess. One of my detectives took her into an interrogation room. He said she was cooperative, laid out every detail of her crime but, all the while, kept checking her watch. After signing her confession, she got up to leave, telling him she didn't want to be late for a dentist's appointment. It never dawned on her that she'd be arrested.

I've always envied those people who live in such tidy little worlds. Everything is simple there; all problems have easy solutions. Mine has always been on the messy side. But I'd never change places with any of them.

My stomach told me it was time to eat. I imagined E.T. must also be hungry, so I stopped at the nearest chicken place. Fried chicken—Sunday comfort food. I was five minutes into the menu when I remembered my friend was a vegetarian and ended up ordering the large family meal, complete with three sides of vegetables, biscuits, and dessert. There was no way we'd finish it all; I didn't expect we would. I was just making sure there would be leftovers for the next day when Lizzie and the kids got home.

As I pulled into the driveway, E.T. drove in behind me. When he saw the bags of food I unloaded, he laughed.

"Is there going to be a party? Looks like you have enough food there for ten people."

"Some for now, some for later," I said as I unlocked the door.

We set the table and dished out our dinner quickly. Neither of us said much other than what we wanted to drink and where we wanted to sit. It was like we were saving our words so we could take time to digest them along with our meal. When we were finally ready, I picked up a chicken wing and said, "Okay, E.T., you go first. Tell me what happened out at the Larkin house."

"Before we go any further, I have to tell you that my given name is Eastwood Theodore Goodman . . . the third. The boss thought it sounded too . . . too rich . . . too fancy. Even though I told him I come from working-class parents and there isn't anything rich about me, he said it might alienate the clients. And he also wanted me to have a nickname, like he'd given every member of the crew. Personally, I think he just likes coming up with crazy names. Maybe it's a memory thing and makes it easier to remember all of us." He grimaced. "But every time someone calls me E.T., I feel like some funny alien creature."

"Have you ever told Nathan how you feel?"

"Naw. No reason to make waves. But you can keep calling me E.T. like everyone else does. I just wanted you to know my real name. It seemed important."

"Helps us to bond, I guess. Thank you for telling me. Sorry I don't have a nickname to share."

"That's fine." He picked up a biscuit, pulled it apart, and buttered half. I dished out green beans onto my plate, then pushed the bowl toward him.

"So tell me about your day."

"I called Polly and asked her to send a photo of Mrs. Larkin to my phone."

"And did she?"

"Yes. So I went to the construction site to show it around, but you were right. The place was quiet. Guess Sunday is their day of rest. Next I drove down to the house and waited."

"See anything?"

His face lit up with a huge smile. "Oh yes. I saw Mrs. Larkin. Plain as day. She drove right past me, up the driveway, opened one of the garage doors with her remote, and went inside."

I stopped chewing. "Was she driving a Porsche? A blue Porsche?"

"I'm not a car guy. I believe that cars are just chunks of steel and glass—nothing more. Certainly not things to be collected or go into a lifetime of debt for. But I do know that she was definitely not driving a sports car. And her vehicle was red."

"You're sure it was her, though?"

"One and the same."

"What did you do then? After she was in the garage?"

"First I knocked on the door, shouted her name a few times. But I got nothing. So I went to the house and banged on that door. And finally . . . she answered."

Suddenly my appetite was gone. Picking up a napkin, I wiped my fingers and waited.

E.T. speared a green bean.

"Don't stop. Tell me what she said. How did your conversation go?"

"It didn't . . . that's the problem. When she asked who I was and what I wanted, I was stumped. I didn't know what to say or how much to tell her. I fumbled for a minute and then decided to just say I was with Walker Securities and wanted to start installing the additional cameras her husband ordered. It was a good thing she didn't take me up on that because I didn't have any equipment in the car with me."

"Did she act like she knew what you were talking about?"

"No expression of any kind. She said she'd been out of town and didn't know what her husband had ordered. That I'd have to wait for him to come back, and couldn't we set up an appointment for Monday. Then she asked why I was working on Sunday. I made up some excuse, told her it was the only time we could fit her in. By this time, I had my wits about me and told her our sales rep would stop by tomorrow and asked if she would be home."

"Your instincts were good, but I hope you didn't make her suspicious. I'll pay her a visit in the morning. Keep your fingers crossed she's still there."

"I'm planning to watch her all night, if I have to. She's not getting away this time."

"But while you're here, she could have left."

"Before I took off, I called Brock. But I couldn't get him, so I called Rosie. She's there now. I'll get a few hours' sleep, a quick shower, and relieve her later tonight."

I was impressed. But why should I have been? E.T. was a trained professional.

Then it was my turn to report what had happened at Ashley Knight's house that afternoon. I took my time, careful not to miss a single fact or impression I'd gotten. E.T. listened and nodded while starting in on the sweet potatoes. I threw in some descriptions of the strange woman to give my story texture and color. There were even moments he laughed. The more time we spent together, the more comfortable we became with each other. By the time we got to dessert, I felt as though we'd gotten to the point of friendship.

"I have cherry pie for dessert. Would you like coffee?"

"I prefer tea . . . if you have it. And green tea would be perfect."

He insisted on loading the dishwasher when we were done. As I watched, I wondered if he'd ever been married. But it wasn't the right time to ask.

I found a legal pad in Lizzie's office and, to get the facts clear and in some kind of order, began writing. E.T. listened and added details as we worked together at the kitchen table. It took almost an hour to fill a page with what we knew so far.

Mrs. Larkin had hired Charlie Kerrigan to kill her husband's mistress, Carolyn Watson. Her trip to New York probably served as an alibi, taking suspicion off her for the murder.

Ashley Knight could have intentionally run down and killed Charlie. But why would she do that? For the twelve thousand dollars? To keep him quiet so he wouldn't tell the police about her involvement in the murder? She had the means and the opportunity, but I wasn't sure about her motive. It just didn't feel right.

If not Ashley, then someone else killed Charlie. But why? Who had something to gain from his death? Maybe an old acquaintance with an old grudge had come for revenge?

Could Mr. Larkin have found out who murdered his lover? But then why would he hire Charlie to kidnap Nathan?

We kept reminding ourselves to stay focused and not get sidetracked. All too often the supporting cast in a mystery only clouds up the case. Nathan had been kidnapped. Mr. Larkin had hired Charlie to help him hold Nathan against his will. Now Charlie was dead. He'd been run down by someone driving a blue car. Mrs. Larkin was seen driving a blue car. Maybe it was her husband's, and she was borrowing it? Maybe she wanted to be seen in it to draw attention to her husband. Mr. Larkin could have killed Charlie to shut him up about the kidnapping. Ashley Knight drove a blue truck. She could have killed her boyfriend for a number of reasons. Or . . . Charlie's death was an accident.

E.T. studied the list we'd just made. "Carolyn Watson's murder is a real shame. You're going to call Chief Bostwick so he can bring Ashley in for questioning, aren't you?"

"I called him on the way here. We're meeting at his office tomorrow morning."

"Good," he said, looking satisfied, until a thought occurred to him. "But even if they get her to talk and the case is wrapped up, it still doesn't tell us why the boss was snatched like that."

"Each clue is like a puzzle piece. But in this case, there're just a lot more pieces than usual. All we need now is for a couple of them to slide into place, and everything will make sense."

"I've always had the patience to put together those two-thousand-piece monsters. So bring it on," E.T. said.

Chapter Thirty-Eight

E.T. had been gone only a few minutes when my phone rang.

"Katie! He's here! They're both in the house. What do ya want me to do?"

"Rosie?"

"Yeah. I thought I should call you. E.T. needed some R an' R. The poor guy's a wreck. So just tell me what you want me to do and I'll—"

"Don't get out of your car. I can be there in twenty minutes."

"Okay, I'll make like a statue. I'm parked near a dumpster in a black Ford pickup."

As much as I hurried, I knew twenty minutes was wishful thinking. It would probably be more like thirty.

* * *

The construction site was well lit, and thanks to a full moon, the residential area wasn't totally dark. As I got closer to the Larkin house, I switched my headlights off. There was only one dumpster near it, which made finding Rosie easy.

When I pulled up alongside her, my phone immediately went off.

"I checked out the back. It's still all dirt. Ain't no way they're gettin' outta there without us seein'. The old dude has met you before, and I might spook him, so you'll have to go in alone. But for the life of me, I can't think of an excuse why you'd be out here this time of night and on a weekend."

I held up my hand to her through the window. "Hold on. There's no reason for us to be taking any chances here. I'm calling for backup."

"It's your call, Katie." I could see her nod.

Fortunately, Bostwick picked up on the first ring this time. "What is it now?"

"I'm at Everett Larkin's house, out on Excelsior. He's the man who kidnapped Nathan. Remember? He and his wife are both here."

"Of course I remember. My men located the wife, but she ran. Their house is being staked out—"

"I've had someone out here for days now. They haven't seen a sign of your men. And FYI, the wife is with him."

"Well . . . this murder has taken priority."

"For you and your detectives, I'm sure it has. But what about the patrolmen who were assigned to watch this house? If they're out here, they must be invisible, because I don't see a sign of a car or a cop."

"Look, Walker hasn't been in here to file any complaints, as far as I know. I'm trying to keep ten balls in the air at the same time. You remember how it is . . ."

I didn't feel like sympathizing with him, but to keep up good relations, I did.

He was calmer when he told me, "As soon as we hang up, I'll call in a car to go out there. Then tomorrow . . ."

Suddenly the front door of the Larkin house flew open.

"I gotta go."

The next thing I knew, Rosie was out of her truck and hunched behind the dumpster. I couldn't let her be out there alone and eased myself onto the ground.

"Is Bostwick comin'?" Rosie whispered.

"He's sending a car."

Ornate lights, on either side of the door, flooded the yard. Then a suitcase came flying through the air, spilling clothes across the driveway.

"Get out!" a woman screamed.

Mr. Larkin came rushing outside and headed for the case.

A woman, who I assumed was Mrs. Larkin, followed him. Waving her arms, she continued to yell. "You've lived off of me long enough! I buy this beautiful house—our dream home. Do you remember that, Everett?" Now she was leaning over him while he stooped to gather his clothing. "This was supposed to be our perfect place. You swore there'd be no more cheating. And like a fool, I believed you."

As her husband folded a shirt, he spoke in a calm voice. "I have a disease, Diana. Go ask my therapist; he'll tell you I can't help myself. It's an addiction."

"I'm through with therapists, and I'm through with you, my darling, good-for-nothing husband. Unlike you, I've worked damn hard for my money. And what I have means something to me. Like Mama's furniture. And you threw it away! How could you? I've worked hard to decorate this place, so we can be proud, and what do I find when I get home? The carpet all ripped up, Mama's three-piece set gone, and that hideous stuff sitting in our beautiful house. Have you gone crazy?"

Now Larkin was standing, his suitcase packed and in his hand. He straightened up and addressed his wife. "I told you, I was protecting you. Do you want us both to be put away for the rest of our lives? I've apologized for the carpet so many times, I've lost track. But I had to get rid of it. It was evidence. Why can't you see I was only trying to protect you?"

He looked so forlorn, standing there with his suitcase, apologizing. And she looked so cold and detached.

"She's a real ice princess, ain't she?" Rosie asked.

A few words passed between them that we were too far away to hear. Whatever Larkin had said, though, it made his wife slowly melt until she was crying.

Rosie grabbed my arm. "Can you believe this?"

Larkin dropped his suitcase, and the couple embraced. I couldn't be positive, but I think they were both crying. Next came a passionate kiss. They must have been so confident no one would see them that they lingered, in a long embrace, there on the lawn, for all the world to see.

"Well, chalk another one up for love."

"This isn't love," I told her. "We're watching a power struggle here. Played out by two master manipulators."

Chapter Thirty-Nine

By the time a squad car arrived, the Larkins had gone inside. The show was over.

I briefed the officers about my call to Bostwick. They were both young and confused, thinking they had been called out to a crime scene. When Rosie got frustrated, trying to explain the situation, I asked her to wait for me in her vehicle. After a few more go-arounds, they finally understood that all they had to do was watch the house and advise their chief of any activity.

"All night?" one complained. "I go off duty in an hour."

Was it really necessary to tell him to call for someone to relieve him? Each year, they got younger and seemed to need more guidance. There must have been a time when I was like that. But at that moment, I couldn't remember back that far.

As the patrolmen drove to a less conspicuous spot, I walked over to Rosie's truck and got into the passenger's seat.

"Cops ain't never been my favorite people," she explained. "They don't like me, an' I don't have much use for them. Know what I mean?"

I nodded.

"So why do you think Diana was so upset about some lousy furniture an' carpet? What was that all about?"

I explained everything to her—the murder, the hit-and-run. Not sure how much she knew at that point, I talked her through all of it. When I was finished, she rested her chin on the steering wheel, silently processing all the facts she'd just heard.

"So because the boss saw somethin' he shouldn't have, this Larkin character snatched him. An' I'll bet the bastard was probably plannin' on killin' him so he wouldn't talk. But he didn't have nothin' to talk about, right?"

"At that point, no. But suppose they were both in on it. Then things begin to make sense."

This time Rosie looked shocked. "Wait a minute! You think that dude in there had his girl-on-the-side snuffed out? On purpose?"

"Not exactly. I'm thinking that somehow he found out what his wife had done and wanted to protect her."

"Or his reputation."

* * *

I left the police on surveillance and felt that between the two of them, Mr. and Mrs. Larkin's whereabouts would be known until Bostwick could bring the couple in for questioning and get a warrant to search the house. Lizzie's plane was due to arrive at 2:10 the next afternoon. Her assistant, Josh, would pick her up. She wanted to be there when the kids got home from school. It was eleven by the time I sunk into the bed. But I had to use my old test-pattern technique to fall asleep.

The next day, I didn't know what or who I'd find at the office. When I walked in, things seemed normal; it was back to business as if nothing had ever happened. Polly had her headset on and was talking to someone. She smiled and waved when she saw me. Rosie, with her feet up on her desk, was leafing through something that looked like a catalog. Brock told me E.T. would be in later, and the boss was back in his office.

After getting a cup of coffee, I went to see Nathan.

He seemed to be trying too hard when he greeted me. The smile plastered across his face looked way out of proportion. He fussed with a chair, rolled it around, and ordered me to get comfortable and sit.

"You've spent so much time here, Kathy. Too much, in fact. I'm sure you want to get home." He sat on the edge of his desk as he spoke, then picked up a pen and clicked the top. *Click . . . click . . . click . . . click.* "Everything's back to normal now . . ."

While he spoke, I hung up my jacket. After settling into the chair he'd offered, I couldn't take it anymore and had to ask, "What are you doing?"

"What do you mean?"

"You think I don't see the way you're overcompensating?" I untied the scarf around my neck, giving him a moment to think about what I'd just said.

"Now why would I be doing that?" *Clickclickclickclick.*

"Because you're scared, Nathan."

He scoffed. "I'm fine." *Clickclick.* "Really."

Over the years, I've wasted a lot of words and time before learning that when a person's not ready to listen, there's no use talking. "I'm just worried, that's all."

"And I appreciate your concern." He spoke to me like I was a business acquaintance, and I didn't like it. "But it seems to me, from what I've been hearing, that I should be concerned about *you*." *Click . . . click . . . click . . .* "So tell me all about your little adventure last night with Rosie."

Before I could say a word, he lit into me.

"What the hell were you thinking? Going out to that house alone—"

"Rosie was with me."

He put his pen down and folded his hands in his lap, still smiling.

"Come on, Kathy. Rosie can be a loose cannon. That's why I try to keep her in the office. And you were both out there, unarmed. There's no telling what that maniac might do next. Just because he didn't hurt me doesn't mean he isn't capable of murder." His hands suddenly became animated, chopping at the air the more agitated he became. "What if something would have happened to you . . . or Rosie? What if he grabbed you, and we never saw either one of you again? Did you stop to think about that? Did you?"

Ahh, the real Nathan was back! What I'd thought was indifference when I first came in was concern mixed with a little anger. I'd never seen him angry before.

"I'm waiting."

I led off with a peace offering. "I hate to admit it, but in this instance, what you say about there being no coincidences in a murder investigation is probably true."

His pleasure in hearing my words was genuine. "I won't bother to say I told you so. But . . . I told you so."

"While you gloat, I'll tell you how I think the Watson murder, Kerrigan's death, and your kidnapping are all connected."

Nathan pulled a chair up and sat next to me. "First, let me tell you my theory."

"I'm all ears."

"That day I went out to the Larkin house early and screwed up his timing, I saw something I wasn't supposed to see—or he thought I did."

"Charlie Kerrigan."

"Right. He must have just come from burying the Watson woman. He was angry. He wanted his money. Maybe he was even drunk. When he finally got it through that thick head of his that he wasn't getting paid, anger got the best of him. So while he tracked dirt and blood all over the house, he spilled the beans to Mr. Larkin."

"But it's the wife who has all the money." I couldn't hold back adding my two cents.

Nathan nodded. "I haven't got it all figured out, but somehow Kerrigan got roped into helping get rid of the evidence he'd just brought into the house."

"The Larkins have a complicated relationship. One of those love-hate things," I said.

"That would explain why, after just finding out that his lover had been murdered, he wanted to protect his wife while he must have been hating her."

"Or afraid of her."

"And also afraid I'd seen too much," Nathan said. "So he promised he'd get Kerrigan his money if he'd do one more job."

"Bring you back to the house."

Nathan slid forward in his chair. "And once she put the plan in motion, Mrs. Larkin took off."

"She thought she was so smart and wouldn't have to pay Charlie at all. He'd committed murder. He couldn't just walk into the police station and report her for lack of payment. But . . . he thought he was smarter."

"And after grabbing me, hanging around the house for a few days, there was no money. Maybe he tried to blackmail them. 'Pay up or I'm taking the two of you down with me.'"

"So they had to eliminate Charlie," I said.

"You know, I've been wondering why they didn't kill me," Nathan said. His smile had now vanished.

"Charlie's girlfriend must have told him that we were looking for you. I didn't make a secret of it."

"Then why would they come back?" Nathan wondered out loud.

"Think about who these people are. Two strong individuals, used to getting their own way either by legal means or with money. They think they have all the bases covered. Diana Larkin was in New York when her husband's lover was killed. No way the police can arrest her for that. Her husband threw away any incriminating evidence linking either one of them to Carolyn Watson. And with Charlie dead . . ."

"One of them killed him, to shut him up," Nathan said.

"Did I tell you Ashley Knight drives a blue truck? A scorned woman and all that, maybe she was involved somehow."

"Well, except for that one detail, I'd say we've got this all figured out." Nathan looked satisfied that he'd finally been able to make sense of everything.

I hated to spoil his mood but asked, "What about the painting? Do you think it's connected somehow?"

"I really don't see the importance of it."

"It's a loose end and it's driving me crazy."

Polly stuck her head in the door. "I hate to bother you guys, but it's all over the Internet. Mr. Watson, Carolyn's husband, just confessed to killing her."

Chapter Forty

After Nathan digested the news about Mr. Watson's confession, he decided to call Dean Bostwick himself.

"He's not too happy with you right now. Let's hope he'll feel a little kinder toward me."

"Whatever works," I said and waited while Nathan dialed.

"I'll put you on speaker so you won't miss anything." He winked.

After five minutes or so, Dean Bostwick answered.

"Chief, Nathan Walker here."

"Oh hey, how're you doing?" To his credit, he sounded truly concerned.

"Better, thanks."

"Good . . . good."

"I know you're a busy man—"

"Things seemed to have calmed down a bit around here. What can I do for you, Walker?"

"I'm checking up on the status of the Larkins. What's going on out there?"

"As a matter of fact, the wife just left. There's no way she could have been involved in your kidnapping. She has a solid alibi. Dozens of people were with her in New York. There was no reason to hold her for further questioning."

"Where's the husband?"

"The forensics guys went to the house with a warrant bright and early this morning. From what I've heard, they had to send for help. There was just too much evidence to carry out in one trip. Guess it was the housekeeper's week off, huh? Or the mister didn't know which end of a mop to use." Bostwick laughed at his own joke.

"And Larkin was there while they processed everything?" Nathan asked.

"No, no, he's resting comfortably in a cell until we have something definite to pin on him."

"And if his only crime is kidnapping and I, the victim, am alive and well, what exactly are you looking for out there?"

"Well, for starters, your DNA, hair, proof that you were in that house."

"But I told you I was there on a job."

"Yes, you did," Bostwick sounded irritated. "You also told me that you were held upstairs. If that's what happened, my men will find evidence upstairs, too. Correct?"

"Yes," Nathan agreed.

"The forensic team is also looking for traces of Charles Kerrigan's blood."

We were both stunned.

"It's my theory," Bostwick continued, obviously eager to share his brilliance, "that he was doing odd jobs for the couple, and for some reason, they killed him. Maybe he knew things he wasn't supposed to know. Maybe he made a pass at the wife. She's a real looker. A man would have to be dead not to get ideas around her." He paused, probably waiting for Nathan to join in with a remark of his own about Mrs. Larkin. "Whatever the motive, I'm sure they're guilty."

"But Kerrigan was killed by a car. His body was left by the side of the road. Why would his blood be in the house?"

"Try to follow me, Walker. I'm thinking that Kerrigan was killed in the house, then his body was dumped off on that road and run over a few times to make it look like a hit and run."

"The only vehicle I'm aware of that the Larkins owned was a sports car. I don't see how they could have fit the body inside a sardine can like that."

"We found a Cadillac in the garage. A person could fit three bodies in that trunk."

I couldn't believe how off track Bostwick was about Charlie's murder. But evidence never lies. The autopsy report would take at least another week to be completed. He'd find out then that he'd been wrong.

I waved to get Nathan's attention and hoped he understood when I mouthed the words for him to ask about Sid Watson's confession. I knew he got it when he steered the conversation that way.

"Well, Chief, looks like you got everything under control."

"You take care now, Walker."

"Thanks, I will. Oh, Chief . . ."

"Yeah?"

"I understand Carolyn Watson was a personal friend. To both you and your wife. Her passing that way must have been a shock. I wanted to extend my condolences for your loss."

"That's very kind, Walker. My wife and I are having a hard time dealing with it. She was a wonderful woman."

"Who's looking after their son . . . now that her husband confessed?"

"Carolyn's sister has taken them in for now. It's for the court to decide where they'll end up."

"Why do you think her husband would have hurt her?"

"Apparently he found out she was having an affair and went off the deep end."

"And you believe him?" Nathan said.

"Just between you and me, he doesn't seem the type. Sid's always been so even-tempered. In all the years I've known him, never once did I even hear him raise his voice. But then . . . I would have never pegged Carolyn as an adulteress."

"Well, maybe now you can take a vacation or something," Nathan said.

"Not until I get the report from forensics. But it's all a formality. I know what they'll find. Then my wife and I are going to Arizona to visit my folks for Thanksgiving."

"I hope you have a good time, Chief."

"I'll do that. And Walker?"

"Yeah?"

"Next time you see Mrs. Sullivan, tell her from me that she can go back to her retirement community. I have every-thing under control here."

I almost gave myself away and laughed out loud.

After hanging up, Nathan said, "Did you hear that, Mrs. Sullivan? You better get yourself on the next train outta Dodge."

"No way. Now that I'm sure you're back to your old self, I have a whole new reason for staying. I have to see Bostwick's reaction when he finds out that Charlie killed Carolyn Watson. Imagine his surprise when that report shows traces of her DNA in the Larkin house."

"But what if Mr. Watson did kill his wife? His confession could be genuine. That girlfriend of Charlie's . . . what's her name?"

"Ashley Knight."

"What makes you think this Ashley was being honest with you? From your description, I don't know that I'd take everything she says as gospel."

"I'm eighty-percent sure she was truthful. But I think I know how to fill in the other twenty percent."

Chapter Forty-One

Lizzie was changing her clothes when I got home.

"Hey, sweetie, I didn't expect you. Thought you'd go to the office first."

She hugged me. "I missed the kids. And you're not around that much. I wanted us to spend some time together before you leave. So . . . tell me your news. I especially want to hear the part about Ashley Knight . . . whoever she is."

As we walked to the couch, I couldn't hide my surprise. "How on earth do you know her?"

"She's left me three voicemails. And two texts. You gave her my card?"

"It's a long, complicated story, but I think she's going to need a lawyer. And you're the best in the state."

"Come on, Mother, spare me the flattery. What's going on?"

"How long do we have before the kids get home?"

Lizzie checked the tiny watch hanging around her neck on a long chain. "About an hour."

"Well," I began, "remember that woman they found at the Coleman place?"

"Of course, but what does this have to do with Nathan's kidnapping?"

I took a deep breath. "You'll see."

* * *

After I'd filled her in, I decided to broach another subject before the kids got home.

"I talked with Tom," I said.

"Did you, now?"

"Has he changed, or am I looking at him differently?"

"I'm sure I don't know," Lizzie said. "How do you see he's changed?"

"He seems . . . I don't know . . . more responsible now, when it comes to the kids."

"Well," Lizzie said, "he's around. Mother, don't tell me you like him now."

"As a husband for you, no," I said, "but he seems to be a good father. Or, at least, he's trying."

Lizzie sighed and said, "I hate to admit it, but you might be right."

At that moment, we heard car doors slam outside.

"Dad's outside," Chloe said as she burst through the door. "He says to tell you he hoped you had a good trip and hi to Grandma."

Lizzie raised her eyebrows. "That was nice of him. Now where's my kiss? Don't tell me I haven't been missed around here."

"I missed you, Mom," Cam stepped up and grabbed his mother around the neck. "A lot." Then, looking over at me, he said, "No offense, Grammy."

"None taken, Cam."

Chloe came and sat down beside me, kissing me on the cheek. "There's my Chloe Girl."

Cam stayed close to his mother but looked over at me. "How come Chloe gets a nickname and I don't? You just call me Cameron or Cam, nothing extra."

I had a flashback of my conversation with E.T. Nathan had saddled him with that nickname, thinking he was doing a good thing. Unfortunately, Nathan's good intentions had backfired. Now here was my darling grandson asking for a nickname that would make him feel he was on equal footing with his sister.

"So what nickname would you like?"

"Call him Camzilla, Grandma!" Chloe shouted. "Because he's such a monster."

"That's not nice," Lizzie scolded. "Be nice to your brother."

"I'll think about it and get back to you," Cam said seriously. I had to smile at his somber attitude. "Take your time."

Lizzie stood up. "Guess I should start thinking about dinner."

"All taken care of. There's a chicken dinner for four in the refrigerator," I told her.

"You're an angel, Mother. Are you sure you don't want to come live with us full time?"

The kids chimed in their approval, but we all knew it was just a game and I'd be leaving soon.

Lizzie and I cleaned the kitchen while Chloe and Cam went to their rooms to do homework.

"Have you been reading all the articles lately about false confessions?" Lizzie asked.

I nodded. "I caught that documentary on WGN a while ago."

"Maybe that's what's going on with Mr. Watson."

"I know for a fact that the detectives in this town would never strong-arm anyone to get a confession. And as much as I complain about Dean, I'm sure he'd never condone any violence in his station."

"There's also Mr. Watson's mental state to be considered," Lizzie reasoned. "He could have been so distraught after learning of his wife's murder that he didn't know what he was saying."

"Or didn't care," I said. "We'll have to find out if he's on any medication—antidepressants—anything that would affect his mental capacity. He could have been feeling suicidal without his wife and just didn't have enough strength to put up a fight."

"We? You said 'we'll have to find out.' I guess that means you want me to pay Mr. Watson a visit?"

"Maybe you should call Ashley back first. Then we can go talk to Mr. Watson."

"You did it again," Lizzie laughed. "You said 'we.'"

"Well, I'm not going to let you go without me."

Lizzie closed the dishwasher. "Remind me again how finding Carolyn Watson's killer helps Nathan."

Closure, there it was again. But as overused as it had become, it explained everything. Right down to the fact that until the Larkins were locked up, Nathan wouldn't feel completely safe.

Chapter Forty-Two

I've always been impressed with my daughter. And I suppose all parents think their child is the smartest, kindest, most talented kid around. But when Lizzie walked into the kitchen the next morning, I got a flash of the way others might see her. There she stood, all five feet six inches of her, a halo of blonde hair complementing those striking green eyes. She had a closet full of power suits, but that day she wore a black dress beneath a gray blazer. Chic and elegant. She wanted to project a no-nonsense image and had succeeded.

"You look great, Mother. I love that sweater."

"And you look professional and competent."

"I try." She finished her coffee. "The kids are on their way to school, and I called the office and told Josh to remind me to call Ashley Knight. My first appointment's at two. Looks like we're set."

When she picked up her black suede briefcase, I was even more impressed.

* * *

Sidney Watson looked like he wouldn't harm a fly, let alone a person. The few hairs he had left on his head were combed over to the right side. His eyes were big and brown, reminding me of Quincy, the basset hound I'd had when I was six. There didn't appear to be any muscle definition beneath his white T-shirt. As he walked sluggishly into the meeting room, he had to keep pulling up his gray sweatpants. When the guard told him to sit at the table, opposite Lizzie and me, he obediently plopped down.

Lizzie stuck out her hand to him. "Mr. Watson, I'm Elizabeth Farina. I'm a family lawyer."

Watson shook her hand then looked at me. "And you are?"

"Katherine Sullivan," I said, shaking his hand. "I used to be the—"

"—chief of police here. I know. Your name's been all over the paper for years."

"So you're originally from here?" I asked.

"There's been three generations of us Watsons in Edina." Then he looked down at his hands, never asking why we were there.

"The reason we're here," Lizzie began, "is because it's come to my attention that another man might be responsible for the death of your wife."

"Look, Ms. Farina, the police have my signed confession. I guess the court will appoint a lawyer if I need one. So I don't understand why either of you are here."

I gave it a try. "Dean Bostwick was telling me the other day that he and his wife are close friends. He thinks very highly of you. Carolyn's death hit them very hard."

"The four of us had some good times."

"And your children," I pushed on, "were close too."

"Yeah, they were."

"Have you ever heard of or met Charles Kerrigan?" Lizzie asked, forcing Sid to deal with the moment.

The confusion on his face gave us the answer before his words did. "No. Never."

"And you won't get the chance to ever make Mr. Kerrigan's acquaintance," I said, "because he's dead, Mr. Watson. Run down like a dog, left by the side of the highway. So if you're worried that he'll come back to harm your son, there's no need. Charlie Kerrigan can't hurt anyone again."

"You think this guy hurt Carol?"

"Come on, why don't you tell us why you confessed to a murder you didn't commit," Lizzie asked. "I came here today because I need your help."

"But you think the real killer's dead, so what can I do?"

"There's a couple in town, Everett and Diana Larkin . . ." I stopped when he jerked up in his chair.

"Now that's a name I recognize," he said. "Everett Larkin was the man having an affair with Carolyn."

"Did you ever meet him?" Lizzie asked.

"I caught them together once—just one time. Right out in public, for all the world to see. I was meeting a client at the Sheraton in Bloomington. As I was going in, they were coming out. All over each other. They didn't care who saw. So I walked over and asked what was going on. Carol made up some excuse about a job interview. She was unhappy working part-time and wanted a place that would give her more hours. All the time she's chattering away, this Larkin guy is smiling and nodding. But he didn't fool me."

I watched Sid closely as he spoke and could detect the control he held over his anger. He just didn't seem the type that would explode into a rage.

"Did you and your wife discuss it again?" Lizzie asked.

"She apologized for not telling me about their meeting. She swore there was nothing going on between her and Larkin. But I'm not stupid, you know."

"No one said you were," I assured him. "But confessing to a murder that Mr. or Mrs. Larkin choreographed isn't a good idea."

"Wait . . . I thought you said this Kerrigan guy killed my wife."

I looked him in the eyes. "Charlie had no grudge against your family. He needed money, that's all. To him it was just a business transaction."

It was obvious he was weakening. Lizzie could read the signs as well as I could and made a move.

"Don't you want to go home to your son, Mr. Watson? There are so many events you'll miss out on. Graduations, weddings . . . grandchildren. And all for what?"

At the mention of his family, he started to sob.

When the discomfort level was unbearable, I said, as gently as I could, "You're not alone, Sid. People confess to crimes they never committed all the time. Maybe they think it'll fix things—get some answers for their family so they're not left wondering for the rest of their lives. They offer themselves up like a sacrificial lamb."

He picked up the front of his shirt and wiped his eyes. "They didn't deserve this. They're great kids. And I wasn't Dad of the Year. Maybe it was all my fault that Carol cheated the way she did. If that's what got her killed, then it's all my fault and I should pay. I could have given her more attention. But I tried. I can always say I tried my best."

"So you'll let us help get you out of here?" Lizzie asked.

"I can't afford a lawyer. There's no savings. And I don't want my kids to suffer because there's no money. They deserve better than I can give them right now."

"This is about giving you a second chance," Lizzie said. "Forget about a public defender. All you have to say is that I'm your lawyer, and I'll start the paperwork. I work a lot of cases pro bono. I'll just add you to the list. I'm your lawyer now, and we're going to get you out of this."

Chapter
Forty-Three

While Lizzie drove, I called Ashley Knight to tell her we were coming.

"I have to warn you," I said as we got closer to her neighborhood. "This woman is a little . . . odd. And from what I could tell, she's an alcoholic and admits to having done drugs with her boyfriend. Now that he's gone, I'm sure she still does."

"Mother . . . please." Lizzie gave me that look. "I've been out in the world for many years. I've seen odd, strange, and crazy. My only concern here is that Ms. Knight makes a credible witness. And remember, we have to be careful not to mislead her about the possibility that she might serve some time for her part in a murder."

"Lizzie . . . please." I couldn't resist giving her my own look. The one that told her I'd been around the block a few times myself. "Have you ever had a client who just didn't understand the repercussions of what they were saying? It's like Ashley thinks she's not a participant in her own life. Like she's someone outside of it, eating popcorn and watching as everything unfolds."

"I know exactly what you're talking about. But ignorance of the law excuses no man."

"Ahh, spoken like a true lawyer."

I didn't expect her to, but Lizzie laughed. "Let's see if I can rack up one more pro bono case today, and my life will be perfect." Her sarcasm wasn't lost on me.

"Not to worry, love, Ashley's family can afford to pay her legal fees and then some. She comes from the Knight Construction dynasty."

Lizzie parked the car. "Don't tell me that her father's the man in those silly commercials."

"That's him."

"Now I'm really eager to meet this woman."

We hadn't gotten halfway to the door when Ashley opened it and shouted for us to come inside.

"Well," she looked Lizzie up and down, "you must be Wonder-Daughter." I could see her liquor cart parked against a wall but didn't detect the smell of alcohol coming from our hostess.

Lizzie smiled and introduced herself.

"Have a seat. I made some munchies for us to have while we talk. Would you care for a drink, Mrs. Farina?"

"Call me Lizzie, please, and a Coke would be nice."

"Sure, Lizzie. And what about you, Mrs. Sullivan?"

"I'll have the same."

"Think I'll join you. Can't have a fuzzy head while we talk over important matters. Get comfortable and I'll be right back."

Lizzie and I sat next to each other on the large couch. "This is going to be interesting," she said, opening her briefcase and removing a minirecorder.

Ashley had poured our sodas into crystal champagne flutes in the kitchen. Standing in front of us now, she set them down on the low table. Then she pulled a large chair closer.

"Do you like this table?"

"It's very attractive," I said.

"Daddy found the wood on a trip to Ecuador and had it made for me. Cost a fortune. He said nothing was too good for me . . . but that was when he liked me. Before Charlie. I haven't had the nerve to call and tell him the mess I'm in. I guess he'll have to learn about it the same way everyone else will. And then he'll either hate me more or feel sorry for me. He's a real take-charge guy, you know. If he thinks I'm out in the hard, cold world, helpless, he'd like nothing better than to swoop down and make everything better. But after he does, every word out of my mouth has to be thank you . . . thank you, Daddy, I love you, Daddy . . . until the day I die."

"Ms. Knight," Lizzie tried to get a word while Ashley took a breath. "I'm sorry about you and your father, but if we can get started please?"

"Oh, sure . . . sorry." Ashley held her glass with both hands and rested it on her lap.

It was Lizzie's show now; she was in complete charge. I sat back and watched.

"My mother tells me that your boyfriend, Charles Kerrigan, worked for Everett Larkin on the side. That Mr. Larkin asked him to do some unscrupulous things. Would you have any proof of that?"

"Proof? Let me think." Ashley drank her Coke while staring at the ceiling. "We mostly had conversations, just the two of us, here in the house. No one was ever around to hear."

"And you never told anyone about these conversations?"

"No. I didn't want to get him in trouble. I loved Charlie—then. I don't now."

"You said he called you from the Watson house, after he'd murdered Carolyn. Is that true?"

"Just once."

"Was it to a cell phone?"

"Yes." She put down her glass and fished around in her bra. Smiling, she brought out a slim smartphone. "This one to be exact."

"Good, good, at least we have that on record."

"Am I going to be arrested?" Ashley suddenly wanted to know. "I didn't kill anyone. I didn't kill Charlie. I swear he was alive after I threw him out of my truck. When he called, he was furious but alive."

I put my glass down. "He called you? After you drove away?"

"Yes." Then a light went off in her head. "Wouldn't that be in my phone, too?"

"Definitely," Lizzie said. "And it would give us a timeline to help pinpoint the exact time of his death. But first we'll have to let the police go over your truck."

Ashley looked panicked. "They'll find the Watson woman's blood in it, and Charlie's of course. I told you that he loaded her body into it and took it out to that farm, Mrs. Sullivan." She looked at me frantically.

"She did." I looked at Lizzie and nodded. "But you can arrange for a polygraph to prove everything she's saying is true. That should help her credibility."

"Even though it's not admissible in a court of law, it'll help convince the authorities you're innocent. But before we get too far ahead of ourselves," Lizzie told Ashley, "let's start at the beginning. No detail is too small. Tell me everything . . ."

Talking was Ashley's strong suit. I just hoped the battery in Lizzie's recorder would last that long.

It took the rest of the morning and an hour into the afternoon, but Ashley Knight was finally talked out. When Lizzie and I suggested that the three of us go directly to the police station, we got no argument.

Chapter Forty-Four

Lizzie had to stay with Ashley Knight while she gave her statement, but it wasn't necessary for me to be there, especially since I'd have to wait outside the room. Ashley was calm now, distracted, watching a detective set up the polygraph. I wouldn't be missed; everything was under control. So I excused myself, telling my daughter that Nathan was coming to take me out for lunch. But in truth, I'd called E.T. to drive me back to the Larkin place.

This time the blue Porsche was parked in the driveway, out in plain sight. E.T. seemed nervous as he handed me the wire and told me how to string it under my sweater. But in the confines of his car, it was difficult.

Making sure the earpiece was hidden by my hair, he asked, "You sure you want to do this? I can go in there, make up some story about the cameras—"

"You have to stay out here and listen. If I need help—come running. But your job now is to make sure everything said in there gets recorded."

"I'm all set up."

Standing on the pavement, I bent down to close the car door.

"Be careful, Kate."

"You, too, Ted."

As I walked to the front door, I looked back over my shoulder and could see him putting on a headset.

"Can you hear me?"

"Loud and clear," I said into my chest.

I was getting ready to use the door knocker when I noticed a white button had been installed. Pressing it, I could hear chimes ringing like they were announcing the pope.

A small woman, dressed in a maid's uniform, let me in. She asked my name and said that Mrs. Larkin was upstairs and she'd go up and announce that I was here.

"A maid? There wasn't a maid when I was there," E.T. said in my ear.

"She's new to me, too," I whispered.

The maid took her time, which gave me a chance to inspect the spot where the missing painting had been. But this time, I was surprised to see it hanging there. The same one that had been in the construction trailer behind Ray DeYoung's desk. Was he connected to all this? Before I could dwell on that any further, the maid came back down.

"You're the policewoman, right?" she asked.

"I was."

"Then you can go up now."

"Thank you."

"At the top of the stairs, make a left. That's the Missus's bedroom, the one with the pink door. If you need anything, just call."

E.T. laughed in my ear. "As if she's going to help you."

The plush carpet felt heavenly beneath my feet. The last time I'd been there, looking for Nathan, I couldn't afford to waste time admiring the decor. But now I appreciated the tasteful touches.

Somehow she knew I was at the top of the stairs, even though I hadn't made a sound. "I'm in here, Mrs. Sullivan!"

It was like walking into a rose. I'd never seen so many shades of red and pink, except in an artist's supply catalog. Petal-pink carpeting, rose-patterned duvet with matching pillows on the bed. Garden prints were hung around the room, all framed in simple white. The curtains were white lace with pink-dipped edges. The room had been decorated to resemble an old-fashion lady's boudoir. And there was the lady herself, sitting at a small writing desk, picture-perfect.

"Mrs. Sullivan, how nice to meet you," she said graciously as she stood.

My hostess was breathtaking. Tall and statuesque, platinum hair curly and shiny, tumbling down to her back. Flawless skin, teeth straight and perfect. From her black stilettos to her skintight leggings, up to her mink vest, she was gorgeous.

"Thank you for seeing me, Mrs. Larkin," I began.

"No, no, you must call me Diana, please."

"Then you can call me Katherine."

We smiled politely, sizing each other up. Then she guided me to a dainty floral chair while she sat in its twin. "Are you hungry? I can have Sebina bring us a snack."

"Don't bother. I'm fine."

"Then how about we get straight to business? I'm sure you already know that I've been interrogated by the police. After watching them put Everett in jail, I took a meeting with my lawyer, who advised me not to speak to anyone about my case or my husband's any further. I could have sent you away, but to tell the truth, I wanted to meet you. You're very respected in this town. So out of courtesy, I'm talking to you today. But please understand this will be the last time. Now, if you don't mind, can we make this quick? I'm dead on my feet."

How quickly her mood had changed! She had transformed from Mrs. Pretty and Pink to Serious Business Gal right before my eyes.

"I've been talking to Ashley Knight."

No reaction. Diana just smiled and waited for more.

"She was Charles Kerrigan's girlfriend."

"If you say so. But I don't see why this should matter to me."

"She said you hired him to kill Carolyn Watson because she was having an affair with your husband."

A big laugh. So big it brought tears to her eyes.

"My husband has been trying to tell the police that Charles Kerrigan was a dope fiend, but they don't want to hear it. It's our money that alienates us; it's got to be. Some poor cop trying to make his mortgage payment on a two-bedroom shack on the edge of town hates us because we have all this." She opened her arms wide.

I assumed she included me in her theory . . . and I didn't like it. "The officers I know joined the force to uphold the law," I said, hoping I didn't sound as angry as I felt. "They knew going in that the job was not only dangerous, but they weren't going to get rich doing it."

"According to your theory," she said, "the police would want to help us then. But even after my husband explained how Mr. Kerrigan came here trying to blackmail him, claiming that I'd hired him to kill some woman I didn't even know, they wouldn't listen. And if you'll check, as they did, I was out of town. And . . . I had never met that horrible man in my life."

"The foreman of the construction site over there"—I pointed toward the front of the subdivision—"claims that you drove over, in the car that's parked out front, and talked to Charlie. There were other witnesses, too. You don't exactly fade into the background, Mrs. Larkin."

She didn't know what to say to that, so I continued.

"I'm thinking that you found out about your husband's affair, hired someone with a criminal record to kill her, then promptly left town. But you didn't pay him. I believe the standard procedure when hiring a hitman is half up front and half after the job's done." I made a show of looking around the room. "Seems to me, with all of this"—I opened my arms as she had done—"that you would certainly have enough to pay him off before leaving town. To ensure his silence. If only you would have seen to that one little detail, none of this would be happening now. Was it an oversight? Or maybe you're so used to having your people take care of the incidental details? Were you trying to cut back on your household expenses?"

"What an extraordinary imagination you have, Katherine! Someday you should write down all your little stories. There are so many books out there written by ex-cops and detectives. A best seller would add some money to your social security check. Every little bit helps, you know."

If she thought ageism was going to get to me, she'd have to try harder.

"So you didn't pay up," I continued, never missing a beat. "Charlie was mad and came to your husband for the money and told him the whole story. Can you imagine poor Everett's surprise? But he isn't the rich one here, is he? He's the nice one who only wanted to protect you. Realizing that he had a killer in his house, threatening him, he had to stall until he could get the money. So he promised Charlie a bonus if he'd do a little job for him."

"Which was?" Her eyes sparkled. In some strange way, she was enjoying our back and forth. It was a game to her.

"To go after my friend, Nathan Walker. His company installed your security cameras, remember?"

"Vaguely."

"Nathan had come because of some additional work Mr. Larkin wanted done. But because he arrived early, he saw Charlie. And your husband was afraid that sooner or later, Nathan, being an ex-cop, might get suspicious and figure things out."

"I was out of town," she insisted. "I cannot be held responsible for what my husband did when I was hundreds of miles away!"

I ignored her protest. "Poor Charlie didn't have transportation of his own, so your sweet husband lent him the car. But a blue Porsche? Really? He never thought it would stick out like a neon sign? Charlie followed Nathan to a dark parking lot and forced him to drive his own car back to your house. I know neither of you are experienced criminals, at least I hope not, but surely Mr. Larkin had to realize that Nathan would be missed."

"I can't speak for my husband. And . . . I was out—"

"—of town, I know. And that's how I got involved with all this," I told her. "I came to track Nathan down. Funny thing, you both might have gotten away with two murders if Nathan hadn't been kidnapped."

"Two murders?"

"I'm assuming Mr. Larkin was the person who ran Charlie down. But don't be mad at your thoughtful husband. He was just cleaning up your mess. Probably like he's always done."

"Again, Katherine, I wasn't here."

I knew she had a temper from what I'd seen on the lawn the other night. People with tempers lose control quickly. She just needed one more shove.

"It's such a shame, really. You being so very beautiful. Not to mention running your own company, living in this magnificent home. And all that money on top of everything!"

She purred. "I've been very blessed."

"But even with all that you have, you couldn't keep your older . . . much older husband . . . from cheating on you. I wonder what Mrs. Watson, an average-looking woman in her midforties, had that you don't? Whatever it was, your husband kept going back for more."

Chapter Forty-Five

"Sebina!" Diana shouted. "Come show Mrs. Sullivan out, please!" Turning to me, she calmly said, "I think we're finished here. You can call my lawyer if you have any further questions."

I didn't bother asking for his name and number; she didn't bother giving it to me. We both knew I'd never have use for either.

"Tell her you're going to check out the Porsche," E.T. buzzed in my ear.

"There's no need to call Sebina," I said as I stood up. "I know the way to the door." I got halfway across the large room and stopped, as if suddenly remembering something. "Oh, I hope you don't mind if I take a look at your beautiful car. I assume the police already have. But just in case . . ."

That got her up and moving. "You're on private property, and my car is on private property."

I walked quickly toward the stairs. She chased after me and would have caught me on the landing if it weren't for those outrageous shoes of hers. Sebina stood holding the front door open for me, unaware her employer was hot on my heels. But suddenly, I turned and she came up short, surprised. I pointed at the wall with the Molly Hartung paintings.

"What about that? Funny how that painting disappears and reappears."

"It's none of your business what I have in my house."

"I'm thinking it was a payoff of some kind. Or maybe Ray was blackmailing you? I think I'll go see him now."

I turned and almost made it outside when Diana grabbed me around the waist, and we both tumbled to the gravel.

E.T. must have moved his car farther away from the house because I couldn't spot him anywhere. As Diana and I rolled around on the ground, my first concern was keeping my wire from being discovered. My second was getting her off of me.

She had attacked from behind, locking her arms around my waist. With my back protecting her face, she tried to scrape my face on the gravel that was laid over the driveway. Somehow, I managed to hold my head up while rolling her over onto her back, surprising myself at how easily I'd done the maneuver.

Breaking the grip she had across my chest, I sat up while she clawed at my back with her long nails. Then with all my weight, I came down onto her stomach.

Miraculously the small earpiece hadn't come loose. "Now check the Porsche over for chips and dents." E.T. instructed.

"You've got to be kidding," I told him, but Diana thought I was talking to her.

"You came here to harass me," She said, lying on her back. "When it comes to protecting myself, and my husband, I never kid around."

"Are you okay?" E.T. asked. "Do you need help?"

"I'm fine," I said under my breath.

"Let me up!" Diana screamed. "I can't breathe."

I leaned over. "That was a stupid thing to do, Mrs. Larkin. I should call the police and file charges against you for assault and battery."

"Please don't do that. I'm just very upset."

I stood up, brushed the dirt off myself, then reached down and pulled her back onto her feet.

"Police?" E.T. squawked. "They'll probably book us for just being here."

"Lucky for you neither one of us was hurt, or I'd call so fast, it would make your head spin. And I'll take into consideration that we're both upset. But if you ever do anything like that again, I'll not only be calling the police, but my lawyer as well."

"Thank you, Katherine. Thank you," Diana said, still trying to catch her breath.

I walked to the Porsche, hoping neither of the Larkins had taken their sports car to the body shop yet.

Diana followed. "I can't believe you're still obsessed with this damn car. That thing's two years old, and the first night we spent in the house, someone broke into it. What with the gravel and heavy equipment around here, all hours of the night and day, that poor baby's taken a real beating."

"She's scared," E.T. whispered.

If I could have reacted, I would have told him I was well aware of Diana's anxiety. It was not only written on her face but obvious by the way her hands were shaking.

Slowly, I ran my hand over the hood, then across the front fender. Squatting, I got close to inspect the area that most likely had come in contact with Charlie Kerrigan's body. As I looked, I tried to think of something I could do to force Diana to trip up.

She stood watching me. When I stretched my legs, she smirked. "See? I told you there isn't anything to look at."

"Just one more thing," I pushed.

She looked at her watch, ignoring me.

"Was it you or your husband who drove out, in this car, to Ashley Knight's home with a gun? Hasn't that poor woman been through enough? She and Charlie were so in love. She'll probably never get over this death. They were such a charming couple," I went on, painting a picture of the two as if I knew the couple intimately.

She couldn't hold back her laughter. "Are you kidding me? That woman's a drunk, just like he was. Charming? There was nothing charming about either one of them."

"So you *have* met her?" I asked.

"Ahh . . . no . . . But I've met those kinds before."

"Those kinds? In the house, you said you hadn't met Charlie either." I took out my phone and snapped a shot of the car. "I think I have everything I need."

She made a grab for my phone. "Give me that!" she screeched.

E.T. pulled into the driveway and got out of his car. "Is there a problem, Mrs. Sullivan?" he asked so politely.

"No—"

"Well, she might not have a problem, but I do! I want you both off of my property now! And if I ever see either one of you again, I'll have you thrown in jail."

In his best chauffeur impersonation, E.T. held the passenger door open for me. I walked to the car and got in. As we drove away, I could see Mrs. Larkin staring in our direction.

"Well, that could have gone better," E.T. said.

"At least she admitted she knew Charlie and that she's familiar with Ashley Knight. That's something. You did hear it all?"

"Every word. But what was all that scuffling about? All I got was some muffled grunts."

"She attacked me. Nothing serious; we just rolled around in the driveway a few minutes."

"If they're turned on, those security cameras will help land Mrs. Larkin in jail."

"Do you need to get back into the house to check?" I asked.

"Not to worry," E.T. laughed. "Mr. Larkin didn't understand how to operate his system and was worried he might erase something important or shut it off accidentally. So he had the deluxe system installed."

"What's that?"

Proudly he took out his phone. "We can monitor his home back in our office. And I can tap into that system like this." He tapped through a few screens. "Ahh. There it is. Your scuffle with Mrs. Larkin was recorded. A nice bit of evidence to take to the cops, with my compliments."

Chapter Forty-Six

A text from Lizzie came in while we drove. She wrote that she was still in the police station, waiting for the results of Ashley's polygraph, but she thought it went well. I told her I'd see her at home.

"Where to now?" E.T. asked.

"Maybe we should find Nathan and tell him what's going on. We did agree to keep him updated."

"According to Polly, he's in the office and looks good. But the boss is a proud man," E.T. said. "Let's just hope he knows we're coming from a place of love and not trying to undermine him in any way."

* * *

The scene at the office was chaotic. Rosie was shouting into the phone on her desk; Polly talked nonstop into her headset. Our presence there didn't seem to calm them.

"I gotta go," Rosie told the person on the other end and hung up without another word of explanation.

"Calm down," E.T. started.

"Don't give me any of your peace-and-love routine right now. They're saying the boss killed someone!"

"Who's saying that? Where is he?" I asked, hoping my panic wouldn't show on my face or come through in my voice.

"That Larkin dude? The one who grabbed the boss? He's sayin' it, that's who."

Polly had finished her call and was now standing with us around Rosie's desk.

"Did you know that Mr. Larkin was arrested today?" Polly asked.

"Yes, I was at the station earlier," I told her. "But what does his arrest have to do with Nathan?"

"Mr. Larkin claims that the boss ran Charlie down."

I couldn't think of anything to say to that.

But luckily E.T. found his words. "Why would Mr. Walker do that? And how could he, if he was being held against his will?" He waited for Polly to answer.

"All we know is the police chief said if Mr. Walker didn't come down for questioning, he'd send an officer to bring him. Out of professional courtesy, the boss has until five."

"So he grabbed Brock, and the two of them went to see what the hell is goin' on," Rosie finished. "How are we gonna fix this mess, Katie? Tell us what to do."

"Relax," I told her. "One step at a time. E.T. and I'll go down there while you and Polly take care of business here. If the press calls, you have no comment. Got it?"

Polly and Rosie both nodded.

"And you'll keep us in the loop?" Rosie asked. "This waitin' is killin' me."

"Me, too," Polly said. "Please, Kate, don't leave us hanging."

"I won't," I promised.

* * *

"I want you to meet Dr. Turney," Bostwick said after E.T. and I were seated in his office. "He's a psychotherapist who's been working with the force for two years now. We called the doctor in to observe Mr. Larkin."

"Nathan Walker would never—could never—kill anyone," I said, agitated. "Come on, Dean, you know that."

"Calm down, Katherine," Bostwick said in an unusually gentle voice.

Dr. Turney was a serious-looking man who appeared to be analyzing all of us in the room. While he pushed his glasses back up his nose, he frowned. And that frown brought out the wrinkles across his forehead.

"I understand you were colleagues?" He looked at me. "And you are employed by Mr. Walker as a security expert?" he asked E.T.

"Why does my employment have any bearing on this?" E.T. asked.

"I'm just trying to get a mental image of Mr. Walker. Any pertinent facts I might gather help."

It was my turn, so I spoke. "Nathan and I were in the force together. Now that we're both retired, we've maintained our friendship. I trust him with my life."

Dr. Turney nodded. "I see."

Dean looked uncomfortable. "Katherine, this is more about Larkin than Walker."

"I was asked to observe Everett when he was brought in," Turney said. "The officers who escorted him from his home reported that he seemed to be suffering from hallucinations. I sat in on his interrogation. He answered every question to the best of his ability, without one outburst. But after he was left alone in a cell, he broke down."

"I'm sure you've seen this before, Doctor. Because I have. These types of people always think they can fool the most highly trained professionals into believing they're having a psychotic episode."

"That's certainly true, Mrs. Sullivan."

"Do you think it's the case here?" E.T. asked.

"Too early to tell," the doctor said thoughtfully. "But I've arranged to give Everett a complete examination tomorrow."

"Where's Nathan now?" I asked Bostwick.

"Interrogation Room Two."

"This is all so stupid," I told whoever was listening. "When would Nathan have had the opportunity to kill anyone? He was bound, gagged, and locked up. Besides, he told me that Charlie wasn't even in the house after the second or third day. So supposing he got away from Larkin and wanted to hunt Charlie down, how would he begin looking for him? And if he did manage to find the address of a man whose name he didn't know, how would he get there? Nathan's car had been taken away and hidden at the park."

Bostwick smiled slightly at me. "You know how this goes. Nathan will be here a few hours while we question him.

Standard procedure. As of this moment, we have no evidence to hold him. It's just the ravings of a crazy man against a retired cop with a spotless record. The Larkins have a boatload of money and are lining up some of the top lawyers in the state to handle their defense. I just have to make sure I'm protecting my men and the department. Every i has to be dotted, every t crossed."

"I know . . . you're right. But I don't have to like any of this." I had to admit—to myself, not Dean—that he was handling things exactly as I would have. Accusations, false or true, were being tried in the media before even half the facts were collected. It was the curse of the technology age we lived in.

"Can we at least wait for the boss?" E.T. asked the chief.

"Of course. It shouldn't be much longer."

I was halfway to the door when Bostwick reassured me that he knew Nathan was an honest and decent man.

"Thanks, Dean," I said, trying not to embarrass him.

* * *

E.T. and I positioned ourselves on a bench in the hallway and waited. We must have been there twenty minutes when Brock came walking toward us.

"This is really somethin', ain't it? The boss, a killer?" He snickered. "Ain't that about the dumbest thing ya ever heard?" There was plenty of room on the long bench to allow him to sit next to me. When he started to unwrap the Hershey bar in his hand, he stopped to ask if we'd like a piece.

"None for me," E.T. said. "All you're eating there is processed sugar."

"An' it sure tastes great." Brock turned to me. "We might be sittin' here a long time. Are ya sure ya don't want some?"

In the face of E.T.'s disapproval, I took a few pieces that Brock snapped off the large candy bar. Nothing made the world a little brighter like chocolate.

The three of us sat in silence, watching traffic flow in and out of the station. Those officers who knew me smiled and nodded as they passed. Those who'd been hired after my departure talked to each other or hurried by. A civilian would walk in occasionally to make a complaint or file a report. It would have been entertaining if we weren't so concerned about Nathan.

According to the large clock over the front desk, it was almost seven. I'd called Lizzie at six, telling her I wasn't sure when I'd be home. We had to wait another half hour before we spotted Nathan exiting Interrogation Room Two.

He stood in the hallway awhile, talking to an officer. They laughed then slapped each other on the back. A few more words were exchanged before he turned and started walking. His gait was light, his face relaxed; an observer would have thought he had come from a visit with a friend. As he got close, he realized the three of us were there, waiting for him.

Brock was the first to reach him. "Ya all right, boss? Ya look okay."

"What are you two doing here?" He asked E.T., then me.

"Oh, we were just passing by and . . . why do you think we're here?" I asked.

"We were worried," E.T. said. "It isn't every day my employer gets hauled into jail."

"I wasn't exactly 'hauled,' and I'm not in jail. Relax, son."

"Easy for you to say," E.T. quipped.

Nathan patted E.T.'s shoulder. "You fellas can take off. Kathy'll drive me home."

"Sure," E.T. said. "Katherine, we can talk tomorrow."

"Good. I'll see you at the office."

As Nathan and I watched the two walk away, he asked, "How about I buy you dinner? There's a gourmet burger place I've been wanting to try."

Chapter Forty-Seven

I wouldn't call the menu at Burger-ama gourmet. It was more eclectic than anything else. But the place was empty and quiet, which was nice on both counts. While trying to decide what to order, we both had a beer.

"Are you all right?" I asked Nathan. "Today must have been so . . . so traumatic."

"Nothing I can't handle. Look at me, Kathy, don't I look fine?"

"Yes, you do. I'm just concerned, that's all."

"Well you can get unconcerned and tell me what you and E.T. have been doing."

I gave him my best innocent look.

"Come on, I know something's going on. And I bet it has to do with me."

"Well, aren't you full of yourself?"

The waiter interrupted to take our order. When he finally left, Nathan came right back to where he'd left off.

"You know, I don't have to be in the office to keep track of what goes on down there. My employees are loyal, and it is, after all, a security business."

"You mean . . ."

"State of the art. Cameras throughout."

"Does your crew know?" I asked. "Isn't that an invasion of their privacy?"

"It would be if I hadn't told them—E.T. even designed the setup. I have a lot of valuable equipment there, and those spaces in that strip mall keep changing hands. When I first moved in, there was a bar at the end. Some nights it was party central. And you know how people get when it's last call. Some don't want to go home. So they go outside and look for trouble. Remember how it was, Kathy? You and I drove our fair share of Saturday-night drunks to the station."

"I remember." I picked up the heavy glass beer stein and took a sip.

"So here's what I know," Nathan continued. "Feel free to stop me if I have my facts wrong or add something I don't know. But from what I've gathered, you and E.T. have spent a lot of time watching the Larkins."

"They should both be in jail, not just him."

"Oh, I agree. But the only thing connecting the missus to Kerrigan's death is that girlfriend of his. We'll just have to wait and see who's more convincing. The lady with money and a spotless reputation or the lady who's been in and out of rehab, lived with a bum, and recently been cut off by her father."

"I've talked with Ashley Knight three times now. She's a little odd, but I believe her, Nathan. Lizzie and I took her to the station, and she gave a statement. Her testimony will probably put Mrs. Larkin away for a few years and get Sid Watson released."

"But you've probably put Ashley in danger now. People with money can buy their way out of trouble and add on a little more to get some revenge."

"I hope you're wrong. But at least you should have the satisfaction that Mr. Larkin will pay for what he put you through."

"That fool didn't have a clue what to do with me. All he wanted was to make things right for that wife of his."

"Dr. Turney thinks Mr. Larkin's lying about his hallucinations—"

"Hold up," Nathan put down his stein. "What's this about hallucinations?"

* * *

By the time I had finished my goat cheese and sunflower seed burger and Nathan was chewing the last of his green olive and bacon burger, I'd also finished my story. We slowed down over the last of our fries and, after they were gone, ordered a piece of turtle pie to share with coffee.

"You've been a busy girl," Nathan said.

"I was worried about you. E.T. felt so guilty that he hadn't gone with you on the call that day. They all adore you."

"Well, I feel the same about them. But this guilt stuff, it's all just made up to control people."

I stirred cream into my coffee. "You've never felt guilty about anything?"

"Every once in a while there's this twinge, but I tell myself it's a trick. I think back to how my mother used guilt when I was a boy, how Terry used it to get me to do things, little things like take out the garbage. It's a device, a tool of manipulation."

"Wow, you've given this so much thought. I'm surprised."

"And if I had any kids," Nathan said, wagging a finger, "I'd teach them not to let anyone manipulate them with guilt."

As long as I'd known Nathan, we'd never discussed topics that could potentially lead to an argument. No talk of religion or politics—ever. But there were times I wanted to debate something more serious than family or the weather. Now he'd opened the door, and I rushed through it. For the next hour, we talked about ethics. Not one thought was given to the Larkins or Ashley Knight, Charlie Kerrigan or Carolyn Watson. We were in the moment for a short time, just enjoying each other's company. And our relationship grew a little richer for it.

The waiter filled our cups for a third time, looking uneasy. It was closing time at Burger-ama.

"We better go," Nathan said.

"I'll drive you home."

"That's real nice of you, but I can drive myself," he said as we stood in the parking lot.

"Yes, it is nice of me," I kidded, "and yes, I do have to because you don't have your car here. Remember?"

He looked embarrassed. "With all that's been going on lately, forgetting a car is small potatoes."

Chapter Forty-Eight

Chloe was texting, thumbs moving across the keys of her phone so quickly they were a blur. When I came into the kitchen for breakfast, she stopped immediately, making Lizzie laugh.

"She's afraid you'll take it away again." Lizzie nodded toward the phone Chloe now held behind her back.

I hugged my granddaughter. "That was then, Chloe. This time around I haven't had to fight for your attention. Thanks."

"So I can finish?" she asked. "Just this one and I'll put it away. Promise."

"She's been a lot better, Mother," Lizzie vouched for her daughter.

I kissed Chloe on the top of her head. "Be my guest."

Cam came into the room, plopped down at the table, and picked up a piece of toast. "I've been thinking about my nickname, and I've got it down to three, but I can't decide which one is the best."

"Lay 'em on me," I said.

He looked confused.

Lizzie translated. "Grammy wants you to tell her what the names are."

"Oh. Okay. I've got Camster."

Chloe laughed hysterically. "Sounds like hamster. Like you're this giant animal running around on a big squeaky wheel."

Cam was not amused. "Or Caminator," he continued as though his sister hadn't said a word. "You know, like the movie, *Terminator*?"

"And what's the third?" I asked.

"Cam the Man," he said proudly.

While I thought over his suggestions, I looked at Lizzie who, instead of helping me, took a big bite out of her toast.

"Well . . ." I began, trying to be as diplomatic as I could, "you already have a nickname. Cam is short for Cameron. And since you're the oldest, you've had it longer than Chloe's had hers."

He scrunched up his face. "I like Caminator."

The determination in his eyes made me understand how important a nickname was to him. "Okay then, how about we try it out for the rest of my visit and see how it fits?"

He gave one big nod. "Fair."

"So what's on your agenda for today?" I asked Lizzie while she packed lunchboxes.

"I've been working with a mediator on a custody case for months. Keep your fingers crossed that this is the last time we have to go into court. I have to be in the office in forty-five minutes to gather up all the paperwork and brief my client. How about you? You'll probably be going home now that everything's wrapped up here."

I didn't want to tell her about my scuffle with Diana Larkin. No need to worry her. Nathan and his crew had things under control. Lizzie would get Ashley Knight through the legalities of her case. "Well, maybe I could stay a few more days . . ."

"We haven't had our painting time," Cam said. "And . . . Mom . . . did you tell Grammy about the play?"

"What play?" I asked.

"Chloe's in a play at her school Friday night," Lizzie said proudly. "I got a ticket for you, just in case you were still here."

I turned to my granddaughter. "I didn't know you were an actress. What's the name of the play?"

"Our math teacher, Mr. Jacobs wrote it. It's called *The Princess and the Dragon.*"

"Chloe plays a lady-in-waiting," Lizzie said coming over to hug her daughter. "I sat in on a rehearsal. She's very good."

"Well, I wouldn't miss this for the world."

"I know you've seen real plays in London, even on Broadway. Don't expect this to be good like that," Chloe said seriously. "Just a warning."

"But this is special because you're in it. I'm so proud of you."

"Don't get too excited until you see her," Cam said. "Her name is Lady Devonshire, and she has to wear this dumb dress."

"Well, the Caminator will have to just suck it up and be happy for his sister," I told him.

At the sound of his nickname, he changed instantly from taunting big brother to delighted little boy.

I was enjoying myself—comfortable in my robe and slippers, happy in the kitchen with my family, not particularly eager to start my day—when Lizzie's phone rang.

"Josh, calm down," she said, looking alarmed. "I can't understand a word when you talk so fast."

The serenity instantly evaporated. The kids knew the routine and grabbed their dirty dishes as they waved good-bye, trying to make a quiet exit while their mother talked business. Putting the phone on speaker, Lizzie tossed a small bag of chips into each lunchbox and snapped them shut. The day had suddenly shifted from first to second gear.

Still I tried to delay moving from my chair and poured myself a second cup of coffee from the pot in the middle of the table. As I watched a small gray squirrel lounge on the low branch of the backyard maple, I couldn't help hearing Josh's frantic voice.

"She's pacing all over the place. I put her in your office—I hope that's okay. But she's acting like a crazy person and I'm worried. Not only for her safety, but we just had the new carpeting installed and she's dripping the coffee everywhere. How soon are you coming in, Mrs. Farina? She says she won't leave until she sees you."

"I have to finish getting dressed, and then I'm on my way, Josh. Relax. We can always get new carpeting. Take it easy."

"But she says someone's trying to kill her."

Lizzie turned to me. "It's Ashley Knight. She says Mrs. Larkin threatened to kill her."

"Hello?" Josh screamed. "Are you still there?"

"Yes. I was talking to my mother. She's staying with me."

"Oh, hi, Mrs. Sullivan!"

"Hey, Josh. Don't worry about Ms. Knight. She's just a little high strung."

"Potatoes—potaatoes, it's all the same," he said. "The woman needs a keeper."

"Just tell her we'll be right there."

"Okay, but hurry."

Lizzie hung up. "Go get dressed. We'll drop the kids off at school and head for the office. You can handle Ashley while I get ready for court. Thank goodness you're here, Mother."

Chapter
Forty-Nine

I was shocked when I saw Ashley Knight. Her hair was almost completely gone. All that was left were two inch spikes, covering her head like a cap. Before I could say anything, she ran the fingers of her right hand across the top.

"I needed a change. I always do something rash when I'm stressed out. First Charlie, then I had to talk to the cops, and now this. Before it's all over, I'll be bald or . . . dead."

"Well, I think your new do is becoming," I said. But I thought she looked like a woman trying to hang on to the last of her sanity. "And we're here to keep you safe."

Lizzie stood behind me and nodded.

"Now, you and I are going to go sit in another office while you tell me what happened. Lizzie needs this one back."

"Sorry." With hands at her side, Ashley grabbed her caftan du jour and twisted. "I didn't mean to barge in here. I know this is a place of business, but I didn't have your address, Mrs. Sullivan, or else I would have gone there."

Thank goodness for small favors, I thought.

"You're here now, and that's all that counts," I said as I led her to a small office across the hall.

After we got comfortable, Ashley began:

Late last night, Oscar, one of Charlie's buddies from work, stopped by. He was agitated, saying over and over that he couldn't believe the nerve of that woman in the fancy house. What would have given that broad the idea she could buy him the way she did Charlie? He might be a lot of things, but no amount of money could ever make him bump someone off. When he told her, "No! No way," she said she'd have to do it herself.

Ashley made some coffee and tried to calm him down. Oscar was a jerk, but she owed it to Charlie to be cordial. So they talked, and that's when he told her the person Mrs. Larkin wanted dead was her—Ashley Knight.

He liked Charlie, and Charlie loved Ashley, so Oscar felt he owed it to his friend's memory to tell her that her life was in danger. She could do whatever she wanted with the information. After this, he was done. He didn't want trouble with the police or that rich chick. No job was worth getting killed over. He had a brother in Dallas, and they were always looking for men down there.

"Then without even a good-bye, he left."

"Did Oscar say when Mrs. Larkin wanted the job done? Did she give any indication of a timeline?"

Ashley looked at me like I was out of my mind. "Timeline? The woman wants me dead, and you talk like we're all just consulting our datebooks to plan a tea party."

"Believe it or not, people like her tend to do things very methodically. I certainly didn't mean to trivialize the situation. I suggest we go to your house right now, you can grab a few things, and we'll get you to a motel. Somewhere safe."

She jumped up. "Then we better hurry."

Josh was seated at the reception desk. "Are we all better now?" He looked up at Ashley.

"Fine," I answered. "Tell my daughter that Ms. Knight and I are going to her place to pack a bag and I'll talk to her later."

"I'll write her a note. When her door's closed, she's not to be disturbed. That's one of the rules around here."

"I know I can be a handful," Ashley told him. "Sorry for any trouble."

Josh put down his pen. "You're forgiven."

* * *

Ashley parked in her driveway, and we sat in the car for a moment, listening and searching for anything that felt wrong.

"I don't see her. Do you think we were followed? I didn't mean to lead her to your daughter's office . . . but she could have found out the address on her own. I was just crazy scared."

"You didn't do anything wrong, Ashley, relax. Now let's just go inside so you can pack. The faster you can do that, the faster we're out of here."

"Do you think we were followed? I tried watching while I drove, but there's always so much traffic this early."

"I didn't see anyone." I waited impatiently while she unlocked the front door.

"But that doesn't mean they weren't there. If she got a professional, he could be waiting inside right now." At the thought of a hitman on the other side of her door, Ashley jumped back, leaving her key ring dangling from the lock.

"She's a smart woman," I said as I reached out to turn her key. "She knows the police are watching her. There's been one trip to the station already. I don't think she'll try to hire anyone else after Oscar turned her down. She's got to assume he'll tell someone." *But*, I thought, *she's certainly capable of doing the job herself.*

Everything seemed undisturbed as I led the way into the house.

"Sit tight. I'll be right back," Ashley told me over her shoulder as she rushed back to what I assumed was her bedroom.

I could see an elderly woman walking her matching Pomeranians as I looked through the gauzy curtains. A mailman stopped to talk to her. It was a beautiful, typical autumn day.

A tiny clock on an end table showed the time to be 9:10. If I were in Taos now, it would be an hour earlier, and I'd still be in bed. The thought of it made me yawn.

"Ready!" Ashley announced. She held up two large bags. "This should hold me for a few days. And what I didn't pack, I suppose I can always buy. Right? Or do you think I should have packed more?" She didn't give me a chance to answer. "Maybe just a few more—"

Tires squealed. Then a car door slammed shut.

I peeked through the curtains again and saw Diana Larkin. She looked ready to explode.

"Oh God," Ashley whined. "It's her."

"Do you own a gun?" I asked.

"No, Charlie had one, but I made him get rid of it. How dumb was that? If only I wouldn't have done that. But how was I to know some whacked-out woman would want to kill me?"

"You stay here. When she sees me, she'll know you called, and that means the police have been alerted."

"You're going out there by yourself? Without any protection? I could get a knife. How about one of those andirons?" She pointed toward the fireplace.

"Just call nine-one-one and wait here."

Chapter Fifty

It wasn't that I was brave or blind to the fact that she had murder in her heart. I knew Diana wasn't crazy enough to kill me on the front steps of Ashley Knight's house for everyone to see.

"You?" she asked disgustedly. "Why can't you just mind your own stinkin' business?"

"What do you want, Diana?"

"I came to see what's-her-face, Charlie's girlfriend. Is there some law I don't know about that says I can't see her?"

"She's not home right now," I said. "If you tell me what you—"

"Liar! I just want to tell her how sorry I am for her loss." She stood in front of her car, feet apart, hands on her hips, in a defiant stance.

"I'll tell her when I see her," I smiled.

"If she's not inside, then what are you doing here? Huh?"

Thank goodness I've always been quick on my feet and could talk myself out of most situations. "I came to get some papers her lawyer needs. Then she'll be heading for the police department."

"Papers? What kind of papers?"

"Look, all you need to know is that she's not here, and there's no reason for you to be."

Slowly Diana walked over to Ashley's truck. "Has anyone noticed that this piece of junk is almost the same color as my car? Did it ever occur to anyone that a bitter girlfriend might have gotten angry enough to run her cheating boyfriend down? Has anyone bothered to check it out?"

I refused to be tricked into getting any closer to her and stayed where I was.

"Are you saying that you and Charlie were having an affair?" I asked.

"You know, underneath all that dirt and uncouth exterior, he wasn't that bad."

I hoped Ashley wasn't taking the bait Diana tossed out to get her to show herself.

"You're not the type of woman who would ever get familiar with the hired help. You consider yourself in an entirely different class. Isn't that right? Even if you had to buy yourself into the inner circle. What does it matter how you got there . . . as long as you're there, front and center."

"I started with nothing!" she shouted. "I put myself through college, earned two degrees by the time I was twenty-two . . ."

"Come on, I've heard your story a dozen times. Do you think you're the only person who worked hard to get ahead in life? Everyone struggles. But not everyone kills."

"Charles Kerrigan was a nobody. A criminal. A worth-less, lying man who couldn't take care of himself, let alone that girlfriend of his. And the way he complained about her? He was always going on about how all she was good for was money. He was going to ditch her as soon as he—"

The front door flew open with such force that I could feel splinters hit my back.

"Is that why you came here, Diana? To bad-mouth my dead boyfriend? The boyfriend that you killed? Because if that's why, then go right ahead. Because Mrs. Sullivan and I will be listening very carefully to every word, just hoping you'll say something that we can use against you at your trial."

I couldn't have said it better myself, I thought in admiration.

"I better be quick," Diana said, "because I'm sure you called the police."

"They'll be here any minute." I looked over my shoulder. "You did, didn't you?" I asked under my breath.

Ashley looked embarrassed. "I was afraid I'd miss something."

My cell phone was in my purse, in the house. The two of us had nothing to defend ourselves with. My only hope was that Diana wouldn't be foolish enough to hurt us out in public. But then I remembered our fight in front of her house. And as I scanned the desolate street, my stomach sank.

Diana reached into her Gucci bag that hung off her left shoulder, taking out what looked like a .38 special. She held it down by her side, just for effect. "Now let's go into the house and have a nice chat."

Ashley was frightened, and even though I stood shield-ing her, not daring to take my eyes off of Diana, I heard her whimper and turn for the door. "We're not getting in there alone with her," I said.

"But she said to—"

"We're not moving," I shouted to Diana. "Just get in your car and drive away before the police come," I bluffed.

I didn't want to scream, to agitate her any further, or to get any innocent bystander hurt. So I turned to that good old standby: reason. "So far the only thing you're guilty of—"

"Today," Ashley added.

I continued. "The only thing you've done today is cause a scene. You haven't touched either one of us or made a threat. Even if the police came, they'd have nothing to charge you with. But that gun just turned this situation into a felony."

"I haven't hurt either one of you," she protested.

"But the intention is there. So just put that gun away and get in your car."

I thought I had everything under control at that point. Diana's shoulders slumped; she looked like a woman defeated. When she stared down at the gun, I sensed she was trying to figure out how to get rid of it. And I think I could have gotten her to leave if Ashley had just waited a moment before shouting, "And if you talk any more trash about Charlie, I'll sue you for defamation of character!"

That got Diana going again. "Get in that house! Both of you," she growled.

Ashley turned and ran inside. But still I didn't move, blocking her entrance.

"No," I said.

"I don't have any argument with you, Mrs. Sullivan. Honest. And all I wanted to do when I came here was to talk with her." She motioned toward the front door that now stood open.

"About what?" I demanded.

"I thought that maybe I could convince her that whatever that creep told her was all lies. That he was a professional con man. Naturally he'd try to blame everyone else for what he did. Charles Kerrigan couldn't be trusted with the truth. Not ever."

"If you leave now," I bargained, "I'll arrange a meeting someplace where the three of us can sit down and—"

"I still don't understand why you have to be there," she said. "None of this ever should have involved you."

"When your husband kidnapped Nathan Walker, I got involved."

I was preparing for another struggle with this woman when a white van stopped in the middle of the street. The driver got out and ran around to the other side.

"Are you all right?" Nathan shouted to me.

Chapter Fifty-One

Diana reeled around and shot at Nathan. The first time, I would have sworn that the gun went off by itself. But the second bullet pinged into the van, and I knew she was intentionally aiming for him.

Nathan pulled his revolver out of his breast pocket and held it on the woman. "Get inside, Kathy!"

Diana stood there, confused for a millisecond, then turned the gun on me. "You wanted to stay out here in the open, so stay."

I didn't have time to react when I heard a third shot. But it hadn't come from Diana's gun.

Like a water balloon dropped from a five story building, blood sprayed from Diana Larkin's knee. Startled, in pain, and bewildered, she dropped her gun and fell backward, down the three steps, landing on her side on the pavement.

As the woman shrieked in agony, Nathan raced up the stairs to see if I was all right.

"Forget her!" Diana screamed. "I'm the one hurt here. Call an ambulance."

I could hear sirens before I saw an ambulance, followed by a squad car, rounding the corner.

Ashley opened her door a crack. "I thought they'd never get here. Are you okay?"

"Fine."

"You sure?" Nathan asked.

I nodded and forced a smile.

Nathan picked up Diana's gun, then walked to the officers and handed it over to them, along with his own. Which was standard procedure, since he had fired it as well. One of the EMTs examined her wound while the other wheeled over the folding stretcher.

"Wow!" Ashley said, coming to stand by me. "Shootout on Dover Street. I can see the headlines now. This is bad."

I half expected Diana to shout threats or obscenities at me as they wheeled her away. But she only turned her head and cried. I had nothing to say to her, but Ashley couldn't resist.

"You're going down, Mrs. High and Mighty! Kiss that fancy house of yours good-bye. I'm going to laugh all the way to court."

After loading Mrs. Larkin into the back of the ambulance, it drove off, and we were left with the two officers.

I told Ashley to give her statement for their report while I called Lizzie, hoping to catch her before she went to court.

But I was too late. Josh asked if I wanted to leave a message with him or with voicemail. Choosing the less emotional of the two, I tried making it brief.

"Mrs. Larkin showed up at Ashley's house. There was a minor . . . altercation. But I'm okay. So are Ashley and Nathan. I'll tell you all about it later. Oh, this is your mother."

I hung up and walked over to Nathan. I was more shaken than I'd thought and regretted calling. My message sounded so cryptic. But the way news travels at light speed now, she would have freaked out hearing it from another source.

"This is Officer Carlson," Nathan told me, motioning to the short man in front of him.

"And that's my partner, Sanders."

I looked at the man on the porch, talking to Ashley.

"It's nice to meet you, Mrs. Sullivan."

We shook hands.

"As I was telling Mr. Walker here, the three of you will have to come down to the station. . . . but you're more familiar with procedure than anyone."

"I told him we used to work with Chief Bostwick," Nathan said.

"He's a good man," I said and meant it. Personality aside, Dean was an asset to the force. He just needed some fine-tuning.

Carlson raised his eyebrows so slightly I doubted if he thought I'd caught the gesture. "We'll take Ms. Knight with us, and you two can follow in your car."

Nathan zipped his jacket up. "Will do."

Sanders allowed Ashley to get her coat, then followed her down the stairs to the patrol car. "The neighbors must be enjoying this. They've always hated me," she told me as she got in the backseat.

* * *

In the time it took us to make the short drive to the police station, more than a dozen videos and pictures had hit the Internet. One even came from the old lady with the Pomeranians—at least that's what Polly told me later.

E.T. had obviously ignored the "Reserved" sign and was parked in front.

When he saw us, he jumped out of his car and almost tackled Nathan as he got out of the van. "Larkin's wife's the crazy one in that family. When I heard she had a gun . . . I was so . . . thank God, you're okay."

"How on earth did you hear about it?" Nathan asked, looking at E.T. with alarm.

"You know I have a police scanner in my car, right?"

"I know we have one at the office. I didn't know you had your own."

E.T. cracked a smile. "Come on, boss, you used to be a Boy Scout like me. We're always prepared. Right?"

Nathan smiled back. "You never cease to surprise me, man. I'm just glad you're on my side."

When we entered the station, we were told Ashley had been taken back already and were asked to wait.

"Can I get either one of you anything?" E.T. asked. "Coffee? Soft drink? I think they have—"

"I'm good," I told him, hoping he'd settle down.

"Me, too," Nathan said.

E.T. calmed down a bit and took his place on the bench across from us. "We have to stop meeting like this." His attempt at humor was endearing.

The muscles in my legs twitched. My arms ached from the tension brought on by Diana Larkin. Sitting there, my back against the brick wall, felt relaxing in an odd way. I closed my eyes and hoped no one would ask anything of me for a few minutes. Taking deep breaths, I willed my brain to slow down. Mentally reviewing the contents of my purse, I was glad I'd packed some Tylenol for the headache I feared would come next.

But all the pain relievers in the world couldn't stop the biggest headache that was marching down the hall.

"Katherine Sullivan," Dean Bostwick said, "sorry to disturb your beauty sleep, but I'd like to talk to you for a few minutes."

Chapter Fifty-Two

"Why is it that everyone coming and going out of this office in the last week is connected to you somehow?"

"I'm sure not everyone—"

"Let's start with Sid Watson."

"Carolyn's husband."

"One and the same." His face was getting red as he tried to speak calmly. "My friend Sid, who, of his own free will, confessed to murdering his wife. Understand, this was something that none of my men coerced out of him. In fact, I wished it weren't true. I spoke with him for hours, giving him every opportunity to rescind that confession. But he insisted he was guilty. He demanded we take his confession. It was my duty to lock him up and call the DA."

"But then he changed his story."

"After you talked to him. You, a stranger, convinced him to come clean. Not me, a friend for years—a friend of the family. You."

I was getting annoyed. "You should be happy."

"Happy? I should be happy that you made me and my detectives look like fools? Can't you see that we looked like we were trying to railroad the guy? The climate out there, in case you haven't noticed, is not very favorable toward the police."

"Don't you think you're exaggerating, Dean? Going public with the news that Nathan had been found, alive and well, made the department look good. Letting Diana Larkin go home after questioning made you look fair. And bringing in Carolyn Watson's killer . . . even though it was the wrong person . . . was the only thing you could have done at the time. The public felt safe for a while."

Dean cracked his knuckles. "So I haul Everett Larkin and his wife in here. Two upstanding, well-respected members of our community. And I tell Mrs. Larkin that some alcoholic daughter of the Construction Knight says she heard from her boyfriend, also an alcoholic and a dope head, that she hired him to kill Carolyn, who . . . get this . . . I'm supposed to believe was having an affair with Mr. Larkin."

"Are you upset because Carolyn was being unfaithful? Is that what you're having a hard time believing? You can't think that everyone who comes in here is a scumbag and everyone out there is nice and clean. No one's perfect, Dean. No matter how hard you want them to be."

He put his elbows on his desk and rested his head in his hands. "I know. It's just that . . . it was Carolyn and Sid."

I felt badly for him. Every officer I'd known, including myself, had that moment of clarity. A revelation that there's not one perfect standard to judge people by. It would be so easy if there was. No, there isn't a pure breed among us.

Dean sat up straight and cleared his throat. "So Carolyn's dead. Sid has to get on with his life, at least make an effort for the kids. But how's he supposed to do that? My wife and I don't know how to help him."

I told Dean what someone had told me after Sully died. "Normal will never be normal again. They have to begin a new life."

He sat a moment, digesting my words. Then it was back to business. "After her leg is taken care of, Diana Larkin will be booked and charged with the murder of Charles Kerrigan. The paint found on his body was a perfect match with her car. Then we'll tack on a few more charges: attempted murder of you, Ms. Knight, and Walker, conspiracy to commit murder resulting in Carolyn's death . . . the list goes on. She'll be in prison longer than her looks will hold out. That husband of hers has been charged with the federal offense of kidnapping, aiding and abetting, and aggravated assault with a deadly weapon."

"Assault?" I asked. "But he never hurt Nathan."

"True, but he almost hurt you. I've got the report right here on my desk. The shells my guys pulled out of the Knight house matched up with a weapon we found at Larkin's place. He was the one keeping tabs on Walker, and it was Mr. Larkin who shot at the three of you that day."

"Forever trying to clean up his wife's messes."

"What a pair, huh?"

"And Ashley? She's been cooperative. Never hurt a soul—intentionally. She doesn't belong in prison."

"We both know that," he said, "but the law feels differently. She interfered with a police investigation. But with your daughter as her lawyer, I'm sure she'll be out on bail until her trial. The judge will be lenient. Hey, maybe this might even scare her sober."

"Let's hope so. And what about Ray DeYoung? Did your guys go ask him what he was doing with the painting from the Larkin house?"

"Good catch, Katherine. After Charlie was found dead, he put two and two together and told her it was either pay him off or he was going to the police. So she gave him the painting as collateral until she could get the cash. He'll face charges, too."

"Too bad for his brother, Jim. He's a clean cop. Hate to see him have to go through this."

Bostwick nodded. "Walker will have to testify against Larkin. You'll have to testify against his wife—looks like the three of us are going to be tied up with the two of them for a while."

"Afraid so."

"But there's no reason you can't go home," he said. "Winter's coming, and you don't want to be stuck here in the frozen tundra. You know how long these things can drag on. We probably won't need you back here until the spring thaw."

"I'd wish there was a better reason for me to come visit my family," I told him.

As he sat there, looking worn out, I wanted to say something to comfort him. He needed some kind words, and I could certainly afford to give him a few.

"You know, Dean, it took me two years to feel comfortable in that chair. Just because you made the grade and achieved the rank of chief doesn't mean it fits right at first. You have to grow into the job. Give it time and go easier on yourself."

"So how am I doing so far?" he asked, surprising me that he would leave himself open to criticism.

"After the month you've had, one of the most complicated cases I've ever seen, you're almost there."

"A compliment? Retirement has softened you up."

"Couldn't resist one more shot, could you?"

Chapter
Fifty-Three

If Nathan hadn't been with me, Lizzie would have gotten hysterical. But the kids were there too, so she had to hold back her tears.

"I was so worried. Why can't you be like other mothers?" she asked as she squeezed me so tight I thought I'd break something.

"Come on now," Nathan told her as she ran over to embrace him. "Your mother has never been like anyone else. It's too late for her to change now."

"Your shootout's gotten 3,212 hits so far. My friends can't believe it's really you," Chloe said holding her phone up to me as verification.

"Grammy, Grammy," Cam was so excited. "Way cool video! Lewis's brother got on America's Home Videos once, but it was for something stupid. He jumped off a roof with his skateboard glued to his shoes. But yours is awesome, not dumb. Were you scared when that lady pulled a gun on you? 'Cause you didn't look like it." Cam couldn't help himself from chattering on.

Lizzie walked over to rub his back, which always seemed to calm him down. "Give Grammy a chance to breathe, sweetie."

"Sure." He looked at us, embarrassed. "Wanna stay for dinner, Mr. Walker?"

"Nothing special," Lizzie said. "Just spaghetti. But there's plenty."

"You don't have plans, do you?" I asked.

"No. Are you sure I'm not in the way?"

"Chloe, show Mr. Walker where he can wash up."

"Don't argue with a lawyer," I teased him. "You'll eat spaghetti and like it."

* * *

It must have been difficult for her, but Chloe resisted the urge to check her phone for more videos during dinner. Instead, she told us all about her part in the school play, which was a very nice distraction from all the day had brought.

"Daddy helps me with my lines whenever I'm there, and Mom helps when I'm here. My teacher, Mr. Black, says I'm really good, and when I get to high school, maybe I could try out for a play there. They even have acting lessons at this place downtown. Do you think I could take some during summer vacation, Mom?"

"We'll see."

Lizzie didn't seem to be enjoying herself as much as I was. "How did your case go today?" I changed the subject to give Chloe a chance to eat and Nathan a more interesting topic to listen to.

"Another continuance; this makes the third. But as they say, 'The wheels of justice grind slow.'"

"'But grind fine,'" Cam finished the quote.

"How did you know that?" Nathan asked.

"Sun Tzu wrote it in *The Art of War*. I did a paper on him for English," Cam said.

"How old are you, boy?" Nathan asked.

"Fourteen."

"Going on thirty," I said proudly.

Lizzie smiled at her son. "Well, whoever said it, I'm going crazy. It seems all I do is hurry up and wait."

"'They also serve who only stand and wait,'" Nathan said.

"Did you just make that up?" Cam asked.

"No, Milton did," Nathan told him. "Someday you should read his sonnets."

Nathan Walker read poetry?

*　*　*

After dinner, the kids cleared off the table while the three adults took their coffee into the living room. Lizzie grabbed the remote.

"Let's see if you guys made the news again. Pretty soon a producer will be coming to ask if you'll be interested in doing a reality show."

"My TV days are long behind me," Nathan said.

"Don't tell me you've been on television?" I asked incredulously. "Is that what you're saying?"

Once he started laughing, he couldn't stop.

"I was just pulling your leg. But I see lawyers doing ads all the time now. So when is our Elizabeth going to make her debut?"

"Never. Josh keeps asking though. He's a frustrated actor. Just to humor him, I tell him that if I ever change my mind, he can be our spokesperson. That keeps him quiet for a few months."

Lizzie channel surfed, trying to find a mention of the shootout on Dover Street, but the local news was wrapping with tomorrow's forecast. While she seemed disappointed, I was happy. Enough was enough for one day.

"Maybe there's something you two would like to watch," she said, tossing the remote in my lap. "I have work to do. Nathan, I'm so glad everything worked out okay. And please, stop by anytime. I know Mother always loves seeing you. Don't you, Mother?"

Could she have been more obvious?

Nathan played along. "And I love seeing her, too."

After Lizzie left the room, we changed channels until finding a movie. But we talked through the whole thing.

"So when do you plan on going back West?"

"In a few days."

"You'll need time to rest up after all this excitement."

"So will you," I said.

Nathan laughed. "Listen to us. We sound like we're ready for the home."

"I guess it's all where you're standing. Did you notice that Bostwick and a few of the cops referred to Mr. Larkin as an 'old coot'?"

"I did. And I didn't like it. That guy must be at least five years younger than me and no way, no how, am I an old coot."

"Not from where I'm standing."

Chapter Fifty-Four

The only place we could work on the mural was in the back of the house. Thankfully, there was little wind and the sun was bright. Cam and I had light jackets over our sweat shirts so we wouldn't be too encumbered by the bulk. It had taken a good two hours to finally decide on the flattest surface. The garage had a few windows, which would make the surface too bumpy. The side of the house was in the shade, so the back would have to do. One of us had to hold and tape while the other unrolled the heavy paper. But we'd used the wrong tape to begin with, and as the edges curled and released, we had to stop and find the right adhesive. Finally, we were ready to start.

But the beginning meant making trips in and out of the house to gather paints, brushes, and rags. I kept glancing at Cam to see if his enthusiasm was running low, but he seemed fully charged. He'd always been so focused when creating. Today he was in charge of our project, and I was his eager assistant.

"It should be bright," he told me when I picked up a small jar labeled Baby Blue #3. "Try the lapis."

"Whatever the Caminator wants."

From the look on his face, I could tell he was in heaven.

I painted bright-red poppies next to tangerine daisies. Purple lilacs hanging from chartreuse leaves. Gardens of flowers, as authentically reproduced as I could make them, growing next to varieties I made up. And I even managed to sneak my baby blue into the background for contrast.

While I painted the foreground, Cam worked on the buildings in the back. At one point, I had to stop and get him a step ladder. When he dabbed on silver stars in the daytime sky, I applauded him. Our time together was wonderful. But as the hours went by, my back and the cramps in my knees reminded me I had to sit down.

Maybe he was getting tired, too. "How're you doing?" I shouted over to him.

"I'm thirsty."

"I'll go get some sodas. We can drink them on the deck."

"Cool."

Lizzie was at the office, and Chloe would be having dinner at Jennifer's house. I looked at the clock and saw we had at least three more hours before it would start to get too dark to paint.

Cam was stretched out on the lounger when I returned.

"So how do you think it's going?"

He took the soda I offered. "It's okay."

I sat and put my feet up. "I've never worked on something this large before; have you?"

"Once."

"When was that?"

"When I was four. Mom said I painted my whole room. Walls, floor, dresser—everything."

"I remember. You didn't like the Star Wars wallpaper."

"I didn't mean to be destructive. There's just something inside me that makes me want to draw and make things."

"My brother, your uncle Nick, was like that. But my parents weren't as understanding as yours are. When he'd scribble on the furniture, which was a lot, they'd punish him. Once, when he was around ten, he got grounded for the whole summer. But he didn't care. He'd rather be in his room, painting, than outside playing with the other kids."

"All the kids around here think I'm weird. Not Lewis. But he's the only one."

"Well, when they see that"—I motioned toward the mural—"they'll change their minds."

He shrugged. "Maybe."

I could feel the temperature was starting to dip. "Guess we better finish up."

"Do you think I could meet Uncle Nick someday?"

"Last I heard, he's thinking of coming back to the states for Christmas."

"Why did he move to Ireland anyway?" Cam wanted to know.

"He said our homeland inspires him. You know how temperamental artists are." I winked.

Cam smiled and winked back.

* * *

Holding a white basket of roses, Lizzie struggled to take off her coat.

I had just finished washing paint off my hands and was walking to my room to change clothes when I saw her.

"These are for you," she said, handing the basket to me. "I ran into the delivery man as I was coming in."

I took the flowers and searched for a note.

Her grin was enormous. "Think they're from Nathan?"

"No." We'd gotten closer this visit, but there was still a long way to go before we started with gifts.

I set the basket on the low coffee table and unwrapped the cellophane. The fragrance hit my nose first, then filled the room. It reminded me of summertime and prom dates, weddings, and garden parties. I picked through the stems for a card and finally found one in a small white envelope, attached with a green ribbon.

Lizzie sat on the couch, eagerly waiting. "Well? What does it say?"

I opened the card and read:

Thank you for stopping your life and coming to our rescue. We don't know what we would have done without you.

Love,
Rosie, Brock, Polly, and Ted

"Who's Ted?" Lizzie asked.

Chapter Fifty-Five

"Good thing I had Josh save seats for us. I've never seen this place so crowded," Lizzie said as we walked through the auditorium. "Do you see him, Mother? Cam, do you see Josh?"

"Is that him in the tuxedo?" Cam pointed.

Lizzie waved to her assistant.

"Tuxedo?" I asked. "Isn't he a little . . . overdressed?"

"Josh says he dresses according to his mood. I never know what to expect when he walks into the office. He's fun. And doing what I do, fun is nice."

We made our way to the front, where Josh stood guard over our seats. "Well, Mrs. Sullivan, so glad you could make it. And Mr. Farina, Cam, looks like the whole family's here for Chloe's acting debut. Isn't it exciting?"

"It's wonderful," Tom said. "Who knows? Maybe we have a future Academy Award winner in our midst."

It was all those things: exciting and wonderful. Plus unbelievable that my Chloe Girl was so grown up and starring in her first production. How lucky was I to be there and share the evening with my talented grandchildren?

After getting out of our coats and settling into the folding chairs, we sat and waited.

At eight o'clock on the button, a man walked out and took center stage. Introducing himself as Mr. Black, he acknowledged the efforts of the students and parents. He mentioned each child in the play, by name, whether they had a major role or were just standing in a crowd scene. Then he went on to introduce the members of the band. How I wished he'd hurry up and allow the play to begin. But wishing didn't make it so.

They say you can always tell if you've lost the attention of an audience when they start to cough. Mr. Black must have never heard that observation because five coughs, several sneezes, and a loud crying baby later, he was still talking.

But by 8:30, act one of *The Princess and the Dragon* began.

As the curtain slowly opened, the lights hit Cam's mural, which lined the entire back of the stage. He'd painted the castle a silver metallic and tossed a few handfuls of gold glitter on top while the paint was still wet. It looked magical. Tom, who was sitting between me and Cam, squeezed his son's hand.

"Outstanding job," he whispered.

"Grammy did the flowers and grass," he told his father.

Tom seemed truly impressed with our joint effort. "Awesome."

Of course, Chloe shined in the role of Lady Devonshire. She had a few minor slip-ups, forgetting a word here and there, but otherwise, she was perfect. I noticed that Cam was mouthing her dialogue and, by the second act, realized he'd memorized all her lines.

Bradley O'Toole, the tallest boy in the class, did a great job in the part of the dragon. His aluminum foil tail only tripped the wizard once. Princess Moonshine was played by Mary Sweeney, a pretty little girl with a very grown-up voice. No one in the back row had any trouble hearing her every word. Even after the microphone went out for a few minutes during the last act, we could all hear Mary.

I looked around the audience at faces lit by the reflected stage lights. Mothers and fathers all so proud, smaller children enchanted with the fairytale being acted out right in front of them. After what I'd gone through the past few days, it seemed almost surreal to be sitting there. What a bizarre contrast, I thought, from what I'd been doing just a few days ago. Tracking down Nathan, dodging bullets, fighting with Diana Larkin. Who said retirement was boring?

After three curtain calls, the play was finally over. Lizzie led the way to the lemonade and cake reception that had been set up in the back of the room while the audience watched the play. The curtain suddenly opened, and all the children who had been in the play stood lined up, still in costume. Lizzie ran to get a spot while the rest of us headed for the cake.

There was already a long line when we got there.

"I really can't stay much longer," Tom said. "I have to make rounds with some med students tomorrow. But I have to see Chloe before I leave. She was great, wasn't she?" he asked me. "And it's not just because she's my daughter. That girl has real talent."

I agreed wholeheartedly.

"If I don't see you again, Kate, have a safe trip home."

I hugged him. "I will, and I'm looking forward to you and the kids coming out to see me. Anytime."

His smile was genuine. "We'll be there. Let's stay in touch, okay?"

"You got it."

Cam tugged at the back of my sweater. "That woman over there is waving at you, Grammy."

I looked in the direction he was pointing, and there stood Barbara Nylander.

"Stay with your father, sweetie. I'll be right back."

She'd traded in her white lab coat for a white apron. "When John told me about the job he was doing for the school, I knew you'd be here to see the play, so I volunteered to help. I thought it would probably be my last chance to see you for a while, before you fly back to that godforsaken desert of yours."

I'd tried, several times, telling her how beautiful Taos was, but she'd have none of it. "Well, I'm glad you're here. Where's John? I've never met him."

Barbara pointed to a man with short gray hair who obviously enjoyed sampling his own baked goods. She grabbed my hand and pulled me toward her husband.

"Honey, this is the famous Katherine Sullivan."

His smile was infectious, and when he took my hand in both of his, coming closer to me, I got a whiff of vanilla and sugar. I loved this man immediately.

"Barb's told me so much about you over the years. It's great to meet finally, face-to-face." Looking at his wife, he asked, "Did you tell her?"

"No," Barbara said. "I thought we'd just show her."

"What's going on?"

The two of them grinned as they guided me back to the large cafeteria kitchen. There in the middle of a stainless steel table was a two layer cake that had been slathered with lavender icing. Piped across the top, in pale-green icing were the words: "Case Closed."

I didn't know what to say as they stood, waiting for my reaction.

"I told you I'd have my baker man whip up something when you found Nathan."

"This is so nice of you, John. Thank you."

"And don't worry, it's chocolate, your fave," Barbara said.

I hugged her. "Can we cut into it later? After you're done with the reception?" I asked.

"Positively, absolutely," John said. "Barb here is an expert at cutting up things."

"That was gross, John. I told you not to joke about my work." But while she tried looking stern, her husband and I knew she was kidding.

Chapter Fifty-Six

The next morning, after I'd packed, I went to Walker Securities to say good-bye to everyone and especially thank the crew for the roses. "And if this guy ever goes missing again"—I pointed to Nathan—"you're on your own."

"Yeah." Rosie winked. "An' if there is a next time, we'll just have to run the business without him. Think you can handle the boss's job, Brock?"

"No sweat."

"What about you, Pol?"

Polly twisted her thumb ring. "Hey, if I can handle you clowns, I can handle anything."

Not exactly what I'd describe as the lighthearted type, E.T. stood off to the side. After the laughter subsided, he said, "Seriously, Katherine, thank you from the bottom of my heart."

When he walked over and hugged me, I whispered in his ear, "As long as you're okay, Ted."

That got a smile out of him. "I am now."

Nathan walked me to my jeep. "I'll miss you, Kathy. But I always do when you leave."

"You heard them in there. They can handle the office a few days while you hop a jet and come see me. And please, stop thinking up reasons to make me come back here."

He stood back and took a good look at me. "You're really something, you know that?"

"So I've been told."

I expected a hug or kiss . . . something. But he kept his distance. Maybe it was because his crew were watching us through the window. Maybe it was because . . . no . . . I wasn't going to analyze it. We knew how we felt, and that would have to hold me until I saw him again.